PASS IT ON!

In the [REAL LIFE] series, four girls are brought together through the power of a mysterious book that helps them sort through the issues of their very real lives. In each of these stories, the girls find the mysterious RL book exactly when they need it. Each girl leaves the RL book for someone else to find, knowing it will help the next person who reads it.

While the RL book is magical, this book could be left in the same way for the next reader. Maybe this book needs to be read by someone you don't even know, or maybe you already know of someone who would really enjoy this book. Simply write a note with READ ME on it, stick it on the front of the book, and then get creative. Give the book to a friend, or leave this book at your church, school, local coffee shop, train station, on the bus, or wherever you know someone else will find it and read it.

No matter what your plan, we want to hear about it. Log on to the Zondervan Good Teen Reads Facebook page (*www.facebook.com/goodteenreads*—look under the Discussion tab) and tell us where you left the book, or how you found it. Or, let us know how you plan to "pass it on." You can also let your friends know about Pass It On by talking about it on your Facebook page.

To join others in the Pass It On campaign, pick up extra copies from the [REAL LIFE] series at your local Christian bookstores and favorite online retailers.

Other books in the Real Life series:

Motorcycles, Sushi & One Strange Book (Book One)

Boyfriends, Burritos & an Ocean of Trouble (Book Two)

Tournaments, Cocoa & One Wrong Move (Book Three)

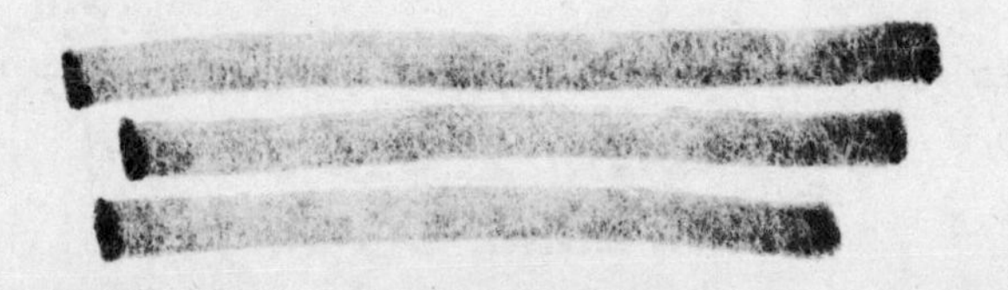

Limos, Lattes & My Life on the Fringe

[REAL LIFE]

book four

Nancy Rue

We want to hear from you. Please send your comments about this book to us in care of zreview@zondervan.com. Thank you.

ZONDERVAN

Limos, Lattes & My Life on the Fringe

This title is also available as a Zondervan ebook.
Visit www.zondervan.com/ebooks.

Requests for information should be addressed to:

Zondervan, *Grand Rapids, Michigan 49530*

ISBN 978-0-310-71487-3

Published in association with the literary agency of Alive Communications, Inc., 7680 Goddard Street, Suite 200, Colorado Springs, CO 80920. www.alivecommunications.com

Cover design: Rule 29
Cover photography: © iStockphoto
Interior design: Patrice Sheridan & Carlos Eluterio Estrada
Interior composition: Greg Johnson/Textbook Perfect

Printed in the United States of America

11 12 13 14 15 16 /DCI/ 23 22 21 20 19 18 17 16 15 14 13 12 11 10 9 8 7 6 5 4 3 2 1

CHAPTER ONE

Before I even start to tell you what happened to me my junior year in high school, let me just say I've changed a whole lot since then. As in, if my outer self had changed as much as my inner self, I'd have to constantly show my ID, because nobody would recognize me.

As a matter of fact, this whole *story* is about me practically changing into somebody else — which is why I have to show you who I was back then. The problem is, you might not like that girl I used to be. *I* wasn't even that crazy about me. But if you promise to stick it out, I promise to make it worth your while. It was definitely worth mine.

It all started to change that spring afternoon. Up until that day — that hour — I was used to the reactions I got when I walked down the hall at Castle Heights High.

I could always predict that the Kmart Kids — not *my* name for them, even when I was so critical I could filet a person with my tongue — would cut a wide path around me, like caring about grades made me an alien. Make that tall, gawky, black, and intelligent. They didn't get me, and I was really okay with that.

And it was also a safe bet that the Ruling Class would ignore me, even though I was in every honors class known to adolescence with them. Well, at least the four honors classes the school actually offered. And I knew that the African Americans — my "people" as my parents insisted on calling them — would say, "Hey, Tyler," with Crest-commercial smiles and then move on, because we really didn't have much in common beyond the color of our skin. According to them.

My actual friends—a group I referred to in my mind as the Fringe—were also predictable. From them I could expect things like, "You're looking enigmatic today, Tyler." At which point any passing Kmart Kid would scurry away as if vocabulary was a contagious disease.

I had come to expect all of that. It was like the way I ate a raspberry Pop-Tart for breakfast every day. It might not be that interesting, but at least I knew what I was getting.

But then there was that day in April, when the snow had all melted for the first time since late November and I had walked to school without a ten-pound down jacket. Like I said, that was the day it changed—the way people were looking at me, I mean. Three steps from my locker on the way to the lunchroom, I was already wondering what high school I'd been teleported to.

I hiked my black-and-white plaid messenger bag over my shoulder, stuffed with all the research I'd done the night before on Andrew Jackson for my group history project. I was thinking about what an egotistical bigot the man was and how we could possibly present that in our report, since Mr. Linkhart was from Mississippi or someplace and probably thought Jackson should be canonized as a saint. My head was totally wrapped around that when three girls in too-tight sweaters and too-skinny jeans planted themselves right in front of me. I tried to steer around them, the way they would have steered around *me* any other day, but they shimmied themselves into that path too and stared at me. It was like they were waiting for me to, I don't know, transform into another life form.

"*What?*" I said.

Apparently that was hilarious, because they spewed giggles and looked at each other and giggled again, all the way down the hall. I decided that couldn't possibly have anything to do with me, and I proceeded another five steps toward the cafeteria, where two-thirds of my group was supposedly waiting with their own bags bulging with fascinating facts about our seventh president. I was thinking they'd probably want to mooch off of *my* facts, as well as my lunch money, when another trio of girls slowed down to gape at me and then sidled off, tittering. I've never "tittered" in my life, but I knew even the kids who thought studying was hazardous to their health didn't collapse into that kind of hilarity without a reason, however lame it might be.

I took a detour into the girls' restroom and examined my face in one of the mirrors generations of girls had clouded with clandestine cigarette smoke. My brown eyes stared back at me as if to say, *What are* you *looking at?* Yeah, in those days, I even looked at my*self* that way.

I expected to see ink smeared across my cheek, or at the very least a large wart blossoming on my forehead. But I looked the same as I had that morning when I brushed my teeth. Hair cut into a close cap on what my mother referred to as a "nicely shaped head"—like that was every girl's goal—skin still the color of pancake syrup, mouth still big enough for several people, nose still the only accusing hint that all my ancestral "people" had not come from Africa. There was nothing in the mirror that all those kids in the hall hadn't seen before. Definitely nothing worth "tittering" over, unless you counted the map of red lines in the whites of my eyes from studying until midnight. Did they think I was on drugs? Were *they* on drugs?

"Oops," somebody said from the doorway.

I looked at her from the mirror. Alyssa Hampton, a senior. Pretty blonde girl. If you liked big teeth. Half the males in the senior class apparently did.

Another girl came in behind Alyssa, nearly plowing into her. Hayley Barr, a junior of thick ponytail fame. The two of them were normally attached right about where their jeans hugged their hips. Jeans that cost more than the entire wardrobe of those six girls in the hall. Combined.

"Hi, Tyler," Hayley said in a voice about two keys higher than her usual voice. "You going to lunch?"

She looked at Alyssa and, to their credit, they visibly stifled the laughter that was so clearly about to explode out of them.

"I usually go to lunch," I said. "Why? Are they serving botulism again today?"

They did explode then, and I knew it wasn't my humor that sent them diving into a stall. Together.

Seriously—what was making me such a source of endless amusement?

I transferred my bag to my other shoulder and hauled Andrew Jackson back out into the hall, where I set out again for the lunchroom. But when I saw my second cousin Kenny at the drinking fountain, I swerved and caught up to him before he could take off to join the other professional slackers at the Jiff-E-Mart.

"Do you have any idea why every girl in this school suddenly thinks I'm funnier than Tina Fey?" I said.

He raised his head and blinked. I could see him taking a full five seconds to recognize me, which made sense. We hadn't actually spoken since Christmas dinner.

"Who's Tina Fey?" he said.

I should have known. Whenever I did try to have a conversation with the boy, he never had any idea what I was talking about. I'd suspected for some time that he was hatched from an egg every morning.

"I don't think you're that funny," he said.

A girl materialized. Candace, Kenny's older sister. Also my second cousin.

"Come on, Kenny," she said, wrapping her fingers around his arm. "You don't want to get into this."

"Into what, Candace?" I said.

"Into nothing." With her hands on Kenny and her eyes warily on me, she dragged him away.

All right. Enough. I charged down the hall, through the looks and the snickers and the snippets of conversation, like I was traveling in a tunnel. I went straight to the table in the corner by the "salad bar" nobody ever ate from, and when I arrived I knew at least things were still normal over here.

Matthew sat, as usual, with his enormous feet propped on a chair, which meant the teacher/cop of the day hadn't been by yet to tell him to get them off. Scrawny Yuri was across from him, frowning at the ingredients printed on an energy drink bottle. Deidre, the only senior in our group of juniors, was standing up, digging through a vintage purse suitable for a bag lady, which probably contained items she hadn't seen since seventh grade. She was talking. Nobody was listening. I sank into the plastic chair next to her and plunked my own bag on the table.

"Does anybody know what's going on?"

"Are we talking globally?" Matthew said. "We're pretty sure Pakistan's harboring Osama Bin Laden. We have a black president—"

"Mercury's in retrograde," Deidre said into her purse.

"No, I mean here," I said.

Yuri looked up from the drink bottle and squinted at me through his wire-rimmed glasses. "Who cares what's going on here?"

"Not me, usually," I said. "But people I don't even know are walking up to me and losing it."

Deidre dragged her eyes from the bottomless bag and pulled her dark I-refuse-to-tweeze eyebrows together over her yes-it's-big-so-sue-me nose.

"They know something you don't?" she said. "Hard to believe."

"Maybe it's about that," Matthew said.

"About what?" I said. Matthew's currently raven-black hair hung over his eyes, so it was hard to tell what, if anything, he was seeing.

"That." He jerked his square chin toward the opposite wall of the lunchroom.

I followed his jerk. Our cafeteria was long and narrow and an even uglier green than any other part of the over-fifty-year-old school. To make it look even longer—and uglier—rectangular tables were placed in rows all the way from one end to the other. Green, yellow, and orange plastic chairs always started out tucked into the tables at the beginning of lunch period but were quickly scattered and regrouped and often overturned, until by the end, the place looked like those prison scenes you see in movies where the inmates start banging their cups and somebody gets thrown into the chow line. One teacher/monitor was only enough to keep that to a minimum.

One of the advantages of being a junior or senior at Castle Heights High was getting to sit at the round tables that skirted the room. We — that would be the Fringe and I — had claimed ours in September, and like most groups we were pretty territorial about it. Which meant we seldom ventured to the other end, where the bulletin board hung. The Ruling Class had their three tables down there so they could preside over the significant events posted on it. Homecoming queen. Roles in the current theatrical production. Starting lineup for the next basketball game. If I'd had the slightest interest in any of that, I might have wandered past it now and then. Since, however, I could very possibly live my entire life successfully without ever going to a homecoming dance or cheering at a basketball game, I'd never even glanced in that direction.

But at the moment, everybody else in the student body appeared to be absolutely fascinated by it. The crowd in front of the board was four people deep.

"Let me guess," Deidre said. "They posted the results of the 'Most Shallow' competition."

"Oh." Matthew sat upright in the chair. "Do you think I won?"

Deidre shook her head. "Although I have known puddles deeper than you, Matthew, I'm sure you didn't."

"Shucks," he said to Yuri.

Yuri cocked a colorless eyebrow that matched his hair. "Define *shucks*."

"That can't be it," I said. "If my name ever appeared on that board it would be for 'Most Unknown.'"

"Isn't that an oxymoron?" Matthew said.

"Is that what they call *this*?"

We looked up at a wildly curly brunette who'd appeared at the salad bar and was poking the tongs into a stainless steel pan full of brown lettuce.

I studied her for a few seconds. She didn't immediately fall into any of the categories of people I passed in the halls. In fact,

I didn't think I'd ever seen her before. It had to be tough being a new kid in April, when all the friend slots had long since been filled. It had been hard enough for me at the beginning of sophomore year, seeing how most of the friend slots here had actually been filled back in preschool.

"Do you know what's going on down there?" I said to her.

She gave the lettuce another dubious look and moved on to the anemic chopped tomatoes.

"I think they posted the nominations for prom queen," she said. "I'm not sure — this is only my second day here."

Yeah, I was good.

"How's that working out for you?" Matthew said.

She passed on the tomatoes too and dumped a spoonful of grated cheese onto her plate. "Is there a microwave we can use?"

Matthew laughed out loud. Yuri scrutinized her as if she were speaking one of the few foreign languages he didn't know.

"No," I told the girl. "We're lucky to have electricity. Where'd you move here from?"

"France," she said.

Deidre stared. "Seriously?"

"My family lived there for five years."

She brought her plate of cheese close to the table, and for the first time I saw that she had incredibly blue eyes, even though her skin was almost as dark as mine.

Deidre kicked Matthew's feet off the extra chair. "Join us," she said, "if you can stand Mr. Crude."

"My stuff's over there," she said. "Thanks, though. Most people here aren't this friendly." She glanced toward the bulletin board again. "They're kind of mean, some of them."

"What do you expect from the low end of the food chain?" Matthew said.

Yuri just glowered.

"No, seriously." French Girl lowered her voice. "A bunch of them are up there laughing their fannies off because somebody's in the top four for prom queen that evidently isn't queen material."

"Did she just say 'fannies'?" Deidre said to Yuri.

"Trust me," I said, "nobody made it to that list that wasn't supposed to be there. We have people who oversee those kinds of things."

"The principal does that?"

Matthew snorted from under his hair. "He never comes out of the office. Nobody's seen him since the Clinton administration."

I shook my head at French Girl. "A bunch of juniors and seniors run everything."

"You'll know them by the vacant look they get in their eyes when you use words of more than three syllables," Matthew said.

"Except 'Abercrombie,'" Deidre said. "They know that."

Yuri was still glowering. "It's all inbreeding."

French Girl had yet to crack a smile. It was time to find out which way she was leaning before we said much more.

"Were you in student government at your school in France?" I said.

She shook her head and pushed a few curls behind her ear. "I was homeschooled."

The three of us exchanged glances.

"What?" she said.

I cleared my throat. "Just a word of warning. Those kids aren't usually outright mean until somebody does something 'different.' Otherwise, they don't really have to be, because they're already in control."

"So start by not telling anybody you've been homeschooled," Deidre said.

The blue eyes blinked. "I don't get that. And I definitely don't get the prom queen thing."

Deidre patted the empty chair. "You absolutely should sit with us. You've found your people, right, Tyler?"

"Huh?" I said.

I'd heard the words, but most of them hadn't sunk in. My eyes and my mind and the sick feeling in the pit of my stomach had wandered back toward the bulletin board. Now the entire cafeteria was alternating between ogling our end of the room and doing some variation on a disbelieving guffaw.

"Tyler?" Deidre said.

"Who is it—do you know?" I said.

French Girl shook her head.

"Will somebody go look?"

"Oh, can I please?" Deidre said. "And can I also poke a fork in my eye?"

"Why do we care who it is?" Matthew said to Yuri, who answered, "We don't."

The girl edged away. "Listen, thanks for talking to me. I better go eat."

"I'll walk with you," I said.

"Oh, yeah," Matthew said. "She could get lost in here. It's a veritable labyrinth."

He gave the whole table an elaborate shrug. I followed French Girl down the aisle, past the freshmen and sophomores, who had also sorted themselves into a caste system early on in their high school careers—if not sooner, since they'd all basically been born in the same hospital. Normally louder and more obnoxious than the crowd at a tractor pull, they practically went into a coma as I went by.

What? I wanted to say to all of them.

But the closer I got to the board, the surer I was that I already knew "what." My mouth felt like sawdust, and my stomach was all the way into the feeling I hadn't had since my first day here a year and a half ago, moments before I made up my mind that fitting in was not my life goal. Even the cafeteria food couldn't wreak this much havoc on my insides.

Still, I kept my head up and, as my father always said, my eyes on the prize. There was no doubt that the object of everybody's attention was a pink sheet of paper stapled to the center of the board and surrounded by a frame of fake roses. Could they have made it any cheesier?

A small sea of people just getting in on the fun parted as I took the final steps. Nobody breathed a word, except the one girl who needlessly said, "Shh!" The silence had the clear sound of people holding back hysteria.

French Girl had been right. It was the list of prom queen nominees, voted on in junior and senior homerooms that very morning and narrowed down by none other than the prom committee, a subset of the Ruling Class.

Alyssa Hampton was the first name. No surprise.

Hayley Barr was the second. To be expected.

Joanna Payne, the third. Ya think?

And there below them, in the same font, the same color, the same size—as if it belonged there—was the fourth one.

Tyler Bonning.

When the room could hold its breath no longer and ripped open in a roar, I realized I'd just read the name out loud.

"Tyler Bonning?" French Girl half yelled to me over the din. "Is that you?"

"Yes," I said. "That's me." I turned to her and plastered a manufactured smile on my face. "Hilarious, isn't it?"

CHAPTER TWO

French Girl shifted her eyes from me to the list and back again, which gave me a chance to adjust my smile to something that felt a little more sarcastic.

Amid the din of laughter that wouldn't die, she said, "Why is this funny?"

"You're kidding, right?" I said.

She shook her head.

"How long did you say you were out of the country?"

She opened her mouth to answer, but I turned to the mob. Although there was still some chortling around the edges, most of the faces were once again bright red from holding back, waiting for me to say something. And obviously hoping for it to be juicy and maybe even profane. The Ruling Class loved profanity. There were some words they could use as every part of speech.

I had no intention of swearing at them. So not my style. The problem at the moment was that my *actual* style wasn't automatically kicking in. It was, in fact, struggling to surface through a hot sheen of embarrassment. I hadn't let myself be embarrassed since the seventh grade.

So I stood there shaking my head at the list until I found a few words they probably wouldn't understand. Just as the roar started to rise again, I turned slowly from the bulletin board and lifted my chin.

"First of all, I'd like to thank the Academy," I said. "It is such an honor to be nominated by my peers and to be placed among my esteemed colleagues. Whoever wins will be worthy of the title—because quite frankly, the title means absolutely nothing." I smiled and waved. "Thank you. Thank you all so much."

Then, pretending to dab happy tears from the corners of my eyes with the pads of my fingers, I walked out of the cafeteria. The stunned silence I left behind was pocked with only a few giggles. Just as I'd hoped, half the people in there didn't get what I meant.

Good job, Tyler. Very effective.

So why did I feel like I'd been slapped across the face with somebody's pom-poms six or seven times? Since when did I care how the Ruling Class treated me?

In case you missed it, that's when things started to change.

I started down the hall, not quite sure where I was going, and blinked back the tears that turned out not to be phony after all. I would analyze this later, of course, and come up with a logical explanation for myself. The only thing I could think to do at the moment was make sure nobody saw.

The bathroom was out of the question—it would be teeming with RCs within the minute. Same with the courtyard, where the guys would go to yuk it up. I finally darted down the hall toward the office. Everybody avoided that area like the whole administration had H1N1.

Everybody except the Fringe, who cut me off at the proverbial pass, just short of the trophy case. They must have ducked out the back door of the lunchroom.

"You kicked some serious tail, Tyler," Deidre said.

She put her hand up, and I slapped half-heartedly at her palm.

Matthew snickered. "I heard, like, three people say, 'What academy?' and some guy goes, 'I thought this was a public school.'"

Only Yuri was sullen. "I wouldn't have wasted my time on those losers."

"It's okay," I said. "That wasn't my best stuff anyway."

"Think what you could've said if you'd had more time to prepare." Deidre put up a hand again. "Not that you weren't amazing on your feet."

I muttered a vague thanks. So far, nobody had commented on my wet eyes, or for that matter asked if I was okay. Which must mean I was successfully hiding the sting I still felt. That was a good thing.

Wasn't it?

"Okay, so it just proves what I've always thought about proms," I said.

"And what's that?"

I blinked at the Fringe for a second before I realized the question hadn't come from them. I turned just as a tall white kid stepped up beside me in that cocky way that says, "Okay, so we've never talked before but I know you want to." The only thing I knew about him was that he was a senior and that he hung out with the RCs. He obviously wasn't there just to get to know me.

"What *have* you always thought about proms?" he said.

Brown eyes sparkled under a messy crop of blond bangs, and his mouth teased. I hated teasing almost as much as I hated—well, a lot of other things, come to think of it.

He was still waiting, hands parked lazily in the pockets of his droopy shorts. Definitely a native New Yorker. The minute the temperature got above fifty degrees, these guys brought out the Bermudas.

"What I've always thought about proms," I said, "is that they make people do stupid things."

"Really," he said. "Like what?"

He leaned against the end of the trophy case like we were about to have a discussion. I opened my mouth to answer, but Yuri nudged me with the camera bag he wore as if it were a life-support system.

"We gotta get to class," he said.

"We've got five minutes 'til the bell," the kid said.

What was his name? I'd seen it during the Student Council elections last year. Sean? Kelly? Something Irish. Corrigan?

"I'm sure this would be a fascinating conversation," Deidre said, "but I've got to go floss."

She gave Irish Boy a long, dark-eyed, you-are-in-way-over-your-head look and drifted off with Matthew lumbering behind her. Yuri went the other way, mumbling something to himself. Probably, "That was five minutes of my life I'll never get back."

Which left me standing there waiting for the kid to say something obnoxious and get it over with.

"Like what stupid things?" he said.

"I have a list," I said, "but I could grow old naming everything on it, so let's cut to the chase: nominating the most unlikely girl in the junior or senior class for prom queen just to try to humiliate her—which, by the way, it didn't."

"I can see that."

Okay, so he was blind. But it felt good to be back on a roll.

"I have to say, though, it took some real organization to make that happen. It was clearly no accident that I got the fourth-largest number of votes."

He shrugged. "Or there could just be that many people who think you should be prom queen."

"Uh, no, because I don't even *know* that many people."

"Maybe they know you."

"Yes—as the girl least likely to be elected, which indicates to me that someone thinks putting me on the ballot gives her a better chance of winning."

His eyebrows went up and for a minute he looked older than seventeen or eighteen. "Interesting possibility," he said.

"Or they just wanted to make me look like the class idiot, which brings me back to my original argument—the prom makes people do stupid things."

"Why would they pick you, though?" he said.

He'd almost had me until he said that. I felt my eyes narrow into the slits Deidre always said were "deliciously demonic."

"I'm sure you'd get your kicks out of listening to me tell you why I am an aberration around here, but I'm not going to accommodate you. The joke's over, so why don't you just move on to somebody else that needs reminding that she is not, nor will she ever be, cool." I smiled, and then I added what my father always told me to say at the end of a pointless debate. "It was a pleasure exchanging ideas with you."

It wasn't, of course, but it caught him off balance long

enough for me to turn on my heel and make a face-saving exit. Back then, I excelled at those.

I was only ten feet down the hall when he said, "Just so you know, I had nothing to do with that."

"What a prince," I said without turning around.

I made myself wait until I was around the corner before I admitted that beneath my I-showed-him expression, my skin was burning.

*

At least there was only a ninety-minute block to get through before the end of the day, and I spent all of that in History with Matthew and Yuri, working on our Andrew Jackson project. Just as I expected, my two smart-but-underachieving friends hadn't seen the point in doing their share of the research, but that just meant I had something else to focus on besides Hayley and Joanna and their ubiquitous buddy Egan Owens continuing the lunchroom fiasco over in the corner. As usual Mr. Linkhart was oblivious to them — and all *over* us.

"Y'all need to balance your report," he said, hanging his bulging form over our circle of desks.

"Define *balance*," Yuri said.

I tried not to look surprised. Yuri didn't usually come out of his sullen-teenager coma around adults.

"You have all this stuff about President Jackson being a bigot and a racist," Mr. Linkhart said, "but nothing about the things the man accomplished in the White House."

Then he stopped to breathe and swab his sweaty forehead with the yellow-looking handkerchief he kept folded in his back pocket. Two sentences was the most he ever spoke without having to mop and wheeze, which meant he never lectured — probably a good thing — and basically made us read the textbook and do group reports. The title "Honors History" was definitely a joke.

"We'll be all about balance," I assured him.

When he'd huffed and puffed himself away, Matthew shook

his shaggy hair at me. "How come you didn't get into a debate with him?"

"Because it would be a waste of breath and mental energy."

"So why'd you talk to Patrick Sykes?"

I looked at Yuri, surprised for the second time in about two minutes.

"Who's Patrick Sykes?" I said.

"That kid in the hall," Matthew said. "President of the student council? Even I know that."

"I make it my business not to know." I looked at Yuri again. "I didn't waste that much breath on him after you left."

"Whatever." He pulled his camera out of its bag and gazed at the digital screen. Once he started doing that ... conversation over.

I went back to Andrew Jackson.

*

So, yeah, I was able to poke the prom queen thing into the back of my mind until dinnertime that night. Then there was the question of how I was going to present it to my parents.

I would, of course. We talked about everything that concerned me, usually over supper in the dining room. I was sure we were the last family in America who sat down to a meal together every night, without a TV on. None of the three of us were allowed to bring a cell phone to the table, and any calls coming in on the landline went straight to voicemail. I'd had Deidre over once, and she completely lost her appetite because she was thinking about how many text messages she was missing.

The only thing different lately was the extra place set across the table from me. My half sister had moved in with us two weeks before, but so far she hadn't joined us at the dinner table. She was wrestling with depression, my father said, after she figured out that the doctorate she was earning wasn't what she wanted *and* having her fiancé suddenly call off their wedding and move to Japan. Her name was Sunny. As far as I could see, it didn't fit her anymore.

As always, the minute the blessing was said, Dad spread his napkin on his lap and looked at Mom and me like a big, eager, curious kid. "All right, high point of the day. Who wants to go first?"

I turned quickly to my mother and said, "Whose suffering did you relieve today?"

Mom was a nurse practitioner, which meant we heard a lot about snot and vomiting when we got to the low points. If we let her go first on the highs, there wasn't always time later for her to elaborate on people's gross symptoms.

"My high point," Mom said, "was having lunch with Sarah Fitzwilliam."

Could I not *win* today? Mrs. Fitzwilliam was the mother of one of the African American males at Castle Heights High. I knew where this was going.

"Let me guess," I said. "You talked about Graham and me."

"Sarah and I do have other things to discuss," Mom said, "but yes, you two did come up."

She smiled at me, displaying the deepest dimples that have ever dipped into a human being's face. Mom was forty but she looked thirty. A petite, shiny-haired thirty. Too bad I didn't get most of my genes from her.

"Okay, just so you know," I said. "There is no 'Graham and me.'"

"Not even as friends?" she said. "I mean, nobody's saying you need to get engaged."

"You've got my vote on that," Dad said.

He was smiling too, although if he'd ever had dimples, they'd long since elongated into the lines on either side of his mouth. He was forty when I was *born*, so I'd never known him without them, or the crinkles around his intense dark eyes. I did get most of my appearance genes from lanky, bony, very-curly-headed him. It all looked better on his body, especially now that the hair around his temples was tipped in gray.

"Just because somebody's black doesn't mean I have to be friends with them automatically," I said. "Have you ever tried to have a conversation with Graham?"

"I have to admit that I haven't," Mom said.

"That's probably because he always has his lips wrapped around the mouthpiece of his tuba."

My dad laughed.

"I'm serious. He owns two of them. The last time I talked to him, he told me his parents refinanced their house to buy him the second one. He *lives* in the band room, and when he comes out ... Let's just say I can only discuss the glories of the brass section for so long."

I didn't add that Graham once accused me of trying too hard to talk like my brainy parents. They were good friends with the Fitzwilliams, so why go there?

"So your high today obviously wasn't a chat with Graham," Dad said, still chuckling in his husky kind of way. "What was it?"

I had to grope for words. Totally unusual for me.

"I guess ... meeting a new girl. She seems nice, actually. A little naïve ..."

My voice trailed off, because my father was no longer hanging on my every word. He was gazing at the doorway behind me, face beaming the way it did when I brought home my report card.

"Now, there's *my* high," he said. "You coming in to sit with us, baby?"

I twisted around to see Sunny lurking in the arched opening, arms wrapped around her slim self, eyes huge in her face. She had barely come out of her room since she moved in, so I'd only really seen her a couple of times. She seemed a lot smaller here in the cavernous formal dining room than she did when we bumped into each other in the upstairs hall. She took after *her* mother, who was tiny like mine, but I was pretty sure it was the lack of food and sunlight and all human contact that made her seem about to disappear.

"Your hair looks nice," Mom said as Dad practically carried Sunny to the chair across from me.

Okay, there was that. She'd arrived wearing a bandana on her head, and as far as I'd been able to tell she hadn't taken it off. Tonight, though, she'd straightened her hair and had it in a curvy bob that must have taken her hours to do. I'd given all of that up and let mine be its mini-Afro self. I was never going to look like Halle Berry anyway.

"It is so good to see you up and around, baby," Dad said to her.

"Let me pop another potato in the microwave," Mom said, already halfway out of her chair.

Sunny shook her head. "This is fine. I'm not that hungry."

"Well, you're here, and we're good with that," Dad said. "Ty, pass your sister the salad."

It still seemed weird, having him call her my "sister." She was ten years older than me and I'd seen her, like, twice a year the whole time I was growing up, because she'd always lived in California with her mother and we were East Coasters. She'd never done the "let's paint our toenails and I'll tell you all about boys" thing, and I was *more* than good with *that*.

"We were just talking about our high points of the day," Dad said.

Sunny gave him a wan smile. "You still do that, huh? I guess mine is that I'm vertical."

"It's a start," Mom said.

Sunny prodded at a carrot curl with her fork and Dad nodded at her for no apparent reason. One thing *was* apparent: we weren't going to be talking about our lows. So much for getting their opinion on the prom queen thing. It would seem sort of lame anyway, compared to Sunny's entire life falling apart. Dad skipped to what was usually the final topic of a meal.

"So what's the most challenging thing you're going to face tomorrow?" he said. "Ty?"

"Challenging?" I said. "At Castle Heights High School?"

"Here it comes," Mom said, dimples fully operational. "There *are* no challenges there, right?"

"Not without a debate team—an orchestra—an AP calculus class. My college applications are going to look anorexic."

Dad twinkled his eyes at Sunny. "We're headed into the 'why can't I go to private school' argument," he said. "You want to take it from here?"

"I went through it enough times with you, didn't I?" Sunny

said. Although she attempted another smile, her voice was flat, like every word was costing her energy. "I'd just give it up, Tyler. Because you'll never convince him that a good education isn't more about what you do than what's done *for* you—"

"And that I can make more of a difference in a community with needs than I can in one that needs nothing."

"That's it," she said. "Word for word."

I looked at my father. "You haven't changed your argument in a decade? Dad, that is sad."

"The truth doesn't change. Now, what about your campaign for more AP classes?"

"I'm presenting it at the student council meeting tomorrow," I said. "I'm going to try to get student signatures on a petition—"

I stopped. Student council. Wonderful. Exquisite. All those kids I was hoping to get on board for more Advanced Placement classes were the same ones who'd nominated me for prom queen. The heat I thought had burned itself out returned to my neck. It was all I could do not to fan myself with the tablecloth.

My father, in the meantime, had already moved back to Sunny.

"How 'bout you, baby?" he was saying. "What's your challenge for tomorrow?"

How about *Get dressed*?

"I'm going to try to find a job," Sunny said. "I need to save some money while I try to figure out what to do with the rest of my life."

If Dad were prone to squealing, I think he would have done it then. As it was, he squeezed Sunny's hand and looked at her like she'd just announced she was running for president.

"You want me to take you to the university?" he said. "I can introduce you—"

"No, thanks," Sunny said. "I don't want you to arrange anything for me."

Okay, so she didn't know him as well as I did. My father was an administrator at the university in Albany, but he always made it clear to me that I was going to have to make my own mark on the world just the way he had to. I felt a little smug.

"It isn't 'arranging' if I just talk to a few people," Dad said.

Okay, so much for smug.

But Sunny shook her head and put down the fork that, as far as I could tell, she hadn't really used. "I'm not even sure I want to teach on the college level anymore, I told you that. It just seems pointless to me—" She pressed her hands on the edge of the table and pushed her chair back. "You know what—I'm exhausted. Good dinner, Rowena," she said to Mom. "But I need to lie down."

"You go ahead, baby," Dad said.

Mom shot him a look and he shot one back, not something I saw often between the Couple of the Century. Seriously—I almost never saw my parents disagree over anything. As Sunny left the table, they were still bulleting each other with their eyes, and I felt resentment nettling at the back of my neck.

"I've got homework," I said. "Excuse me?"

Nobody objected when I slipped out of the dining room.

*

I retreated upstairs to the window seat in my bedroom. It was the only thing I really liked about the hundred-year-old house my parents bought when we moved from Long Island to Castle Heights. Dad always told people it had "character." It was a character all right—with a furnace that groaned like a dying elephant and pipes that complained every time anybody flushed a toilet and doors that swelled and shrank with the weather, so that in summer I could barely close mine and in winter it rattled with every gust of wind. I guess if you were the romantic, poetic type it would be a cool place to live. I was neither.

But the wide seat, padded by Mom and me in black-and-white stripes, curved into the bay window in my room and made a great place to sit and analyze. I conquered geometry on that seat. Analyzed Emily Dickinson and decided she was agoraphobic. Figured out what I believed about God, and what I didn't. Tonight, I was going to sort through the prom queen joke and put it to an end. Period. How "challenging" could it be, considering who I was dealing with?

I arranged the black plaid, the white solid, and the black-and-white-striped pillows behind me on one end of the seat and tossed the pink one onto the floor. Mom had thrown that in to be cute. I kind of loved that about her—the way she knew just when to push my buttons so, as she put it, I didn't take myself too seriously. The pink pillow. The amusing notes in my lunch bag. The random suggestion that I learn to make an angel food cake or try on a pair of stilettos. It worked. My IQ may have been the only thing I had going for me, but because of her, I didn't *really* think it made me all that.

I squirmed against the pillow pile. I never thought it made me a laughingstock either, until today. What was with all the blushing and feeling like a pariah all of a sudden? I hadn't felt that here since the first day when I saw how the school was structured and how I *wasn't* going to find a place in it, so why try?

I might have made an attempt in a public school in Albany, if my parents had chosen to live there, which would have made more sense than Dad's thirty-minute commute every day. But he and Mom wanted a small community, and they wanted to live close to Dad's cousin, Lana Ellis, and her kids, just in case they needed help. Which they never did. And if Candace and Kenny ever did want for anything, they sure wouldn't come to me. Even at Christmas they acted like I was something out of the Ripley's Believe It or Not Museum, because I got tickets to hear the New York Philharmonic and thought it was the best gift ever. Kenny actually wanted to know if Phil Harmonic was an old Motown singer.

So no, I didn't fit in here and it had never mattered before today. It still didn't. It just mattered that it mattered. And that had to stop.

I pulled a legal pad and a sharpened pencil out from under the seat cushion and made two columns. I headed one "what bothers me" and the other one "why it shouldn't." I didn't get further than *people actually organized my humiliation* when my cell phone rang. It was Deidre.

"What are you doing?" she said.

It was what she always said instead of "hi," but I covered the pad as if she could *see* what I was doing. Fortunately she didn't wait for an answer.

"Get on your computer," she said.

"Why?" I said.

"Because you need to see something. Go to Facebook."

Between the verve in her usually I-could-care-less voice and the fact that she knew I felt the same way about Facebook as I did about poison ivy, I was immediately suspicious.

"Not until you tell me why," I said.

Deidre sighed through the phone as only the people in her family can sigh. Her mother could blow out an entire cake full of birthday candles with one.

"Okay—the prom committee has its own Facebook page."

"And I care about this because ..."

"Because right now it's all about you, and you need to get on there and see what you're dealing with."

"I'm *not* dealing with it," I said.

"Even if they're saying—"

"I don't *care* what they're saying."

"Well, whatever," Deidre said. "If it was me, I'd want to know."

"Why?" I said.

"So I could come back at them." She cackled. "I want to see you shut them down. I mean, seriously, they've got absolutely no game when it comes to debating you. Don't you want to watch them fall all over themselves?"

"Not especially," I said. What I really wanted was for the whole thing to die. At that moment I decided *that* was my strategy: to let "Tyler Bonning for Prom Queen" shrivel up from neglect. It might be my most challenging "challenge" yet: to just keep my mouth shut.

But that was what I was going to do.

CHAPTER THREE

The student council meeting was during third block, which meant I had to take my pass to leave class to my English teacher, Ms. Dalloway. She seemed to like me well enough, because I was the only high school student she'd ever had who knew that her name was the same as a character in a novel by Virginia Woolf. Of course, she liked me in the same weary way she did everything else, from calling the roll to, at the moment, checking French Girl into our class. When I walked up, Ms. Dalloway was looking at the form like she was being asked to push toothpaste back into a tube.

"Oh, hi," I said to French Girl. "Are you in here now?"

She nodded her head of massive curls. "They put me in a regular class but the teacher said it would be more challenging for me in here."

That seemed to be everybody's favorite word lately. Ms. Dalloway's Junior Honors English was definitely more demanding than Honors History, mostly because she gave pop quizzes and made us write critical essays. The Ruling Class was always complaining about those like they were lethal injections.

"Do you pronounce this *Valerie*?" Ms. Dalloway said. "Even though it's spelled V-a-l-l-e-r-i?"

"Yes, ma'am," French Girl said. "My mother's creative."

"I bet you can never find it on a keychain."

"That's okay. I don't drive anyway."

"Neither do I," I said. "We might be the only two people in the junior class who don't."

"Here you go." Ms. Dalloway waved the form in Valleri's direction. "Sit wherever you can find a seat."

Yeah, making a seating chart was *way* too much of an effort.

"Where do you sit?" Valleri said.

"Me?" I said.

"Yeah."

I was oddly stunned. "Uh, third row over—there's actually an empty seat behind me. But I'm not in here today. I'm going to a student council meeting." I rolled my eyes. "I think the only reason anybody's in it is so they can get out of their third-block class every other week. No offense, Ms. Dalloway."

She just grunted at me. It must also be too much trouble to get offended.

"I have to take this form back to the office," Valleri said to her.

"Do it," Ms. D said.

"I'll walk with you," I said.

Valleri smiled, the way I guess we did back in kindergarten when somebody said, "Play with me on the playground." There was something so innocent about her. It was sad to think what was going to happen to that after a week here.

"So—are you in it so you can get out of class?" she said as we headed toward the office, which was just down the hall from the library, where the council met.

"What? Student council? No. I'm just making a presentation. It is so not my thing."

"Why not?"

"Because it's lame, in my opinion. As far as I can tell they do things like plan the best ways to make an idiot out of yourself during homecoming week. Which is too bad, because the kind of personal power those kids have? They could do a lot if they gave a flip about anything significant."

"So you're saying it *could* be effective if there was a good enough cause," Valleri said.

I stopped in front of the trophy case and gave her a closer look. Had she actually just used the word *effective* in a sentence?

"Yeah," I said.

She pointed to the folder in my hand. "Then maybe *your* cause will be the one."

"Maybe," I said.

She hitched her shoulders and smiled and bounced her curls into the office. What a strange child. Talked like an adult and thought like a ten-year-old who didn't know yet that the world wasn't fair.

She kind of made me feel like I might be the one who had it wrong.

A feeling which disappeared the minute I walked into the library and half the people at the round tables turned to the other half and whispered like the show was about to begin. Mr. Linkhart, the advisor, looked at me blankly as I handed him my pass.

"You're not on the council," he said.

"No, she's on the agenda."

Patrick—that was what Matthew said his name was, right?—slid a piece of paper across Mr. Linkhart's table and smiled up at me. He must grin all the time, seeing how the last time we'd talked I insulted him right to his face. Either that, or he didn't know I insulted him. There was always that possibility.

"Why don't we have her go first so she can get back to class?" Mr. Linkhart said, crumpling his eyebrows over the agenda.

I didn't tell him I'd be staying to pass around a petition after my presentation. He was already going for a brown paper towel, his backup whenever the hanky lost its ability to absorb.

Patrick banged a gavel on the table and most people got themselves to order. Especially the girls. You'd have thought he was Robert Pattinson the way they looked up at him. I resisted the urge to roll my eyes.

"We're going to start with new business today," he said.

A hand shot up. Alyssa Hampton.

"Lyss?" he said.

"Is the prom committee still going to make its report?"

Her eyes glanced over me, leaving me feeling like I'd just been dusted with eye shadow.

"Yeah," he said. "We'll cover everything after Tyler speaks."

The whole room giggled-snickered-whispered. I fought off the burn. This was about AP, not the stupid prom. I had to stay focused on that.

"Go for it," Patrick said to me.

Taking in my perfected prespeech confident breath, I went to the podium, folder in hand, and made eye contact with my audience. Few of them could look back. The ones who did appeared to be about to cry, they were trying so hard not to laugh. *Give it a minute, Tyler,* I told myself. *They'll get that this is serious.*

"You may not be aware of it," I said, "because I wasn't until I did the research, but only thirty percent of high school students take any Advanced Placement courses at all. And yet major studies indicate that good grades on AP tests significantly increase the chances of earning college degrees. In today's economy, in order to compete for the shrinking number of good jobs, we need to have those degrees."

I nodded at them, prompting them to nod with me. Some *were* actually nodding—off to sleep. Others' eyes were turning to glass. That was okay. I hadn't gotten to my punch yet.

"Statistics like these have led many public schools in disadvantaged neighborhoods to look for ways to increase the number of AP classes they offer. *Disadvantaged* neighborhoods," I said, eyebrows reaching for my hairline. "Alyssa, Hayley, Egan—I'm sure you'll agree that you are not *disadvantaged.*"

"Ya think?" Alyssa said.

She curled her lip as if I'd just suggested she had an average wardrobe. That was exactly the reaction I was going for. Encouraged, I moved on.

"And yet we have only four—*four*—AP classes in our current curriculum. The best schools in this country have as many as sixteen."

I waited for that to sink in. A few more eyelids slammed shut.

"I propose that we, the voice of Castle Heights High School, speak out for enough Advanced Placement courses here to give us the same college-graduation rates enjoyed by students from the country's wealthiest private schools and most selective public schools."

Egan raised his hand. He was a junior who painted his face in Castle Heights' purple and white for basketball games and had run the homecoming queen thing two years in a row. I always imagined him on the cover of GQ someday. Either that or selling cars on TV.

"I'm already going to SUNY in Albany. Why do I need to bust my tail in high school when I'm, like, already accepted?"

"You've been accepted as a junior?" I said.

"No." He shrugged and grinned at Joanna and Hayley, who were, of course, on either side of him. "But I know people."

"You wouldn't rather have a chance at Harvard or Yale or Princeton?" I said.

"Do they have cute guys there?" Hayley said.

Alyssa leaned across the table. "They have *rich* guys there."

"Well, there you go," I said dryly.

"You need to wrap this up," Mr. Linkhart said.

Wrap it up? I'd barely gotten started.

I pressed my hands into the podium. "All I'm saying is that we can be more than we are. We don't have to settle for a mediocre education when we could have a great one—"

"Are you implying that the schooling you're getting here is 'mediocre'?" Mr. Linkhart stood up, simultaneously going after his brow with the already soaking-wet paper towel. "Because if you are, I take exception to that."

A couple of the people who had dozed off woke up as other people poked them and nodded their heads toward Mr. Linkhart and me. I had to take advantage of that.

"What if you had a more challenging class to teach?" I said to him. "What if your students were actually motivated because they were earning college credit for their work?" I craned my neck toward him. "Wouldn't you enjoy that?"

He laughed—but it didn't sound like he was relishing the prospect. He was laughing at *me*.

"Little darlin'," he said, "where do you think you're gon' get all these teachers? Because if we add Advanced Placement courses, we have to subtract some of the regular classes that most of the students here need to take."

"So what you're saying is that the students here aren't smart enough for college." I cast my gaze around the library, eyes deliberately wide. But my "do you *believe* what he's saying about you?" was met with glazed-over stares. It was like talking to a box of Krispy Kreme donuts.

"You're bordering on insubordinate," Mr. Linkhart said. "I think that's enough for this item on the agenda."

"I was just expressing my—"

"Let's move on to other business, Patrick."

Alyssa's hand went straight up, but I turned to Patrick too. "I still need to pass around the petition."

"You don't know when to stop, do you?" Mr. Linkhart said.

He wheezed, reminiscent of the radiators in my house, and waved me on as he groaned into his chair. I took the petition and a pen to the first table, mind reeling. If this had been a discussion between my dad and me, Dad would be salivating at this point—not shutting me down. No wonder these kids were so brain-dead.

"All you have to do," I said, "is sign this if you think you deserve the opportunity to pursue a higher level of education and, subsequently, a better quality of life."

"Are you speaking English?" somebody said.

I said, "My point exactly."

Obviously nobody got it. I sat down in the back and waited. It should take about fifteen seconds for the petition to go around the room—since nobody was even going to look at it, much less sign it—and then I could get out of here.

"Can we please talk about the prom now?" Alyssa said.

Patrick's brown eyes danced. "Are you going to keep bugging me until we do?"

"Yes," she said — apparently unimpressed with the dancing eyes.

"Okay. Knock yourself out."

Patrick leaned against the podium, and Alyssa stood up. I guess. She was one of those miniature girls who could barely see over the steering wheel of her Audi and yet ran her posse of friends like a mafioso. She tossed back her mane of every-shade-of-blonde hair and leveled green eyes at her audience, who had obviously been saving their stash of attention for her. And then she nodded at Egan and said, "Okay. Go for it."

Egan stood up next to her, every spike of his bleached-out hair in place. "First of all, I just want to say that as chairman of the prom committee, I have tried to get the prom moved to someplace cool, but Mr. Baumgarten is still being a — still says no, and now it's too late to reserve a hotel or something anyway."

The juniors and seniors gave a unanimous moan. The sophomores and freshmen went back to sleep, since this had nothing to do with them. It had nothing to do with anybody, as far as I was concerned.

"May I remind you again," Mr. Linkhart said, breathlessly, "that you are lucky to even have a prom after what happened two years ago."

"True," Patrick said. "We didn't have one last year."

"What happened two years ago?" I said.

They all looked at me as if they'd forgotten who I was already. I hadn't actually meant to speak, but I hated to see an obvious question go unasked.

"It was stupid," Alyssa said, flicking her hand at me.

"They had the prom at Birch Hill," Patrick said, "and some parents hired a bus for a bunch of kids to get out there."

"A *nice* bus," Egan put in. "Not a school bus. I actually went with a junior — she's graduated now — "

"Whatever," Alyssa said. "Everybody knows the story — "

"Some kids sneaked alcohol onto the bus," Patrick said to me, "and they got to the prom totally plastered."

"And nearly destroyed two restrooms," Mr. Linkhart said. "Which is why we are no longer welcome at Birch Hill."

"It was kind of cool how they snuck the booze on, though." Egan focused on his hands, held in front of him. "They got these, like, special flip-flops that you can pour liquid into. I mean, I wasn't in on it, but, dude, nobody knew."

"Until Doug Letterman fell off the bus," Alyssa said. "What a moron."

"So where do you get something like that?" a wide-awake freshman said. They were, in fact, all wide awake at that point.

"Moving on," Patrick said to Egan.

"Okay, the deal is we have to have the prom here at the school. Sorry."

"Which will mean a lower ticket price," Mr. Linkhart said.

Alyssa rolled her eyes at the entire council.

"Okay, I don't mean to be disrespectful, Mr. Linkhart," Hayley Barr said. She glanced at me like I was the poster child for disrespect to teachers. "But people *expect* to spend a lot of money on prom. I mean, right?"

She swiveled in her seat for the reaction, ponytail swinging. Everybody nodded — everybody, including the underclassmen. What, had they already set up prom accounts for their junior year?

"Oh, yeah," Egan said. "The tickets are, like, nothin'. You've got the limo, corsage for your date, the tux rental, dinner, stuff for the after-party — "

"The girls spend more, I bet," Alyssa said. She enumerated on her manicured fingers. "The dress — which, if you're going to get anything decent, is going to run you at least five hundred — "

"Are you serious?" I said. "Five hundred dollars for a dress you're going to wear once? That's like a hundred dollars an hour!"

As soon as I said it, I wanted to rip my vocal cords out. Alyssa, Egan, Hayley, Joanna — all of them and more honed in like cats when you bring in the Meow Mix. Every eye glittered.

"What do you plan to spend on *your* dress?" Alyssa said. "You realize you're going to be standing in front of everybody there when they announce — "

"You have a spreadsheet for your expenses, right, Tyler?" Patrick said. "I'm gonna get with you later and see how that works." With another flash of the grin, he turned to Egan. "What else you got, dude? We're burnin' daylight."

I started to label Patrick Sykes a jackal in my mind, until it dawned on me that he had just deflected any mention of me and the prom queen thing. And he'd done it on purpose. Maybe I'd thank him later. Or maybe I'd just grab my petition and get out of here whether it was signed or not. Or maybe I'd tear it up and get back to campaigning for my parents to please, please send me to private school. In Siberia.

While Egan went on about whether people were allowed to bring dates from other schools, I stretched my neck to see where the petition was. I expected to find it at the last table, discarded by the sophomore who had been jabbing her thumbs at her phone ever since the meeting started. But it seemed to have gotten hung up at the RC's table, where a kid they called YouTube was hunkered over, writing, while Joanna whispered in his ear. I just hoped he didn't drool on the paper.

With that in mind, I skirted the tables and crouched at the back edge of theirs.

"I'll go ahead and take that," I whispered.

Joanna jumped and pressed her hand to her lips. She was going to come out of that with a palm full of lip gloss.

Below her at the table, Hayley snatched the petition from YouTube and stuck it under a bunch of other papers.

"I wasn't done!" YouTube said.

"How long does it take to sign your name?" I said. I swallowed back, *Or don't you know how to spell it yet?*

"Shut up!" Joanna hissed at YouTube.

She snatched up the paper and thrust it at me. She couldn't look at me, but YouTube leered openly.

I gave him a cold look and made it out the door and into the hall before I said, out loud, "All of those people are sharing a brain. All of them."

The paper was wrinkled and smeared, and I smoothed it

against the wall so I could slide it back into its folder. The amount of ink on it surprised me—until I looked closer.

It wasn't my petition, but a different sheet of paper. And the writing wasn't signatures. Not unless *She's our token black chick* was somebody's name. *We need somebody butt-ugly to make everybody else look good*, someone else had written. What on *earth*?

I searched the sheet. At the top, someone had written WHY TYLER BONNING SHOULD RUN FOR PROM QUEEN.

I had to believe they'd accidentally given me the wrong paper, because somehow everyone had gotten the message that they were supposed to be as hilarious as possible with their entries.

Because she can't run for king.

She'll give a long acceptance speech and everybody will be able to sneak out and go party.

About halfway down, funny turned to crude. By the end—I didn't even *get* to the end before I crumpled it into a small ball and squeezed it until my fingers hurt. I'd been wrong: they weren't just sharing a brain; they were sharing a purpose, and that, apparently, was to make me look like a complete idiot.

But why? What had I ever done to any of them?

It was a question I wasn't sure even I could figure out an answer for. I didn't even want to. I just wanted to go somewhere and cry. Really cry. And I hadn't done that since ... Since I couldn't remember.

It had been so long I didn't know how to stop it. I blinked and swallowed my way back to Ms. Dalloway's classroom, but I still felt like I was going to lose it any second. I stood in the doorway until she looked up at me.

"Problem?" she said.

"Restroom?" I said.

She started to say something, but I took off before she could. I barely made it to a sink when the tears erupted. The thing about waiting so long to cry? It hurts a lot more when you finally do. Every sob ripped through my chest and burned up my throat and shook my shoulders until they ached. I probably didn't notice the warm hand on my back until it had been there awhile.

"You okay?" someone said.

I raised my head and looked in the mirror at Valleri. Her blue eyes were swimming.

"No," I said. "I'm a mess. I need to blow my nose."

She tore off a paper towel and handed it to me.

"I feel like Mr. Linkhart," I said.

"Is he that teacher that's always sweating?"

"Yeah." I honked.

"There's something wrong with that poor man."

"There's something wrong with me too," I said. "It's called idiocy."

"What happened?"

I honked into the paper towel again. "I let those jackals get to me."

"What's a jackal?"

"It's a wild dog that runs in packs and devours what's left over after the lions eat."

"Oh. Then I know exactly who you mean."

She waited while I splashed my face with cold water, and then handed me another paper towel.

"I bet you never had to put up with people like that when you were homeschooled," I said. "Matter of fact, I think I'm going to opt for that myself."

Valleri shook the curls. "There are jackals everywhere, trust me. We have a lot more in common than you think."

"You and me?" I pulled in my chin. "It isn't the niceness factor, that's for sure."

"You're the only person who's *been* nice to me since I got here."

"Then this place is worse than I thought," I said, "because that is not an adjective most people would apply to me."

My mouth dropped open as she hiked herself up onto the next sink and swung her legs.

"That's because most people think of 'nice' as, like, sickening sweet," she said. "That kind of 'nice' turns around and cuts you down behind your back."

"You can definitely count on me to cut you down to your

face if I think you need cutting, only—" My eyes filled up again. "I don't really do that, either. I've hardly even talked to any of these people in the last year and a half. I don't even know them."

"Me neither," she said. "So, see, we have that in common too."

"You've only been here three days."

"That's long enough to know I *don't* have anything in common with *them*."

I had to nod. "Yeah, I figured that out pretty early on too. Which is why I don't see why they can't just leave me alone." I gazed miserably into the mirror at my swollen eyes. "I just figured it out: I haven't cried since September 11, 2001. That's why I can't believe I let this get to me—I mean, this is not like an attack on the World Trade Center."

"It's an attack on you, though."

"I haven't even told you what they did."

She shook her head. The curls, I was discovering, had a language of their own. "You don't have to," she said. "But maybe we can figure out—"

"Okay—*what* is going on?"

We both turned to the doorway, where Deidre was storming through. She tossed her vintage bag into the third sink and put her hands on her hips. Her wrists jangled with noisy bracelets.

"Yuri texted me that you came back from the council meeting upset and I'm like, 'Tyler doesn't *get* upset.' So I texted him back and he texted *me* and said 'girls' bathroom.' Like I'm supposed to know what that means." She glanced at Valleri. "Hi, by the way."

"Hi."

"So what went down?"

"Just—more harassment," I said.

"About the stupid prom queen thing?"

"Yeah."

I choked back more tears. Valleri put her hand on my arm.

"And you're *crying* about it?" Deidre said. "This is not the Tyler Bonning I know."

I didn't answer. I wasn't the Tyler Bonning I knew, either.

The bell rang, and Valleri squeezed my arm.

"I'm going to go back to class and get my stuff," she said. "You okay?"

"Yeah, thanks," I said.

She hung on for a second longer. "I'm going to pray for you," she said.

When she was gone, Deidre stared at me. "Did she just say she was going to pray for you?"

"That's what I heard."

"Who says that? They are going to eat her alive here—which is so not my problem. *You* are my problem."

"I'm not your—"

"When I come in here and find you crying in the sink because a bunch of brain-free posers played some game with you, *that's* a problem." She hoisted the bag onto her shoulder like we were about to storm the castle. "All right, I'm sorry I even brought up the Facebook thing last night. You're right—we have to just pretend this whole thing isn't happening. So—tomorrow, half day, we're going to lunch. Far away from here, where we can get your mind off all this—garbage. My treat, so don't eat breakfast. Are we clear?"

"Sure," I said.

But nothing was clear to me right now. Nothing at all.

CHAPTER FOUR

Usually on the half days we had so that teachers could do whatever it was they did when we weren't there, I hung out in the chemistry room and helped Mr. Zabaski. But the next day I was happy about the prospect of getting far, far away from Castle Heights High when the bell rang at eleven thirty. The Fringe was waiting for me out in the student parking lot, and Matthew was tossing his car keys from one hand to the other.

"*You're* driving?" I said. "Why can't we take Deidre's car?"

"Because it's in the shop," Deidre said. "The brakes are shot."

"I still think that's safer than riding with Matthew."

"Man, that's harsh," Matthew said.

"No," I said, "that's the truth. How many tickets have you had?"

"Technically, none. On my record, anyway."

"You got stopped twice first semester alone. What happened to those?"

"My mom was dating a cop then. He made them go away." Matthew shrugged his hulking shoulders. "Then *he* went away, so now I have to be a law-abiding citizen."

"That bites," Yuri said.

"Tell me about it."

Deidre folded her arms. "Are we actually going to get in the vehicle, or are we just going to stand here and review your rap sheet?"

Matthew creaked the back door of his ancient Mercedes open and disappeared inside from the waist up. Various articles of clothing, a handful of CDs, and a liter bottle of Mountain Dew were tossed onto the shelf under the back window.

"So it's true," Deidre said. "You do live in your car."

"How are you going to see behind you with all that stuff in the window?" I said.

Matthew emerged from the backseat. "Am I supposed to see behind me?"

"Are you *serious*?"

"No." He jerked his shaggy head and climbed into the driver's seat.

"Tell me again why we're doing this?" I said to Deidre as I joined her in the back.

"Culinary therapy," she said.

"Where are we eating?"

"Five Guys. I love their Fat Burgers."

"I don't think that qualifies as culinary."

"Define *culinary*," Yuri said from the front seat.

"Food that only contains ingredients I can pronounce," I said.

Yuri said something—at least his mouth was moving—but I couldn't hear him over the scream of the car's engine as Matthew revved it into the red zone on the tachometer, with the car, fortunately, still in park.

"Do you have to do that?" Deidre shouted to him.

"Gotta blow the carbon out. It's old."

"What, the carbon or the car?"

"You. You sound like my grandmother back there."

"You're going to blow more than carbon—"

I didn't hear the rest of what Deidre said, because Matthew lurched the Mercedes into gear and peeled out of the parking space. I could actually smell rubber burning.

"This is a bad idea," I said. "Let me out."

He may have ignored me, or he actually may not have heard me over the squeal of brakes as, in a horrible slo-mo moment, a red Jeep turned into the oncoming lane, which Matthew was taking up half of at warp speed. I hadn't even had a chance to buckle my seat belt yet, and I stuck my arms out to keep from colliding with the back of Matthew's seat. As the Mercedes rocked to a violent stop, I was flung backward into my own seat so hard my teeth clacked together. The bottle of Mountain Dew flew between Deidre and me and landed on the console.

The Jeep was now almost sideways, its driver's side fender about a half inch from the Mercedes' left headlight. If the driver hadn't been paying attention, we'd probably have been picking glass shards out of Matthew's face just about then.

"That's it," I said. I fumbled with the handle and got the door open.

"What are you doing?" Matthew said.

"Making sure I live to see graduation," I said.

I got out and tried to pull my bag with me, but it caught on the same handle I'd just wrestled with. Gritting my teeth, I yanked it loose, and both bag and I fell sideways, right into somebody's arms.

"You okay?" the person said.

I looked up and groaned. It was Patrick Sykes.

"Seriously—are you hurt?"

"No," I said, and to prove it I wrenched myself away from him and dumped my bag onto the parking lot. Facedown, of course.

I didn't crouch down to retrieve it when he did. I'd seen enough cheesy movies where two people who couldn't stand each other went for the same dropped book, handbag, contact lens, you name it, and came up miraculously in love. That definitely wasn't happening here.

While Patrick was sticking all my stuff back into my bag, Matthew poked his head out the car window.

"Sorry," he said

"That's it?" I said. "'Sorry?' I was almost decapitated by a liter of Mountain Dew, Matthew. Not to mention the fact that you could have totaled his Jeep." I looked at the top of Patrick's head. "What are we talking—twenty, thirty thousand dollars?"

Patrick stood up and handed me my bag. Papers reached from every pocket like they were begging me to spare them the shame.

"We're good, man," he said to Matthew. "We better move—we're blocking traffic."

Horns had started to blow from all directions. One kid had his head sticking out of his sunroof, yelling obscenities.

Matthew nodded. "You getting in, Tyler?"

"You're kidding, right? No, I am not getting in."

I slammed the door, and Deidre immediately lowered the window.

"You're not coming?"

"You *are*? Do you have a death wish?"

About six more horns blared, and Patrick slapped his hand twice on the top of Matthew's car.

"You're good to go," he said.

Matthew nodded again, gave me one last I-don't-get-you look, and swerved around Patrick's Jeep and out of the parking lot. Deidre was mouthing something out the back window and gesticulating at me. She could do that even better than she could sigh.

"Can I give you a ride someplace?"

I looked at Patrick, who was backing toward his Jeep amid the jeers from all the drivers who had to swerve to avoid smacking into it.

"No," I said.

"You sure? You were headed somewhere."

"Not anymore. But thanks."

He grinned at me. "I'm a better driver than he is."

"Who isn't?" I said. "I'm good, really."

"Okay, well—"

"You better move that thing before somebody succumbs to road rage."

His grin widened. "Can you say that again?"

"Why?"

"Because I like the way you talk."

"Sykes!" somebody yelled from a pickup truck. "What the—"

"Going," Patrick said. "Later, Tyler."

I stepped up onto the curb and watched him maneuver his

car through the motor mob like a sensible human being. He'd actually been pretty decent about the whole thing. But then, he was alone. I had to wonder how he would have acted if he'd had somebody else from the Ruling Class with him.

No, I told myself, I didn't have to wonder that. It wasn't worth my time. I had better things to do. Such as …

Yeah. Such as what to do now that my ride had taken off and I basically didn't have a plan for the afternoon. I could just walk home and get some studying done—except that Sunny was there, and I wasn't up to trying to have a conversation with her. Now that she was emerging from her room more, her being at our house gave new meaning to the word "awkward."

Awkward wasn't what I was feeling at the moment. What I was feeling was lonely, and I couldn't ever remember feeling quite that way in my whole life.

"Hey, Tyler."

I did some kind of spasm thing and turned around to see my cousin Candace standing there. She had her head tilted, looking at me in a way that made me want to check my nose for a booger.

"Something wrong?" I said.

"No. I just don't usually see you standin' there not doin' nothin'."

There was so much wrong with that sentence I didn't even know where to start, so I didn't. Candace shrugged bony shoulders, straining at the knit of a red sweater that looked several sizes too small for her. But, then, so did the black houndstooth microskirt and the black leggings that hit her at her skinny midcalves. If I wasn't mistaken, the outfit was *meant* to look like it belonged to somebody three sizes smaller. Candace saw herself as quite the fashionista. She had perfect skin the color of a latte, and there wasn't an ounce of fat anywhere on her, so she actually could've been a model. Except for the hair. It never looked anything but completely out of control.

"So what are you doin'?" she said.

"Uh, nothing," I said.

"No way."

"What are *you* doing?"

"I'm taking the bus to the mall." Her face brightened. "You want to come with?"

I would rather be taken out and beaten, actually. But she suddenly looked so hopeful, and it came to me that she was probably as lonely as I was. It *would* make my father happy, and it never hurt to score points there ...

Okay, Valleri would definitely not think that was "nice." You can't say I didn't warn you.

"Sure," I said.

"Awesome!" She looped her arm through mine — a move I didn't anticipate, or I would have found a way to avoid it, and pulled me toward the street. "We have to hurry. The bus'll be here in — now!"

Still hanging onto my arm, she broke into a long-legged run across the schoolyard, and I really had no choice but to keep up. We clamored on board just as the driver was closing the doors. Candace didn't stop laughing for the next two miles.

I had to admit, I wished anything was that funny to me.

*

Of course, by the time we had done two stores in the mall in East Greenbush, I was wishing I'd opted for loneliness. Candace never stopped talking, and yet she never seemed to say anything. I didn't have to say anything beyond, "Really?" and "No kidding?" But that didn't make up for the twenty minutes I spent at the earring display in rue21 while she agonized over whether to go for the gaudy green rhinestones or the gaudy blue rhinestones.

"Get them both," I said when I was ready to flush both her and the jewelry down the nearest john.

Her eyes widened to the size of Frisbees. "I can't afford both. You know what?"

"What?" Pray tell.

"I could get the same thing cheaper at Claire's!"

"Why don't you yell that a little louder?" I said between my teeth.

"Huh?"

"Never mind," I said, and nudged her toward the door.

We made three more stops at stores she couldn't afford before we at last reached Claire's, at which point I was ready to climb back into a car with Matthew.

"I need to make a phone call," I said. "I'll wait for you out here."

"I could be in there a while," she said.

"No kidding?" I said.

She scampered into Claire's like a squirrel in search of the perfect rhinestone nut. I sank onto a bench and thought how it was truly incredible that I was related to this person.

Just so I wouldn't be lying to her, I called my dad's cell phone and left a message to let him know where I was. I didn't mention that this little shopping trip should fill my quota of extended family time for pretty much the rest of my natural life.

I then set myself to the task of repacking my bag, which still bore the mark of Patrick's organizational skills. When I was done, it seemed to me that Candace should have made a decision by now. The Louisiana Purchase didn't take this long. One thing was for sure: I was *not* going in there.

I did look from the bench, though, hoping to see her standing at the cash register. But she was still over in a corner, by the window, holding up two pairs of dripping-glitter earrings that I could tell were identical even from where I was sitting. It was all I could do not to yell, "Pick one already!"

Until I saw her drop both of them into her purse.

I squeezed my eyes shut and opened them again. I did not just see that—did I?

I did, because Candace looked over her shoulder and scooped a matching necklace into the bag too. Looking guiltier than anybody on death row, she stitched her way among the displays and headed for the opening out into the mall. I met her at the hair bows and put my lips next to her ear.

"Put them back, Candace," I whispered.

"What?"

"The jewelry. Put it back."

"I don't— "

"Yes, you do." I thrust my hand into her purse and hit cold metal with my fingers. Grasping frantically, I pulled out both sets of earrings and dropped them among the hair bows while I fished for the necklace with my other hand. Candace stood there like she'd fallen into a coma as I yanked it out and threw it into the bow bin with the earrings. She didn't come to life until I dragged her out into the mall. It was, of course, her mouth that regained consciousness first.

"Are you gonna tell on me?" she basically shrieked at me. "'Cause I ain't never done nothin' like that before—I swear—and I'll never do it again. Just don't tell Mama."

"I think 'Mama' is the least of your worries right now," said a deep voice behind us. "Stop right there, ladies."

Candace gasped and whirled around. I didn't have to. I already knew it was probably the biggest security guard in the state of New York.

CHAPTER FIVE

I was wrong. He was the biggest mall cop in the northeastern United *States*. Surely this job was only temporary until he got his big break in the WWE.

That's what I *would* have thought if my brain hadn't been frozen in fear. As I looked up into his suspicious face, anxiety surged through every vein. The more his eyes twitched, the more certain I was that I would die within moments.

"Were you just in Claire's?" he said. His voice had gone even deeper.

Candace shook her head, and I shook *her*, by the arm.

"Yes, we were, Officer," I said.

Candace whimpered.

"Did you take anything without paying for it?"

"Did we take anything out of the store?" I said. "No, sir."

His eyes narrowed at Candace, who was now weeping as if he'd slid bamboo shoots under her fingernails. "How about you?" he said. "Did you take anything out of Claire's without paying for it?"

"No!" she cried. "I put it all back!"

I closed my eyes and wished for that death I'd feared moments before. I hoped Candace hadn't considered spy as a possible career choice.

"You put it back," he said. "Were you *planning* to remove items from the store?"

"I wanted to buy them, but—"

I stepped between them. "Like she said, Officer, everything

went back. I think you'll find the items in question in the hair bow bin."

His lips also twitched. That happened a lot when adults heard me talk for the first time. They usually went from there to either mild amusement or the assumption that I was being a smart aleck. He chose a different route.

"All right—would you ladies mind if I looked in your bags?"

"Not at all," I said. I looked hard at Candace. "You wouldn't either, would you?"

Once again she whimpered like a wet cocker spaniel, and my life in a jail cell took shape in my mind. What had I *not* dug out of the bottom of her purse?

She finally shook her head and handed it over. The officer nodded for us to sit on the bench and then went through the thing, lip gloss by glitter pen by pack of chewing gum. She must have had every flavor known to mankind in there. When he pulled out a battered leather book and leafed through it, Candace flung herself into my arms and wailed. The cop looked at me, eyebrows raised.

"She's a little bit of a drama queen," I said.

He frowned at the book and stuck it back into her purse. By then I was perspiring from places I didn't even know had sweat glands, but when he finally reached the bottom of the bag, he looked at Candace and gave it back to her.

"May I see yours?" he said to me.

On TV, people always said things like, "Not without a search warrant," or "I want my lawyer present," and I'd always told myself I would be that protective of my rights if I were ever a suspect in a crime. Yeah. I handed him that plaid bag so fast, even he looked surprised. Meanwhile, Candace was peeking at him between her fingers and muttering what sounded like some kind of prayer. She was going to *need* prayer when I got through with her.

Mine evidently proved to be more of a chore because I had everything in zippered bags and Velcroed pockets. He inspected every one of them like I was under suspicion of terrorism instead of shoplifting. With Candace now in the clear, I was relieved enough to want to say things like, "If I were going to steal something, it wouldn't be from Claire's. You couldn't even *pay* me to wear that stuff. I mean, do I *look* like the zirconium chandelier earrings type? I barely wear a watch."

Candace stopped crying by the time he'd done everything but test my wallet for gunshot residue.

"All right, ladies," he said. "I can't charge you with anything, but I suggest you stay out of Claire's."

"Oh, not to worry, Officer," I said. "We're leaving the mall."

"Good plan," he said, and then stood there like he was waiting for us to flee.

I curled my fingers around Candace's now-wilted arm and pulled her off the bench and down the mall.

"I'm sorry!" she said over her shoulder.

"Candace," I said in her ear. "Shut up."

Miraculously she did, until we got outside to the bus stop. Then the mouth came open again.

"I was so scared! I thought he was gonna arrest me for sure, and my mama would kill me!"

"Arrest you for what?" I said. "I put the stuff back. The only reason he went through our bags like that was because you were acting so guilty."

"I was scared about that book thing."

"What book thing?"

Smacking the newest tears from her cheeks, she plunged into the purse and pulled out the leather book I'd last seen in Mall Officer's hands. She plunked it onto the seat between us.

"What is this?" I said.

"I don't know."

"What do you mean you don't know? It was in your purse."

"I found it when we were on the bus and I took it."

I could feel my eyes bulging. "What are you, Candace, a kleptomaniac? Do you just rip off anything you want?"

"No! It was there on the seat and I opened it and it said if I found it I should take it. So I did."

"When did you do that? I was sitting right next to you the whole time."

"When you were lookin' out the window not listenin' to a thing I was sayin' like you always do." She jutted out her negligible chin. "You always treat me like I'm nobody."

"Oh—so was that me treating you like nobody back there in the mall when I saved you from being dragged off to jail? If I hadn't caught you, that cop would have, *with* a handful of tacky jewelry in your purse. If I thought you were nobody, Candace, I wouldn't have bothered."

The chin quivered, and I rolled my eyes.

"Okay," I said. "I don't listen to everything you say. Nobody can. You never stop talking. My brain has to take a break now and then."

"I know," she said, bony shoulders shuddering. "And I 'preciate you doin' that for me."

I gave a sigh that would have put Deidre to shame and nodded at the approaching bus. "Come on, I'll ride home with you."

"Maybe we should put that book back when we get on," she said.

"Give it to me," I said. "I'll do it."

She picked it up off the seat and handed it to me with index finger and thumb, pinky extended like it was crawling with lice. I tucked it into my bag for the moment and ushered her onto the bus, where she slunk into a seat and hugged her purse to her chest.

"It's over," I said as I sat down beside her. "You learned a lesson, not gonna happen again, done. Move on."

But she shook her head until the bun she'd fashioned somewhere in her hair sprung and went haywire on the top of her head.

"What?" I said. "Come on, dish. I promise I'll listen to everything you say this time."

"How am I gonna look like somebody at the prom with no jewelry?" she said.

I lifted her hand, which bore a ring on every finger. "What's this?"

"This is cheap stuff. I can't be wearin' this to no prom."

I bit back the obvious reply, which was that jewelry didn't get much cheaper than Claire's. There was something truly pained in her voice.

"Quinn wants to take me—"

"Who's Quinn?"

She turned her once-again-running-over eyes on me, and her voice went up into the stratosphere. "My boyfriend—from Schodack. That's who I was talkin' about all the way to the mall. See, you wasn't listenin'."

"I'm sorry, okay? Seriously. So—Quinn wants to take you."

"Yeah. And he wants it to be special. He's gonna get me a corsage and borrow his uncle's car—he's got him a *nice* Camaro."

"Okay, then, it'll be special."

"'Til I walk in there with ol' nasty jewelry and some ol' tired dress, and all them rich girls start lookin' at me and laughin'."

A part of my heart caved in. "Are you talking about Alyssa Hampton and Hayley—that crowd?"

She nodded.

"Why do you even care what they think?"

"You do!"

"No, I do *not*."

Candace's neck rose like E.T.'s. "Then why did you look like you was gonna start cryin' when they put your name up for prom queen?"

I started to shake my head, but she nodded hers harder.

"Maybe nobody else seen it, but I know because I ain't never seen you look like that before. You always look like you got everything handled—and you didn't that time, now. You look like somebody done stabbed you with a knife."

We stared at each other, probably longer than we'd ever shared a look over a Thanksgiving turkey or an Easter ham. I was the first to turn my eyes away.

"All right," I said. "I'll concede that the Ruling Class can make you feel like you shouldn't even be breathing the same air as them."

"You got that right."

"But you can't let them control you. I mean, seriously—have you ever tried to steal something from a store before?"

"No!" she said, voice shrill again.

"And you wouldn't have this time if you weren't trying to keep up with them."

"I know. Maybe I just won't go. I'll just tell Quinn to forget it."

"Then they really do win," I said.

"So what am I supposed to do?"

"Go to the prom with Quinn and have that special time in what *you* want to wear."

She gave me another long look. "You don't understand, Tyler," she said. "You only just started gettin' laughed at, 'cause you got other things goin' for you. You're smart and you can talk like you some kinda professor—and you're all playin' the violin and all that." She jabbed a ringed thumb into her chest. "I ain't got a whole lot goin' for me except Quinn and my dream that I'm someday gonna be a fashion designer and make all them girls look like they been shoppin' at Walmart." Her voice thickened. "But right now, I don't even see how that's gonna happen, 'cause I can't go to the prom without feelin' like I don't belong there."

It was probably the first time in my life that I ever just opened my mouth and let something important come out without analyzing it from six or seven different angles first.

"You know what, Candace?" I said.

She shook her head.

"I am going to change that."

"How you gonna do that?"

"I don't know," I said. "But if they want to throw the prom in my face and nominate me for queen—then they are just going to see what I can do with it."

A smile spread across Candace's face like melting butter. "They sure are, cousin," she said. "They sure are."

*

By the time I got Candace to her house and dragged myself upstairs in mine, I was exhausted. I thought at first that was the reason my bag felt so heavy when I finally made it to my window seat. Then I remembered the book I was supposed to have left on the seat of the bus. I'd gotten so wrapped up in making my vow about the prom, I'd forgotten about it.

"The way this day is going," I said out loud, "the police will probably come looking for it, now that I'm a known felon. Thank you again, Candace."

Come to think of it, *she* should return the book to the bus. I hardly ever rode it, and I wasn't the one who picked the thing up in the first place.

I couldn't help being a little curious about it, though. Hadn't Candace told me it said if she found it she should keep it? I had a hard time believing that, given her recent penchant for theft, but of course I had to see for myself.

I stuck my hand in the bag—and yanked it out again. Something in there was warm. The words "hot jewelry" popped into my mind.

Okay, I was turning into a worse drama queen than my cousin. I slid my hand back in, tentatively this time, and felt around for where the warmth was coming from. My fingers touched the leather cover, and heat shot instantly up my arm. It didn't burn. In fact, it made me want to hold on.

So, fingertips pressed to its warmth, I eased the book from the bag and rested it on my lap. It was the first time I really had a chance to look at it, and I was immediately fascinated. The leather cover was scarred and scuffed like it had seen some serious miles, and a long crease ran from top to bottom on the left side, probably from people folding it back like a magazine. There was even a watermark along the bottom, maybe from somebody reading it in the bathtub. Whoever had it before Candace discovered it had carved things into the cover—mostly what looked like initials, and in different styles. So it had been in the hands of several different people, then. Definitely fascinating.

The only thing on the cover that looked like it had been there originally were two letters—RL—which were engraved into the leather. *RL*. Did I know any famous authors with those initials? Robert Louis Stevenson? No—the *S* was missing.

You could look inside, Brain Child, I told myself. But my fingers didn't want to leave the warmth of the cover. It was somehow soothing, and I wasn't sure I'd ever needed soothing. I always managed to sort things through logically before I got to the I-need-a-hug stage.

Until now.

Now I wanted to cling to this book. And that scared me.

So for no other reason than that, I shoved it under the cushion of the window seat.

CHAPTER SIX

But I didn't forget the goal I'd announced to Candace, and I spent the next several days fine-tuning it. When I typed the final version on my computer — in official-looking Georgia font — it was exactly what I'd been working toward.

Make the Castle Heights Junior/Senior Prom accessible to everyone who wants to attend.

My dad had taught me that it was always essential to have a firm objective for a campaign. Once you had that, you could maintain your focus. Or, as he put it, you could better "keep your eyes on the prize." Mine was going to be seeing Candace walk into that prom on Quinn's arm with her head held high.

Having that as an objective also kept me from envisioning the Ruling Class being locked out due to lack of character, not to mention manners. It had to be accessible to everyone. That was a bummer, but I didn't see any other choice.

The next step was another thing my father always said: If people knew better, they'd do better. That meant research, and that's where I could kick tail. Even Google feared me.

So I spent all day Saturday sailing around on the Internet and printing out articles on financially out-of-control prom activity. I had so much information, Sunday morning I had to go down to the sunroom and use the long table to spread things out and get organized.

The almost-all-windows room was drenched in delicious light. I hadn't even noticed until then how much spring had crept in. The trees that canopied the backyard were covered in lacy bright-green first leaves, and the walkway that led to Mom's koi pond was lined in daffodils a foot deep on each side. Last spring, she'd called it an embarrassment of riches.

It was kind of inspiring, really, as I ordered my papers into neat piles. That and the fact that I basically had the house to myself. Sunny was in her room. My parents had gone to church as usual, something I'd stopped doing the second Sunday we lived in Castle Heights. It wasn't only because at the church they chose the pastor preached the single most boring sermon I had ever heard, or that the high school class consisted of Kenny, Candace, and another boy and girl who fell just short of making out during the lesson. I'd already started getting restless with religion before we left Long Island, and a new place seemed like the logical point for pulling away from it.

It wasn't that I didn't believe in God, or even that Jesus came, died, rose again, all that, so that somehow we could be sure we'd go to heaven. What I wasn't sure of was what difference that made to me now, and the Castle Heights church didn't show any signs of being able to help me figure that out.

So on that second Sunday morning, I quoted my parents the only Emily Dickinson poem I could actually relate to:

Some keep the Sabbath going to church
I keep it staying home
With a bobolink for a chorister
And an orchard for a dome.

I made the argument that I wanted to explore my spiritual growth myself, even though I wouldn't know a bobolink if it pooped on my head. They agreed, on the condition that I would get up when they left for church and spend that hour intentionally exploring. I always got up. But I couldn't say I did much spiritual excavation. Maybe today, doing a good deed while the daffodils bloomed in the garden—maybe that qualified.

I was about to start a spreadsheet on my laptop—you thought you were being a wise guy, huh, Patrick?—when a slim shadow fell across the table. I hadn't heard Sunny come in, but she was now standing over me, holding a coffee mug. The prickles of resentment stirred on my neck.

"Morning," she said. "You're up early."

"So are you," I said, trying not to *sound* like I hoped her visit to the sunroom would be short.

It evidently wasn't going to be, because she sank onto the flowered-cushioned loveseat and tucked her bare feet up under herself. Her white oversized sweater fell into just the right folds as she snuggled her hands around the mug. Even when she was depressed, she was poised. Although, I had to admit, her face looked a little less pinched-in today.

"Dad and Rowena are at church, huh?" she said.

"Uh-huh." I snuck my gaze over to the computer screen.

"They invited me, but—" She shrugged and took a sip from the mug. "Can I get you a cup?"

I shook my head. I actually liked the stuff, especially if it was loaded with cream and sugar, but I didn't want this to turn into a coffee klatch. I had work to do.

"I just can't do church right now," she said. "When I was in the worst of the depression, I talked to the pastor at the church Will and I went to—I was seeing a therapist, but I thought I should have some spiritual guidance too, you know?"

I didn't, but I nodded anyway. I let my hand wander onto the keyboard.

"I didn't expect him to pray over me and I would be magically healed, but I also didn't expect him to tell me I was only depressed because I had unrepented sin I needed to confess. He actually said seeing a therapist was not only a waste of time, it was unchristian. There I am, bawling my eyes out, and he's telling me I'm just a lousy sinner and I need to fall on my face before God."

"So did you?" I said. I was interested in spite of myself.

"I'd already spent so much time praying and crying I had calluses on my knees and slits for eyes. A little comfort would have been a nice touch." She took another sip of the coffee and closed her eyes as she swallowed. "I'm sure the pastor here isn't like that, but I'm not ready to open myself up to that possibility. I just feel so vulnerable all the time."

"Good word," I said.

"What?"

"Vulnerable. It's a good word."

As Sunny surveyed me over the top of her mug, her eyes filled. This was why I felt so awkward around her; everything I said made her cry. Everything *anybody* said made her cry.

"That's what I admire about you, Tyler," she said. Her voice was fragile. "You see things so, I don't know, objectively. You were always sort of logical as a kid—you never freaked out over things, from what I remember. I thought maybe you'd get a little more emotional when the hormones kicked in, but you're still so analytical." She pointed her chin toward the stacks of papers on the table. "Are you this coolheaded about everything?"

"I try to be," I said.

One of the tears spilled over her lower lashes. "I would love to be more that way. Maybe then I wouldn't get hurt and turn into a basket case."

I didn't know how to respond to that, which turned out to be fine, because she uncurled from the loveseat and headed back into the main part of the house.

I looked at the tidy piles on the table. *Vulnerable* might be a really good word, but I didn't want to be it. It looked painful.

*

Monday I had my spreadsheet ready and my facts in an outline I could speak from extemporaneously—another one of my favorite words. My next step was to make an appointment with Mr. Baumgarten, the principal, and I did that before school. His secretary gave me a pass to get out of Chemistry, which on that day's block schedule was right after lunch.

"Don't plan on this taking all period," she said when she handed it to me.

"I don't want it to," I said. "I like Chemistry."

"Oh," she said. "Well, how refreshing." Then she gave a short laugh. "A little nutty, in my opinion, but refreshing."

And they wondered why so many kids thought school was a waste of time.

I was jazzed about the way my research had turned out, but I wanted to test drive it on somebody before I presented it to Mr. Baumgarten. At lunch, I talked Valleri into joining the Fringe and me for a dry run. She didn't look all that excited about it, but she came.

The Fringe was there, waiting. Matthew and Deidre had gotten over me ditching them on the half day—they weren't into grudges—and Yuri acted like he hadn't even been there. Half the time I suspected Yuri had early Alzheimer's.

I got everybody around my laptop at our table in the corner of the cafeteria and brought up my spreadsheet. "This is how much the average high school student—the *average* kid, now—spends on the prom. Three hundred to three *thousand* dollars." I shook my head. "Isn't the word *recession* in anybody's vocabulary?"

I looked up for nods and agreeing grunts. I got a beige look from Matthew and a clueless one from Yuri. Deidre laughed out loud.

"What?" I said.

"How much *time* did you spend on this? I didn't put this much into my English midterm." She laughed again, from some pointy part of her I didn't know. "I think you've gone OCD or something."

"You don't get what I'm trying to do?" I said.

"I get *what*," Matthew said. "I just don't get *why*."

"Because the way it is now isn't fair."

"What *is*?" Yuri said. "If life was fair, I wouldn't be five foot four. You don't see me getting on the Internet to find out how to get taller."

"That doesn't even make any sense," I said.

Deidre tapped my screen. "Neither does this. I thought we decided to let the whole prom queen thing die, not resurrect it."

"I changed my mind. I think it's important."

"And I think you need medication," Deidre said.

I looked behind me, hoping for some support from Valleri. But she was gone.

"Your new little friend bailed five minutes ago," Deidre said.

"So when's that Andrew Jackson presentation supposed to be?" Matthew said.

"Why don't you find out?" I squinted at him. "I need to go get some medication."

I shut down my laptop and closed the cover. Matthew shrugged and propped his feet up on the table. I didn't even look at Yuri.

"You don't need to get all annoyed, Tyler," Deidre said.

"Who said I was annoyed?" I said.

Annoyed really wasn't what I was feeling as I slid the computer into my bag and left through the back door. Once again, lonely was the word to describe it. I used to be enough company for myself. Now—not so much.

*

I'd never been in Mr. Baumgarten's office before that day, and as I sat on a black leather and chrome seat facing the matching one he lowered himself into, I realized I'd never even had a conversation with the man. A file with my name on it was on the glass coffee table between us, which meant he'd had to look me up. All I knew about him was that he ran the school without being seen that much, and now I knew that his office looked like it belonged to a corporate CEO—at least as they were portrayed in movies. There wasn't so much as a championship trophy or a picture of a team anywhere. Nobody would know this office belonged to a high school principal; that made me think he didn't really want to be one.

"What can I do for you, Miss Bonning?" he said.

He had a bemused look in his eyes. It was like we were playing grown-up or something. That was okay. He'd get it in a minute.

I opened my computer and went over the spreadsheet. He gave me the nods and grunts I'd hoped for from the Fringe, so I went from there to my memorized outline, explaining in detail the dilemma of the less financially privileged student. When I was finished, I sat back and folded my hands and waited, the way my father had taught me. The person who is willing to stay quiet and wait usually gets what he or she wants. I'd lost many a debate at the dinner table before I learned how to do that.

Mr. Baumgarten steepled his fingers under a chin with a cleft you could have parked a Buick in. "This is impressive, Miss Bonning. I can see why you have a four point 0."

I nodded my thanks. He cleared his throat. Good. He wasn't comfortable with silence. He'd have to break it soon, like—

"So let me ask you this."

Now.

"What is it that you want me to do, exactly? You think I should cancel the prom?"

"No, sir," I said. "My goal is to make the prom accessible to everyone. As you can see, the current standard is far beyond the typical student's reach, financially speaking, and—"

He put up a finger and glanced through my file. "Ah," he said. "That's right—you weren't here year before last. I offered discreet assistance then for anyone who couldn't afford to buy tickets, but ..." He dropped the file on the table. "No one ever asked."

"Nobody's going to *ask*!" I said. "How demoralizing would that be?"

His eyebrows came together over his nose. I hadn't noticed until then how precisely man-scaped they were. He actually had more hair in them than he did on his head, so I could see that his scalp was turning red.

"You might want to watch your tone," he said.

What tone? I was confused. I thought we were having an adult discussion.

"I'm still not clear on what it is you're asking me to do," he said. I expected, "So make it snappy, kid," to be the next words out of his mouth.

"I'd like an opportunity to present this to the juniors and seniors," I said. "And I'd like your support in encouraging them not to turn the prom into a competition for who can spend the most money."

"You want to level the playing field, as it were." He tried the amused smile again. "Are you a bit of a socialist, Miss Bonning?"

"No," I said. "I'm a realist. I think part of our education should be in how to spend money wisely and how to treat people decently instead of making them feel less-than because they don't drive to school in a BMW." I tapped the computer screen in the vicinity of the demographics I'd worked up. "This is a blue-collar town, Mr. Baumgarten. Only twenty percent of the student body comes from households that are considered upper middle class, yet the entire school is run by that minority."

His scalp went a deeper shade of red. "The school is run by me," he said.

"Then you are the one to point your students in a more democratic direction. Because right now, they're primed to perpetuate the inequalities that currently threaten the very fabric of our society."

The crimson faded from his scalp, and he gave me what could only be termed a patronizing smile. As in, "That all sounds very good, but when you grow up you'll understand."

"Well, Miss Bonning," he said as he stood up and looked down at me. "I'm sure you'll change the world someday, but I don't think the junior-senior prom is necessarily the place to start."

"I do, sir," I said, "because this is the world I'm stuck in right now."

His eyes flinched as he watched me stand up. "Like I said, Miss Bonning, you might want to watch that tone."

I was still trying to figure out what "tone" he was talking about when I walked out of his inner sanctum and into the main office. I didn't have time to give it too much thought, though, because Egan Owens popped up from a chair and got right into my space.

"They told me you were in here," he said. His eyes darted around like he was watching confetti fall.

"Who's 'they'?" I said.

"Whoever. Here." He stuck a piece of paper at me. "It's about the photo shoot and the interview. It's tomorrow."

"For . . ."

"For the prom queen nominees."

His mouth twitched into a smile and back out of it again. He still didn't seem to be able to look straight at me. If I hadn't known better, I'd have thought he was nervous.

"Is this part of the joke?" I said.

He licked his lips. By then his face was even redder than Mr. Baumgarten's scalp. "I heard what happened with your petition thing at the council meeting. They were just messing around and ended up giving you the wrong paper."

"There's that 'they' again. Have we figured out who 'they' are?"

"Just — some people." He put up his hands, and I saw that his palms were sparkly. He *was* nervous. That made me squint in suspicion, which I was doing a lot lately.

"This is for real," he said, nodding at the paper I was now holding. "Ms. Dalloway will be there. Seriously, it's legit."

"Why is she going to be there?"

"Because it's for the school paper," he said. "She's the advisor."

"Oh, right," I said.

"Great," he said, already backing away. "It's all on there." He took another step back and sent a wastebasket spinning across the floor. I left so he wouldn't hurt himself.

*

When I got to Chemistry, Mr. Zabaski had already started the class on a heat transfer calorimetry experiment. Normally Yuri was my lab partner, but since I was late, he was already playing mad scientist with Matthew, a pairing Mr. Zabaski had outlawed after they heated a hexane on the Bunsen burner during a lab back in November and caused a minor fire. Zabaski never said they did it on purpose, but they were way too smart for it to have been an accident. Which was probably why he was hovering over them when I walked in and didn't see me standing there for a good fifteen seconds.

"Bonning," he said, his eyes still on the dangerous duo.

Mr. Zabaski was a retired army officer, so he called us all by our last names and said things like "fall in" when he sent us to the lab side of the classroom. Guys like YouTube couldn't resist going straight to the floor every single time. Hilarious.

"Can you work with the new girl?" He nodded toward the end of the line of lab stations, where Valleri was staring blankly at a test tube. It occurred to me that they must not mess around much with chemicals in home school.

"Sure," I said, although I wasn't sure Valleri was all that interested in working with *me*. She'd basically ditched me at lunch. I shrugged and made my way through the pairs of people looking cluelessly at their lab workbooks until I got to her.

"I guess you're stuck with me," I said.

She glanced up from the test tube she was still gazing at. "I think it's the other way around. I don't even know where to start with this stuff. That's why I asked for you."

"Seriously? I got the impression you were over me."

"No. I'm over your friends." She put her hand on my arm. I didn't know anybody as touchy-feely as she was. "No offense," she said. "I know you guys always eat together and everything, but— " She shifted her eyes down the row and let her voice drop. "They're kind of rude to you."

"Really," I said. I, too, glanced down the line of stations at Yuri and Matthew, who weren't looking at the lab workbook at all. "They don't get what I'm trying to do with the prom thing, but— "

"They're rude," she said. "Or maybe it's just me."

I wasn't sure. They definitely weren't as warm-fuzzy as she was. I'd have to think about that.

"Okay," I said, "so, if you'll just read the steps to me, I'll do it and you can watch and see how it's done."

"Thank you *so* much," she said. "I don't want to blow something up my first day in here."

I picked up the aluminum and glanced behind me to make sure Mr. Zabaski was out of hearing range.

"I don't think you actually *can* blow anything up," I said. "He makes it sound like we *could* if we don't follow directions, but, seriously, I can't see him giving us anything we could potentially create an explosion with."

"Ohmygosh, do you *hear* her?" someone whispered on the other side of the half wall from us. It was one of those whispers they use on stage—the kind that could be heard in the back row or, in this case, at my lab station. One thing about those whispers; they're always used on purpose.

"She talks like a brain surgeon."

"No, she talks like she's better than everybody else." That was followed by a swear word, but the speaker might as well just have said my name. As for who was talking—it could have been Hayley or Joanna or any other female junior in the Ruling Class. They all sounded the same to me.

"Next step," I said to Valleri.

She looked from me to the half wall. I nodded at the workbook.

"Um—we're supposed to put the aluminum in the water."

"So—a little Al in the H_20."

I wiggled my eyebrows, and just as expected, the RC whispered, "What is she even talking about?"

"She probably doesn't even know. I don't think she's really that smart. I think—"

Whatever she thought was shattered by a blast that shot white smoke into the air. The room erupted in screams and coughing and falling lab stools. I grabbed the fire extinguisher at our station and aimed it at the smoke, but it was already evaporating. Foam spewed out of the hose and drenched the feeble flames—and, it turned out, Hayley and Joanna, who clung to each other in the falling mist, hair plastered to their heads.

"All right, people, fall out!" Mr. Zabaski barked.

Even YouTube scrambled with the mob back to the classroom section. I ran around the end of the bank of lab stations, extinguisher in hand. Mr. Zabaski took it from me and held out his arm to keep me from getting any closer. Hayley and Joanna were still entwined and shaking.

"You all right?" he said.

Neither of them even moved.

"What's the matter, are you paralyzed from the neck up? I said, are you all right?"

"I don't know!" Joanna cried, and burst into tears.

From behind me, Valleri emerged out of the mist and went to her and peeled her off of Hayley. Joanna collapsed in her arms.

"Barr!" Mr. Zabaski said to Hayley. "Are. You. Hurt?"

She looked down at her foam-covered self and shook her head. "It just scared me to death! Ohmygosh—we could've been killed!"

I, meanwhile, was inspecting their station and shook *my* head. "There wasn't even a fire."

Mr. Zabaski peered at Hayley and nodded. "Yeah, it singed your eyebrows a little, but other than that—"

"My *eyebrows*!" she said.

Joanna drew back from Valleri and frantically rubbed her own.

"They're still there," I said.

"I'm glad you weren't hurt," Valleri said, giving Joanna's arm the expected massage. "Thanks be to God."

I was startled—not just because nobody around there mentioned God with anything close to reverence, but because it actually sounded natural coming out of her mouth.

"All right, Bonning and—" Mr. Zabaski looked at Valleri.

"Clare," she said. "My last name's Clare."

"Duly noted. You two take these ladies down to the nurse. McKinney—get a janitor."

A white-faced YouTube nodded and fled from the room.

"I'll take them," Egan said, inserting himself between Valleri and Joanna. He was shaking worse than the girls were.

"Did I say it was up for discussion, Owens?" Mr. Zabaski said. "Bonning—you and Saint Clare take care of that detail."

Two vertical lines cut into the skin between his eyebrows. "The rest of you, turn to chapter twenty-eight and start reading. Now."

Faces went into books, but I would have bet some serious money nobody was comprehending a word. Valleri put her arm around Joanna and moved her to the door. I looked at Hayley, who said, "Don't even think about it."

"Never entered my mind," I said.

Valleri walked ahead of us with Joanna, murmuring to her all the way. I didn't plan on saying anything to Hayley. She, on the other hand—

"Don't even start in on what we must have done wrong to make that explosion," she said.

"I wasn't going to," I said.

"But you were thinking it."

"How do you know what I was thinking?"

"Because you're always thinking you're better than the rest of us."

The last two words came out in the middle of a hiccup. Hayley was crying. She shook her head and hugged her arms around herself and hurried to catch up with Joanna. That saved me from having to answer her, and I didn't know what I would have said. *I don't think I'm better than the rest of you* would have been a lie.

That definitely didn't qualify me as nice, and for the first time, that left me cold.

CHAPTER SEVEN

Dad started dinner that night with Sunny's high point. Now *there* was an oxymoron if I ever heard one. By the time Mom brought out the angel food cake, we still hadn't discovered what could possibly be "high" in my sister's day. Or her life, for that matter. It was clear I wasn't going to get to run the chemistry lab episode or my meeting with Mr. Baumgarten or tomorrow's interview and photo shoot past them. Not tonight. Maybe not before I finished my junior year.

I clearly wasn't the only one who was having a problem with the focus of our entire meal. Mom pretty much dumped the strawberries over the cake, and by the way she stuck a spoon in a tub of Cool Whip and said, "Have at it," I knew she was as done with Sunny's angst as I was.

My father, on the other hand, was so zeroed in on the girl, he never got through his Caesar salad. He didn't even notice that I'd picked out all his croutons and eaten them. When Sunny started in on the wayward fiancé for the fifth time, I offered to help my mother clear the table. We're talking desperate to get away from dinner and a therapy session.

"Is it just me?" I said when Mom and I had escaped to the kitchen, "or is she saying the same thing over and over?"

"I guess she has to," Mom said. She let a handful of silverware clatter into the sink.

"Yeah, but do I have to listen?"

She gave a soft little grunt—her version of sympathy—and turned on the water and the garbage disposal. I got that cold feeling again. Without stopping to analyze it, I blurted out, "Am I a nice person?"

Mom shook her head, which left me even colder, until the strawberry tops disappeared down the drain and she turned off the water and said, "I couldn't hear you."

"I said ..."

She put a hand on her almost nonexistent hip and lifted her brows at me. The dishes waited. A fork fell off the pile. My father's voice soothed on and on beyond the door.

"Never mind," I said.

Mom nodded. "It's okay. I know you have homework. I'll have Sunny help me."

"That's not what I—"

"She owes me," Mom said. And with a withering glance at the door, she went back to the sink.

Nettles prickling at the back of my neck, I made a production out of passing through the dining room on my way to the stairs. If either Sunny or Dad noticed me, they did a great job of hiding it.

I barely hit my room before my phone started ringing. I was surprised to see that it was Deidre, because she usually texted. Besides, I didn't think she was all that thrilled with me right now.

I picked it up, prepared to answer the usual, "What are you doing?"

"Has Yuri called you?" she said instead.

"Yuri?" I said. "No. Not ever, in fact. Why do you sound like you just ran the four-forty?"

"Because I'm, like, flabbergasted. Are you sitting down?"

"Why do people ask that?" I said, although I did plop onto the window seat. "How many people actually fall over when they hear news over the phone?"

"I have no idea—but I almost did when I found *this* out."

I had to admit I was curious. Deidre didn't get this excited about much of anything.

"Did Yuri win the lottery?" I said.

"What? No. Get this: they actually asked him to take pictures for that prom queen photo shoot tomorrow. Can you believe that?"

"Well, yeah—he's a photographer."

"He's not *that* kind of photographer. He takes pictures of light bulbs with paint dripping over them."

"So why did they ask him?" I said. I was losing interest fast. "Who usually takes the pictures for the school paper?"

"Mr. Linkhart, but he's evidently sick or something."

"Ya think? The man sweats like he's in a sauna. Even Valleri noticed it—"

"Who's Valleri?"

"She's the new—"

"The thing is—I think, and so does Yuri—that this is another part of their little campaign to make us look stupid for whatever reason. First it's you with the prom queen thing, now they're trying to make Yuri think they really want him to take pictures, and you *know* there's some kind of prank involved."

I could tell from the jangling of bracelets that she was changing her phone to the other ear. I contemplated hanging up; she probably wouldn't notice for at least five minutes.

"So what's next, is my question," she went on. "I don't know, and that's what scares me."

"So what did Yuri say?"

"Huh?"

"What did Yuri say when they asked him?"

"He said no, of *course*."

"So what's the big deal?"

"The big *deal* is that they are out to get us. Not just you—all of us. You have to give up this stupid prom campaign, Tyler, or we're all going down."

I stiffened on the seat. "I'm trying to effect change, Deidre. That always comes with risks."

"Yeah, well, we're not interested in being martyrs. You could think about somebody besides yourself in this."

"I am! I'm thinking about the Kmart Kids and—"

"People you don't even know. People who are going to forget about the prom the next week."

"Fine — and Yuri will forget they asked him to take pictures by tomorrow morning."

"They're not going to stop with that. They already tried to mess him over in your chemistry lab today."

"What are you even talking about?"

"The experiment that literally blew up in those girls' faces? It's so obvious what happened."

"Yeah. They can't read lab instructions."

"No — one of *them* set it up so Yuri and Matthew would get blamed."

"*What?*"

"Those two guys already got in trouble once for knowing more than Zabaski. You didn't hear that he had them in his office interrogating them the whole rest of the period today? And meanwhile, Egan and YouTube and the rest of them were laughing their butts off."

I was about to laugh *mine* off. "Are you serious? YouTube wouldn't know how to set something like that up if his life depended on it. And why would he do that to his own friends?"

"You know they knew it was going to happen."

"No, I don't. I was there. It totally freaked them out."

"That's what they wanted you to think."

"Okay, you're paranoid, Deidre. Unless there's some kind of evidence — "

"The janitor came in and cleaned up everything while Zabaski had Yuri and Matthew under a naked lightbulb."

"Did they get busted for it or not?"

"No. Which is why I know this isn't the end. You have to call off your campaign — that's all there is to it."

I pulled my knees into my chest and squeezed my eyes shut and pressed my lips together, but I still couldn't keep myself from asking it.

"And what if I don't?" I said.

I heard her catch her breath. The fact that she didn't expect that from me — that made me catch mine.

"I guess we'll have to stay away from you," she said. "And that's not a threat, just so you know. It's self-protection."

"Do what you have to do," I said.

"Really? Really, Tyler? Is that the way you want to play it?"

"No," I said. "That's the way *you* want to play it."

The bracelets jangled again, and this time her voice jangled with them. "You realize you're going to be totally alone, right? Not to be mean, but you don't have a lot of friends."

"That's true," I said. I didn't add, "And it looks like maybe I never did." Instead, I just hung up.

*

I didn't do moods. I'd never even had PMS. But the next day, Tuesday, I put on a black sweatshirt and wore the hood as I walked into English block. If Ms. Dalloway hadn't outlawed sunglasses in class, I'd have worn them too. I basically didn't know how to navigate in a bad mood, so all I could think to do was hide.

That didn't work on Valleri, who sat down behind me and said, "Do you want to talk about it?"

"About what?" I said.

She just looked at me.

"Is that what *you* do when your friends dump you and you're about to go make an idiot out of yourself yet again and you can't stop any of it?" I said. "You talk about it?"

She nodded, bouncing the curls.

"Does it change anything?"

She didn't have a chance to answer, as Ms. Dalloway came up to us, looking at me wearily over the tops of her half-glasses.

"You're wanted in the office, Tyler," she said.

"Do you know why?"

"I didn't get a memo. I hope they make it quick, though. You're out of class more than you're in lately."

I could've argued the statistical accuracy of that, but Ms. Dalloway had already dropped the pass on my desk and was shuffling away. I stood up and leaned over Valleri.

"Lunch?" I murmured.

A delicate line appeared between her eyebrows. "Are you eating with—"

I shook my head.

"Shall I tell the office you're too busy to get down there?" Ms. Dalloway said.

"Going," I said.

A quick mental survey on the way to the office revealed no reason why I should be called in, yet my stomach was still wreaking havoc on the Pop-Tart when I arrived. The secretary pointing me to Mr. Baumgarten's inner sanctum didn't help, but when I saw Mr. Zabaski on the black-leather-and-chrome seat, I calmed stomach acids, half-eaten breakfast, everything. They wanted to know what I knew, and they knew I'd tell them. It was one of the few benefits of being a smart, honest kid.

Mr. Baumgarten's scalp was already pink, and he didn't give me any version of his smile, patronizing or otherwise, as he leaned against his desk, arms folded. Mr. Zabaski's face said what it always did: follow orders and nobody gets hurt.

"Are we here about the incident in the lab yesterday?" I said.

"We are," Mr. Baumgarten said. "What do you know about it?"

"Not much, although from what I could tell, they put sodium into the water instead of aluminum. It all happened too fast for me to see much more than that."

Mr. Baumgarten crumpled his eyebrows at Mr. Zabaski, who was nodding at me.

"That's entirely possible, Bonning," Mr. Z said, "except that there was no container of sodium anywhere near Payne and Barr's lab station."

"Really," I said. I could hear my father telling me to stay quiet and let them talk.

"And why would there be? I set up only the chemicals that were supposed to be involved in the lab at all the stations myself."

Ah. So *he* was the one who was going to take the fall for this. Totally unfair in my opinion.

"He always does that," I said to Mr. Baumgarten. "If anybody messed up, it wasn't Mr. Zabaski."

"Nobody's suggesting it was."

"Then who are you suggesting?" I said. We might as well get to the Yuri/Matthew theory and get it over with.

"Actually, Miss Bonning," Mr. Baumgarten said, "we're suggesting you."

All I could do was stare at him as my mind tried to rearrange itself. Nothing fell into any kind of order—because there was none. This made zero sense.

"Me?" I said.

"Mr. Zabaski says you're the brightest student in that class. You yourself just demonstrated your understanding of what makes things go boom."

I didn't like the sarcasm in his voice, or the chill going up my backbone.

"Be that as it may, sir," I said, "I was here talking to you when the lab started. By the time I got back to class, it was already in progress."

"And who set up that meeting with me?" he said. "It seems to me you initiated it. And if you recall, I cut it short. You'd have argued all afternoon if I had let you."

"If you'll check with your secretary, she'll tell you that I told *her* I didn't want our meeting to take all period. I told her I *liked* Chemistry."

"You certainly covered your bases."

"Ex*cuse* me?"

"If I could interject," Mr. Zabaski said.

He looked at Mr. Baumgarten until he nodded. The scalp colored a shade deeper.

"Look," Mr. Zabaski said. "I'm aware of the undercurrent of tension between your friends and those of, say, Egan Owens. That would naturally indicate that you might know something about the situation."

"And I've told you everything I know. I'd like to go back to English." I looked at Mr. Baumgarten. "I like that class too."

"Did I not call you on your tone yesterday?" he said.

"I don't know what tone to use when I'm suspected of something I had neither opportunity nor motive to commit."

"No motive? What about prom queen?"

"Are you serious ... sir?" I said. "You think I would try to burn someone's face to eliminate the competition for *prom queen*?"

"You were pretty adamant about your cause in here yesterday."

"Adamant, yes. Violent, no."

My heart was slamming so hard I had to take in huge breaths to get the words out. If this was what blowing your cool felt like, I was almost there.

"As for opportunity ..." Mr. Baumgarten jerked his chin at Mr. Zabaski, who looked at me soberly.

"When I tested the containers on the lab station," Mr. Z said, "I discovered that the one that should have contained aluminum had traces of sodium in it. Someone evidently tampered with that container and made sure it went to Barr and Payne's station. There are only three people in the class who would know what would happen if sodium was used instead of aluminum in the experiment. I've already squeezed Marseilles and Connor every way I know how, and I'm inclined to think they had no hand in it. I watch them like a hawk, and I haven't trusted them in the lab except during class ever since the incident last semester. You're a different story." His eyes bored into mine. "You, I could trust."

"And now?" I said.

"You tell me. You come in and study, do extra work, help me out from time to time."

"And you seriously think I would do something like this?"

"I don't want to."

"Then don't. Unless you have solid evidence, you can't charge me with this. And since you don't—because there is none—I'd like to go back to class. Please."

Mr. Baumgarten's arms unfolded. "You *really* don't know when to back off, do you?"

But Mr. Zabaski put his hand up to him, still looking at me. "She's telling the truth," he said. "She can be dismissed."

Mr. Baumgarten's entire head went scarlet, but I was already on my feet.

"I'll just have your secretary sign my pass," I said.

*

I tried to talk myself down on the way back to Ms. Dalloway's room. Mr. Baumgarten wanted me to be guilty because he couldn't make me quake in my Nikes. Mr. Zabaski didn't want me to be guilty, but it would be a whole lot easier for him if I was. But I didn't do it, so I had nothing to worry about ...

Except for the fact that I still didn't know who did, and whoever it was obviously wanted everybody to think it was the Fringe.

I stopped outside the classroom door, hand on the doorknob. Could it be that Deidre was actually right? That they *were* out to take us down? There was no way, unless they'd become chemists overnight, and I just wasn't seeing that.

And did I need to? Did I need to figure it out at all? I wasn't involved. Period. That's what cool-headed, logical Tyler would say. But with my hand shaking on the doorknob, I wasn't sure I was her anymore.

Squaring my shoulders, I pushed the door open. I had to be her if I was going to get through the next "challenge" the Ruling Class had thrown in front of me—namely, the photo session after lunch.

I walked straight to my seat in front of Valleri, and Ms. Dalloway's gaze only trailed across me as she went on about *The Red Badge of Courage* to a dozing class. Good. I could use this time to get my head straight and read up on Stephen Crane later.

I took out my notebook to at least pretend I was writing down her every word about the protagonist's rite of passage—which had nothing whatsoever to do with any of us because we didn't *have* rites of passage anymore, unless you counted getting a driver's license or becoming drunk out of your mind on prom night. When I opened the notebook, I found a folded slip of paper. Nobody ever wrote me a note. Matter of fact, now that we all had texting capability, nobody wrote *anybody* a note anymore. The way this day was going, I was almost afraid to open it. Only the determination not to let the Ruling Class get to me made me unfold it.

Lunch, it said in the kind of pretty handwriting only librarians wrote in anymore.

It was signed *Valleri*.

That actually got me through a whole period of Stephen Crane without being jerked back and forth between visions of myself being photographed next to Alyssa Hampton and images of being placed in handcuffs for attempted eyebrow singeing. Without Valleri's promise to sort it all through, I'd have come out of there feeling like I'd been shell-shocked in the Civil War Crane droned on about.

The minute the bell rang, Valleri had me by the arm, pulling me out of Ms. Dalloway's classroom.

"I'll see you right after lunch, Tyler?" Ms. Dalloway said from her desk. "For the photo shoot?"

I paused at the doorway, Valleri still attached, and nodded.

"You *are* planning to change, I hope."

I looked down at my sweatshirt.

"Oh, yes, ma'am," Valleri said. "That's where we're going right now."

"She doesn't need a total makeover. Just—" Ms. Dalloway ran her hand over the top of her head. "Lose the hood."

My mood plummeted even further.

"Is this why you're so bummed today?" Valleri said when we were out in the hall.

"That's part of it," I said. "And it just got worse. I didn't bring anything to change into."

"I can do more than talk about that," she said. "I have a couple of things in my locker."

"Why?"

"Because sometimes I go straight from here to a church thing or something, so I change in the bathroom. You and I are about the same size."

"Yeah," I said, "but I'm not perky."

She flinched.

"Not that that's a bad thing," I said. "It just isn't me. Of course, at the moment, I don't know what is, which is totally strange, since I usually do." I stopped her at the end of the hall and waited for a bevy of girls to pass before I said, "Can I ask you something?"

"Sure."

"Do I come across as, I don't know, snarky or something? I mean, do I have a 'tone'?"

Valleri looked at me so deeply I almost covered my eyes so she wouldn't see too far. This moment had enough of the unknown in it already.

"No," she said finally. "You come across as honest—as far as you know the truth to be, anyway."

"What does *that* mean?" I said—but I closed my eyes and shook my head. "Never mind. I don't even think I can wrap my mind around that right now."

"I'm sorry—"

"No, it's cool. I'm just freaking out because I hate to have my picture taken anyway. Throw in having to try to look like a beauty queen and I'm a nutcase. I never get this crazy about stuff."

"You already are beautiful."

"And you are a really bad liar."

"I'm serious." Her eyes were, actually, pretty solemn. "In France they say every woman has her own beauty. She just has to discover what it is."

"I don't think I have that kind of time," I said.

"Follow me," she said.

Since I had no other options, I did. We made a stop at her locker and another in a restroom I didn't even know existed, way down in the art wing. There was nobody in there, which gave Valleri room to spread out makeup brushes and blush and lip gloss in packages printed in French. She also hung up several wardrobe choices, all like nothing I'd seen on my shopping trip with Candace.

"You keep all this stuff in your locker?" I said.

"You just never know," she said. "So is it okay if I—"

"Have at it," I said.

While I watched in the mirror, Valleri gave me cheekbones I also didn't know existed and found a curvy lip line I wasn't aware of and coaxed my eyelids out of hiding.

"I know you're not into anything fake," she said as she worked. "This is all just to bring out what's already there. Which is what your outfit should do for your body too."

"So we're going to accentuate gawky and awkward?" I said.

The tiny line appeared between her eyebrows again. "Is that how you see yourself?"

I gave a short laugh. "Actually, I don't look at my physical self any more than I absolutely have to."

"So how do you know what you are?"

"I never thought about it that way."

"Don't think about it," Valleri said. "Just feel it."

I gave a longer laugh. "If I have to 'feel' who I am, I'm never going to find me!"

"You don't feel?"

"I'm just more of a thinker."

"You felt that day I found you crying."

I opened my mouth to argue—and closed it again.

"What are you feeling about the prom, for instance?"

"I think—"

"Feel."

"I feel—uh—kind of angry, I guess? Like there's an injustice and I have to correct it. I thought that was a thought, but if it's a feeling I'd call it ... conviction."

"Passion, even?"

I gave the longest laugh yet, but Valleri didn't smile. It was another one of those moments when she seemed years older under all that little-girl hair.

"Okay, somewhere between conviction and passion," I said.

"Then I think you should wear the red top."

I saw my eyes widen in the mirror. "I've never worn red before."

"Have you ever been passionate before?"

"Uh, no."

"Then there you go." She picked up the red silk blouse and draped it in front of me. I was suddenly somebody I'd never seen before.

"What do you think?" she said.

"I thought I wasn't supposed to think," I said.

"Then how do you feel?"

I watched a slow smile ease onto my face.

"I feel passionate," I said.

CHAPTER EIGHT

Of course, feeling passionate and—okay, a little bit beautiful—in an obscure restroom, and carrying that into a library swarming with the Ruling Class were two entirely different things. For openers, I couldn't take Valleri with me; she had to go to fourth block. Ms. Dalloway was there for the shoot, but she didn't have time to do more than say, "Glad to see you changed." She did actually give me a second look, but by then Egan Owens had edged up to me like coming too close was going to put him in danger of contracting leprosy, and I could feel the lip gloss and the blush and the passion-red top not mattering at all.

"Could I go first?" I said. "I really need to get to class."

"Of course you do," Alyssa said, without taking her eyes from the fingernails she was inspecting. I looked at my own chewed set. Valleri hadn't had time to give me a manicure. Yikes—were our *hands* going to be in these pictures?

"Oh. Wow."

I glanced back at Egan, who had his head pulled back and was staring at me.

"What?" I said.

"Nothing. You look ... good."

"Nice, Owens."

That came from an almost familiar voice. Patrick Sykes slapped Egan playfully on the back of the head.

"What was that for?"

"For making it sound like she doesn't always look good."

"Well ..." Alyssa said. She pulled her made-green-by-contact-lenses eyes up to me, and I saw them startle before she recovered herself. "Oh. You put on makeup. What a concept."

"You should do that all the time," Hayley said, her own eyes wide, though whether that was from surprise or the amount of mascara she was wearing, I couldn't tell. I did notice that her eyebrows were completely intact.

"Y'know what?" Patrick said. "Let's get started before we have to call in a surgeon to get everybody's feet out of their mouths."

The grin was in gear, and the eyes were dancing. This boy had charm down to a serious art form. He'd just kept me from grabbing the nearest Kleenex and smearing all the makeup off my face, and yet all three girls were looking at him as if he'd already crowned each one of them queen.

"We'll take you first, Tyler," Ms. Dalloway said. She held a camera that looked almost as complicated as the one Yuri carried around, and she sounded a little less fatigued than she did when she was anesthetizing us with naturalistic literature.

"We thought we'd have her leaning against the shelves there with the books as a background," Egan said. He looked at Hayley and Joanna, who nodded like dashboard dogs.

"Why?" Patrick said.

I stopped en route to the book shelves and looked at him. Could we not just get this over with?

"Because ... she's smart?" Egan said.

"Everybody knows that." Patrick shrugged. "Show them something they don't know."

"Like what?" Alyssa said.

"I don't remember you being on the newspaper staff," Ms. Dalloway said to her.

"I'm not."

"Then why are you involved in this discussion?"

I wasn't the only one who looked at Ms. Dalloway like she was an imposter. Alyssa made a face behind Ms. D's back and folded her arms.

"Go on, Patrick," Ms. Dalloway said.

"I'm just thinking we should give people something to think about when they vote. Y'know, change it up a little."

"I like it," Egan said.

"You do?" Hayley and Joanna said together, at exactly the same time, with precisely identical inflections.

He nodded, but uneasily.

"Sure he does," Patrick said. "He's like this natural expert on pageants. He doesn't want to just do the same old, same old."

"Okay," Ms. Dalloway said. "Think outside the box, Egan."

"Tyler's definitely outside the box," Alyssa muttered.

Ms. Dalloway gave her a look that could've blistered the paint off a wall. Alyssa snapped her face away.

Meanwhile, I was starting to feel like a painting that nobody could decide where to hang.

"Can I say something?" I said.

"Talk to us," Patrick said.

"I want my picture to convey that I'm passionate—"

Alyssa exploded into a laugh that spewed spit onto the back of Ms. Dalloway's neck. A laugh she didn't even try to disguise.

"All right—you, you, and you," Ms. Dalloway said, pointing at Alyssa, Hayley, and Joanna in turn. "Out in the hall until I call you."

Alyssa nodded to the other two girls, but she didn't leave without giving Egan a hard look. If he made it until the end of the day still in the Ruling Class, I would be dumbfounded.

When they were gone, Egan glanced at me, face so drained every freckle stood out in bas-relief. What did he want *me* to do about it?

"You were saying you're passionate?" Patrick said.

"Yes," I said. I refocused on him. "I'm passionate about making the prom available to everybody, so even if you don't have a bank account the size of Montana you can still go and make it special and not feel like you're pond scum because you didn't arrive in a coach and four."

Patrick grinned at Ms. Dalloway and Egan. "Don't you love the way she talks?"

"Yes," Ms. Dalloway said, voice dry. "It's called being literate."

"Okay, so I have an idea," Patrick said. "Egan, do you mind, buddy?"

"Go ahead," Egan said. His voice cracked.

"Let's put her on that ladder they use to get the books off the top shelves—you know the one I mean?"

Ms. Dalloway nodded. "Go on."

"She could be up there, like, looking down on the way things are with an expression on her face, like, 'I see how it is and it's about to change.'" He grinned at me. "What do you think?"

"No offense, but nobody's gonna get that," Egan said.

"He wasn't asking you," Ms. Dalloway said.

Patrick said again, "What do you think?"

"Actually," I said, "that feels good to me."

Valleri would've been proud.

It was easier to talk about than to pull off, but after a couple of tries, Ms. Dalloway got me and the lighting and the angle just right and took what seemed like fifty shots.

"I'm not as good at this as Mr. Linkhart," she kept saying.

I personally was ecstatic that he wasn't the one doing it. He'd be in a puddle of his own perspiration by now. I was no slouch in the sweat department myself when we were done. Even my hall pass was damp when I handed it to Ms. Dalloway so I could go to History.

"You still have the interview to do," she said.

Ugh. I'd forgotten that part. "Where do I go for that?" I said.

She nodded toward a table. "Over there. Patrick will take care of you."

I looked up to see the eyes practically doing the polka.

"He's doing the interview?" I whispered.

"Yes," she whispered back. "Try not to drool too much." Then she shook her head at me. "I'm sorry, Tyler. You're not the drooling type. Thank you for being a good sport about all this. It'll be over soon."

I felt strangely deflated as I went over to Patrick, which made it easier for Alyssa to nearly mow me down on her way to the camera.

"Well," she said, "were you 'passionate'?"

"Define 'passionate,'" I said.

"Don't you ever give it a rest?"

"What?" I said. "My brain?"

"Alyssa, are we going to do this or not?" Ms. Dalloway said. She was back to her chronic fatigue voice.

Alyssa huffed at me and flounced off. When I turned back to Patrick, he was watching, without the grin. Great. Just when I was thinking he might have an intelligent thought in his head, I had to go and insult one of his women. I was not good at any of this.

I sat down across from him and proceeded to chew off the lip gloss.

"You okay?" he said.

"What?" I said.

"Are you okay? Did Lyssa say something witchy?"

"Witchy?" I said.

He did grin then. "Are we just gonna sit here and ask each other questions?"

"I thought you were supposed to ask the questions," I said. "Isn't this an interview?"

"Yeah. I'm supposed to ask you why you want to be prom queen."

"I don't."

"I know."

My mouth came open.

"So I'm not going to ask you that," he said. "I want to know about your idea of making the prom available for everybody."

"And then what are you going to do with it?" I said.

He blinked. "I'm going to write it up for the article."

"The way I say it, or the way you hear it?"

Patrick sat back, and the grin evolved into what might be an interested expression—although I still wasn't ready to believe it. "Dude—that's a great question. Both, I guess.

I mean, I'll try to make it the way you say it, but it's going to come through me, so my filter will probably show. You want to look at it before I turn it in?"

"Oh," I said. "Is that, like, normal procedure?"

"No. But what about this is 'normal'? That's why I'm diggin' it."

So he was into it because it was outside the box …

Uh, wasn't that what I dug too?

"Okay," I said. "Here's what I'm thinking."

As I went into my spiel, he bent over a spiral notebook and wrote furiously with a ballpoint. Every so often he stopped and chewed the end of it while he watched and nodded and then went back to scribbling. He asked a couple of questions, like—

"Why do you think people spend so much money on one night?"

"Why not just outlaw the prom altogether?"

They were things I had to think about before I answered them. I hated to admit it, but it was the most challenged I'd been in a week—even at my own dinner table.

"Cool," Patrick said when Ms. Dalloway signaled for him to move it along.

She was already photographing Joanna, and Alyssa was visibly fuming several feet away.

"I'll show you this tomorrow," he said to me. "You want to meet at lunch?"

"Hello," Alyssa said. "You have plans for lunch tomorrow."

If she narrowed her eyes any tighter she wouldn't be able to see. I stood up briskly.

"That's okay," I said. "You can just email it to me. Tbonning at gmail dot com."

"How original of you," Alyssa said. "No—how passionate."

I turned to go and almost plowed into Egan. He was holding a clipboard.

"I just need to know who your escort's going to be," he said.

"Escort?" I said.

"You have to have a guy escort you in the prom queen presentation. It's tradition."

"Oh."

"It can just be whoever you're going to prom with."

"Oh," I said again. Was I waxing eloquent or what?

"If you don't know yet, you can just let me know when you do."

"Great," I said. "I'll get back to you."

Alyssa didn't even try to hide her snickers as I escaped from the library. The worst part: somebody else was laughing with her, charming as ever.

I charged down the hall, wondering where my hooded sweatshirt was when I needed it. At least I could hide behind my enormous history textbook this block—especially since we probably had a substitute—

I stopped dead in the classroom doorway and stared at the person standing in front of the room. We definitely had a sub.

"Hi, Tyler," she said.

"Hi," I said, and slid into my seat.

Next to me, Matthew roused himself from slumber and looked through his shaggy hair at me. "Do you know her?" he said.

"Yeah," I said. "She's my sister."

*

At the dinner table, I decided that gravity had taken over the day. Once it had started downhill, it wasn't going to stop on its own, and I obviously had no power to do it.

"That is excellent news, baby," Dad said to Sunny, bobbing his head like a Muppet.

She had just announced her gig as Mr. Linkhart's sub and was basking in the beams coming off my father's face. Even my mother looked pleased. Of course. Sunny wasn't crying into the gravy boat.

"It was just for one day, but it puts me in the system," Sunny said. "And I have to say, it felt good to be in front of a classroom."

"How did it feel to you, Ty?"

I looked at my father. "Are you talking to me?"

He grinned. "You're the only 'Ty' at the table."

"It isn't actually fair to ask her," Sunny said.

Well, thank you.

"She wasn't there for most of the period."

But you shouldn't have.

"Why was that?" Mom said.

"I had to do something in the library," I said quickly. "Could somebody pass the rolls?"

My mother did, still looking at me with one eyebrow raised.

"Well, what I like," Dad said, "is that you have a high point today, baby. Let's raise our glasses to that."

We lifted our water glasses. I thought of dumping mine in my lap so I could excuse myself from the table, but Dad leaned toward me and said, "I want to hear your high, Ty."

I would have taken a pass, but I could feel my mother's eyes still on me. And lying was never an option. It wasn't one of my core competencies.

"I had an interesting conversation," I said.

"With ..." Mom said.

"This guy."

"We need more information," Dad said. His face was still shining with Sunny light, and I was sure he didn't catch the edge in my voice. My mother, on the other hand, apparently did.

"His name is Patrick," I said. "We were discussing equality."

"Excellent. And what conclusion did you come to?"

"We didn't," I said. "We're going to continue by email. Which, I really need to get to. Does anybody mind if I ..."

I nodded toward the door. My father's face fell, and Sunny looked down at her plate.

"It's family time," Mom said. "We'd rather you stayed." She looked at my father. "What was your high?"

Three guesses. I chewed heartily on my salad so I wouldn't hear the answer.

*

One answer I did need was why I was having such a huge problem with Sunny when I already had about six other things to worry about. I tangled with that when I was finally allowed to escape to my room.

She herself said being Mr. Linkhart's sub was just for one day. Even if she got called in regularly, most of my teachers didn't miss days. Mr. Zabaski had never been absent from anything in his life, I was sure.

I flopped down on the window seat and stared dismally at the cherry tree that even in the gathering dusk was bright enough to cheer up Sylvia Plath, the single most depressing poet I had ever read. I wasn't cheered, because I pretty much knew why Sunny was, as Mr. Linkhart himself often drawled, getting on my last nerve.

It wasn't just that she was so emotional and I wasn't. It was because my father was coddling her like she was a motherless puppy, while I was expected to work everything out in my mind and practically put together a PowerPoint presentation for every problem I faced.

But then, wasn't that the way I went about things naturally anyway? Why did I suddenly want him to ask me how I felt about *me*?

Someone knocked lightly on my door.

"Tyler?" Mom said.

"Come in?" I said.

She opened the door a crack. "Was that a question or an answer?"

"Sorry," I said. "I didn't know if you just wanted to tell me something or—"

"No," she said, crossing to my bed. "I want you to tell *me* something."

When were we going to get to the bottom of this day so it couldn't go down any farther?

She sat on the edge of my bed, and I had to look down slightly from the window seat to meet her eye to eye. Even at that, she had control. No wonder people got better when they were in her care. They didn't dare stay sick.

"You want to tell me what's going on with you?" she said.

Funny. Now that somebody was asking, I didn't know how

to answer. I gave it a shot. "Okay—" I said. "Sunny gets on my nerves. But I'll get over it. She has a job now. Kind of. That should help."

"Except that she's encroaching on your territory."

I considered that. "It's not that. I just can't get away from her—and I don't know why it bothers me yet. I'll get back to you on that."

I waited for her to leave. Intimate talks weren't a normal part of our mother-daughter relationship, and she looked as uncomfortable with it as I was. While I was starting to get sweat beads on my upper lip, she was rubbing her arms like she was cold.

"I was thinking more about your general attitude," Mom said.

"Like my 'tone'?" I said—and then wanted to tear my tonsils out.

"We could start with that," she said. "I know there's a fine line between sarcastic wit and disrespect, but you've always stayed on the right side of it."

I closed my eyes, but I couldn't shut out Mr. Baumgarten, and now her, telling me I couldn't express what I felt.

"Tyler." Mom's voice was sharp. "Look at me."

I did. Her skin was taut across the bridge of her nose. The dimples were absent.

"If you're mad about something, let's have it. We don't do the anger-ridden adolescent around here."

"But we do the depressed young adult really well."

Mom sat up tall—and then someone pounded on the door and opened it before I could even think "There's already one too many people in here."

Sunny flew in, eyes shining, smile pushing her cheekbones into points.

"Guess what?" she said.

Do tell.

"Mr. Baumgarten just called." She looked at Mom. "That's—"

"I know who he is," Mom said.

"Mr. Linkhart has to have quadruple bypass surgery. Not that that's good news—

I mean, it's horrible for him. But they want me to be his long-term sub!"

"For how long?" Mom said.

I already knew the answer before Sunny said, "For the rest of the school year!" On a day like this, what else could it be?

"I am so jazzed," Sunny said. I didn't even get to attempt an appropriate reaction, because she turned immediately to me. "I promise I won't cramp your style, Tyler. I even asked Mr. Baumgarten if it was appropriate, since you're in the honors class."

I sucked in air.

"And?" Mom said.

"He said if you gave me any trouble to send you his way." Sunny laughed. "He has kind of a dry sense of humor. Anyway—I think this is a real turning point for me."

"Have you told your father yet?" Mom said.

Now that was a ridiculous question.

Sunny nodded happily. "He's opening a bottle of sparkling cider. He wants us all in his study for a toast."

"I really—" I started to say.

"Tyler's buried in homework," Mom said. "But I'll be right down."

Sunny bounced out of the room and I turned gratefully to my mother.

"Thanks," I said.

"I didn't do it for you," she said. "I thought Sunny's angst dragged on too long too, but now that she's moving in a direction, she needs support. I'm excusing you from the celebration until you can do it without a sour look on your face."

When she was gone I turned to my reflection in the window. Sour. Was that what it looked like on the outside when you were being split open on the inside?

I didn't actually see "sour" in the glass. I saw a sheen of perspiration on my face—and, come to think of it, I felt it on the back of my neck and behind my knees. And it wasn't just frustration oozing from my pores.

I got up and went to the radiator, but it was iron-cold. The air on that side of the room was actually chilly, but the seat of my jeans was so warm you'd have thought I'd been perched on top of the stove.

Still feeling my rump to make sure I wasn't losing it, I went back to the window seat and lifted the cushion. Heat came up in a rush like the explosion in the chemistry lab. I stuck my hand into it, and my palm touched the heat source. Something leathery.

I drew my hand back and peered in. It was that book Candace lifted from the bus. I'd stuck it under there and forgotten about it.

I remembered it being warm before, but why was it now giving off heat like — like nothing I'd ever felt?

Moving with caution, I touched it again, and when it didn't burn my flesh off I pulled it out and sat with it on the seat. Now the warmth was in my hands.

Seriously — there had to be a logical explanation for this. It would only be a matter of time before I discovered it. The first step was obviously to open the thing and see what it said, but I was having a hard time bringing myself to do it. Tyler Bonning, afraid of what she was going to find?

Not likely.

I opened the cover and pressed my palm on the first page. I was surprised — and relieved — to feel coolness against my skin. But there was still something warm in there ...

Curiosity won out over feeling ridiculous. I flipped through the pages until I came to one that exuded the same heat that had previously burned my backside. The words seemed to rise up to meet me.

You like to have things put to you straight, and that's the way you prefer to shoot too.

Despite the warmth, I shivered. That was me to a *T*.

But there are some things that won't be explained in facts and statistics. You can't google them. They're things you can't know until you live them. If you're willing to accept that, this book will help you experience your way into what you want to know.

I stared at the words. Who said I wanted to know something?

YOU did.

When?

When your heart broke.

And this was when?

That's part of what you need to know. We'll start with a story.

I shoved the book onto the seat beside me and shrank away from it. I had just had a conversation with it. I read the words and thought my questions and it answered them. Right? Wasn't that what just happened?

I picked it up again and looked at the page.

You did. When your heart broke. That's part of what you need to know.

That was all gone. But the words had been so clear in my mind, and I hadn't put them there.

The book went back on the seat, and I got up and paced, hands sopping wet with sweat and fear. Either I was losing it, or I'd *already* lost it and had entered a psychotic world where books answered your thoughts with words that disappeared the minute you read them. And yet—I wanted more...

I stopped and looked back at it, still sprawled there on the window seat. I did want more. Even with my heart racing and my hands so wet they left damp prints on my jeans as I wiped them on my thighs, I wanted to know what else it had to say. What if I *was* headed for a crack-up? At least this voice was talking to me and listening to me—and not telling me to watch my tone.

Slowing my breathing, I went back to the window seat and opened the book again. As I'd already seen, most of the "conversation" we'd just had was gone. All that was left was—

They're things you can't know until you live them. If you're willing to accept that, this book will help you experience your way into what you want to know.

"Okay," I said out loud. "What have I got to lose? Besides my mind."

I turned the warm page to printing that didn't look like it would dissolve any second like invisible ink in a Nancy Drew mystery.

Yeshua arrived in Jericho and took a walk through the town.

Yeshua — the Aramaic name for Jesus. Jericho — a town in ancient Israel. I looked at the cover again. The same crease, carvings, and engraved RL looked back at me, so it probably wasn't a Bible. A commentary, maybe? They didn't use this curriculum in any Sunday school I'd ever gone to. I'd figure it out later. For now, I turned back to the page.

There was a guy there named Zacchaeus. I'd normally call him Zach, but since you've already figured out that this is biblical, let's just call him Zacchaeus.

I pressed my hands to my mouth. Okay — I was losing it.

My mind scrambled for an explanation. A lot of people probably read that far and knew it was a Bible story. Probably some of the people whose initials were carved into the cover. It wasn't reading my mind. I was okay.

Zacchaeus was a tax collector, and not just any tax man but the Big Boss of tax men. If this guy audited you, you better hope you had a receipt for every cup of coffee you claimed as a travel expense or you were toast. Burnt toast.

I didn't know that much about the IRS, but I was aware that (a) you didn't want to tangle with them because, in my father's words, you'd think it was their personal money and they were being cheated out of it, and (b) the ones in the Bible were usually in the same camp as Bernie Madoff.

He was worth millions, and you didn't have to be a rocket scientist to figure out where it came from. He wasn't popular, but otherwise, he had it all.

I had to ponder that for a second. The rich people I knew — the Ruling Class — "had it all," *including* popularity. *I* didn't like them, but they were popular with each other, and everybody knew them, thought they were cool, let them run the school — no matter what Mr. Baumgarten thought.

I couldn't untangle it yet so I read on.

The only thing Zacchaeus still wanted was to see Yeshua, and yet despite his wealth and influence — as in, he could usually force anybody to do anything he wanted — he hadn't been able to get in to see him yet. He was actually desperate.

I took a chance with my sanity and thought, "Why?"

Everybody in Jericho had heard about the miracle worker, the healer, who not only claimed to be the Son of God but could do things only God could do. Like possibly help Zacchaeus turn his life around? Who knows?

One thing was for sure — this definitely wasn't the Bible. At least, not the way it had been taught to me. I'd been told it was this perfect book with all the answers and you didn't question it. And it sure didn't tell you it didn't "know."

That actually spurred me to read on.

So the day Yeshua walked through Jericho, Zacchaeus was in the crowd, trying to at least get a glimpse of him. The problem was, all he could see were elbows and backsides. He was a short little dude—interesting, seeing how he was so feared—so his only option was to—

"Climb a tree," I said out loud.

The story was coming back to me now. When I was eight, one wacky Sunday school teacher in Long Island had us all climb trees in the churchyard while she taught the lesson from below. Knees got scraped and Sunday dresses got torn and parents had fits. Except mine. They thought it was creative, until when they quizzed me about it over that afternoon's leg of lamb, I didn't know the point of the lesson. After eight *more* years of Sunday school, I still didn't. Hence my decision to worship with the bobolinks.

But maybe now I'd get an explanation. It couldn't hurt.

Zacchaeus's shrewdness kicked in, and he raced ahead of the crowd, in the direction Yeshua was walking, and shinnied up a sycamore. It was the perfect vantage point for seeing the man when he went by.

That was it? He just wanted to *see* him?

But when Yeshua got to the tree, he looked up and made eye contact with Zacchaeus, which Zacchaeus was NOT expecting. He was expecting even less for him to say, "Zacchaeus, come on down."

"We're going to your house for tea," I said. Those were the words to the song that same wacko teacher had tried to get us to sing. No self-respecting third-grader was doing *that*. Besides, who went to somebody's house for *tea*? Pizza maybe . . .

Zacchaeus didn't care if it was for liver and onions. He was blown away that Yeshua would want to be a guest in his home. He wasn't any more flabbergasted than the people who heard it. What was up with Yeshua wanting to hang out with this crook when they were respectable, churchgoing people?

I could see that, actually. It reminded me of having my pencils all sharpened and my homework all done and my extra credit ready and my hand up in the air to answer the questions practically before the teacher asked them — and she was over there dealing with the fourth-grade version of YouTube McKinney. I always wondered why the kids who stuck crayons into the pencil sharpener and wrote stuff on their desktops with Magic Marker got all the attention. Junior jackals.

Zacchaeus was no doubt asking himself the same question. And then he broke out of his stunned state and said, "I give half my income to the poor, and if I'm caught cheating, I pay four times what I owe the person."

I thought everybody said he was a crook. Was he lying? Or were they?

You like it black and white, don't you?

What isn't black and white about that? Either he wasn't a crook to begin with or he was and he was trying to make Yeshua believe he wasn't.

As if Yeshua didn't already know. In fact, Yeshua said, basically, "Let's go celebrate at your house, Zacchaeus. I came to find and restore the lost."

The rest of the page was blank.

"That's it?" I said. And then realized that, again, I was speaking out loud to somebody who was only there in words on a page in a book. Somehow it didn't feel quite as ridiculous as it had earlier, but I was irritated.

I didn't have a whole lot of time in my everything-crammed-in life. I definitely didn't have time to be figuring out stories that had never made any sense to me before, and yet somehow I'd managed to live without knowing.

But you want to know.

I jumped. Literally. Knocking the warm book sideways on my lap.

They're things you can't know until you live them. If you're willing to accept that, this book will help you experience your way into what you want to know.

Again with that. What I wanted to know was how I was going to go back to school tomorrow—*un*popular, *not* having it all—and stage an equality campaign, avoid being arrested for trying to blow off beauty queens' eyebrows, find an escort for the prom, deal with being friendless, and get through six more weeks of History with my sister as my teacher, not to mention handle my parents, who suddenly didn't get me anymore. *I* didn't even get me anymore. Suddenly I had all these feelings and passions, and all anybody could do when I tried to express them was say, "Watch your tone." What was I supposed to do with all that?

Maybe you should climb a tree.

"Thanks for that," I said.

I closed the book and stuffed it back under the seat. Maybe tomorrow I would take it back to the bus.

CHAPTER NINE

Patrick found me at my locker the next morning before school. He looked sleepy-eyed the way a three-year-old is when he just wakes up and can't wait to get out and play. It might have been cute if I didn't immediately remember him laughing it up with Alyssa in the library the day before. One minute he acted like he might be taking me seriously, and the next he was sharing some sick joke at my expense.

So I greeted him with a cold glance before I worked my combination.

"You okay?" he said.

"Why are you always asking me that?" I said.

His grin spread. "Here we go again with the questions. So—I sent you an email last night. Did you get it?"

I hadn't even checked my email. Too much weirdness going on in my room with the RL book talking to me.

"You sure you're okay?"

"Yeah," I said. I grabbed my health book and shut my locker. "And no, I didn't see your email."

"That's okay. I brought you a hard copy."

I blinked.

"Of the article."

"Right." I took the papers he handed me, two sheets stapled together.

"If you can read it before the end of first block, that would be great. Just text me and I'll come by the health room."

My head spun. "How did you know—"

"I looked up your schedule. Coach Wendover will never know you're sending a text."

"True," I said. "But I leave my phone in my locker—like, uh, we're supposed to."

His eyes did that thing—what was it this time, a tango? "You're the only nongeek I know who actually follows the rules."

"Is that a compliment?" I said.

He parked a hand lazily on the locker above me. "It was supposed to be. So—I'll meet you after first block and you can tell me what you think about the piece."

"Okay," I said.

I waited for him to leave, but he didn't. If anything, he looked even more comfortable standing there. "I like the way it turned out," he said, "and I liked everything you told me in the interview. But here's the thing—"

"I know 'the thing,'" I said. "Everyone has informed me of it, starting with Mr. Baumgarten."

"Have they told you to have a plan ready when the article comes out the day after tomorrow?"

My next words stumbled to a stop.

"You'll see when you read it. The article says you're determined to make this Prom for Everybody thing happen, so people are gonna want to know what you plan to do. I'm just saying be ready for that."

I took a full survey of his face for signs of threat, warning, glee. I didn't see any of that, but then, I hadn't seen him mocking me during the interview either.

"Just so you know," I said—completely without planning to—"I'm aware that it is unlikely anyone is going to ask me to the prom. It's not like that's new material for a stand-up routine."

"Okay—so—I have no idea what you're talking about."

"Egan said I have to have an escort."

"Yeah."

"You and Alyssa seemed to find that hilarious."

"We did?"

This boy was good. His brown eyes were wide and no longer doing the rumba. He had innocence *down*.

Or maybe he *was* innocent and I was a paranoid freak. I could feel the heat rising on my face.

"You know what, forget it," I said.

"You sure?"

"Absolutely. I need to get to class."

"Don't forget to read that. I'll see you after first."

I nodded feebly and turned around. Alyssa was right there. Of course.

"Why are you everywhere I am lately?" she said.

"You mean, in front of *my* locker?" I said.

Patrick laughed. I headed off down the hall, though not before I heard Alyssa say, "Shut up, okay? Just shut. Up."

*

First-block health was my least-favorite class, not only because it wasn't honors or because I'd put off taking it until junior year, which meant hardly anybody I really knew was in there. It was mostly because Coach Wendover never did anything but show videos of things like car wrecks resulting from DUIs and put us in groups to answer the questions at the ends of chapters. That morning, though, I was glad for the inevitable movie so I could read Patrick's article.

It was really good. As in sentences like, *Tyler Bonning's eyes are fiery when she points out that the standards of the prom have skyrocketed to the point where those who can't afford dinner at a five-star restaurant and a coach and four to get them there either opt out of going, or they risk ridicule when they arrive in Dad's car wearing less-than-Prada shoes*.

But I decided he was right. If I couldn't back that up with some kind of action plan by Friday when the Ruling Class read it, I was going to look like nothing more than a whiner.

I wondered what *Patrick* was going to look like when they read it. He didn't cut his friends any slack in there. "Lyssa" would be saying worse than "shut up."

The lights came on, and yawns and stretches erupted all over the classroom.

"All right, people," Coach Wendover said. Unlike Mr. Zabaski or Mr. Baumgarten, with their last names and their Miss So-and-So, he never called us anything but the collective "people." I wasn't sure that applied to the kid next to me, who was lifting his head from a puddle of saliva on his desk.

I stopped myself in midthought. Was I always that judgmental about people?

"I want you to get into groups," Coach Wendover was saying.

Big surprise.

"And do the activity at the end of chapter twenty."

I flipped there in my book and sniffed. The "activity" was ten questions on content.

Normally I would have just done it on my own, but this time I grabbed a spiral notebook out of my bag and crossed over to where my cousin Kenny was forming a group that included himself and three of the Kmart Kids. The drooly kid followed me. What was his name? Dizzy? Tizzy?

"You woke up, Izzy," Kenny said as we approached. "You got to go to bed nights, man."

Izzy grunted and fell into a desk next to the one I pulled into the circle. The other three faces stared at me blankly.

"You guys mind if I join you?" I said.

"Looks like you already did," said a girl with a precise bob and perfect pink lip gloss. Why had I never bothered to learn anybody's name?

"I was thinking I'd answer the questions," I said, "and turn them in for all of us if you'll talk to me about something else."

"I'm in," the other guy said.

The girl beside him punched him in the arm. Had to be his girlfriend. The way she commenced to drawing on his hand with a purple gel pen was a dead giveaway.

"What you wanna talk about, Cuz?" Kenny said.

"Seriously?" Pink Lips said. "She's your cousin?"

"You don't think we look alike, Ryleigh?" Kenny said.

"Not at *all*."

"He's definitely cuter," I said quickly. "Can we talk about the prom?"

Izzy dropped his face on the desktop and was immediately snoring.

Ryleigh and the girlfriend eyed each other the way I'd seen girls do when they were close—as if words were entirely unnecessary in certain situations.

"Is this about you being nominated for prom queen?" the girlfriend said.

"*She* was nominated for prom queen?" the boyfriend said.

"Shut *up*, Fred," she said, and punctuated it with another arm slug. That must be the new romance language.

"I was," I said. "It was totally a joke, but it woke me up to the fact that the prom has gotten completely out of hand in terms of how much people spend on it and how much they expect from it. I want to make it so anybody can go and feel like it's *their* prom—and I just need to know how you feel about that."

"I don't get it," Fred said. "Feel about what?"

"I get it." Ryleigh nodded at the girlfriend, who nodded with her. "You're asking us because we're the ones who can't afford, like, the stretch limo and the weekend party—"

"And the booze," Kenny said.

"I didn't even know you drank," I said.

"I don't. But that's what it's all about. People tryin' to sneak in alcohol and gettin' wasted."

"No, it's not about that," Girlfriend said.

"What's your name, by the way?" I said.

"Noelle. It's so weird that we've been in the same class all year—"

"Yeah," I said. "So, go on—what *is* the prom about?"

"It's about who's gonna be the most glammed out—wear the most expensive dress, have the designer manicure. I'm probably gonna spend three hundred dollars total—that's dress, shoes, everything." She twisted her cute mouth into a knot. "That wouldn't even cover a hair appointment for Alyssa Hampton. Not that I think she's bad or anything."

"You don't?" Ryleigh said. "I do. Okay—this doesn't have anything to do with the prom, but, like, all the time she and her friends will be talking in a class and one of us will say something and she'll just stop and look at us like 'why are you even talking?'"

"More like 'why are you even *here*?'" Noelle said. She leaned against Fred, who wrapped an arm around her neck. They could probably start locking lips right here and Coach Wendover would never notice. Come to think of it, weren't they the couple in the Sunday school class I dropped out of?

"So why would the prom be any different?" Ryleigh said.

"It isn't," Kenny said. "'Cept that it's worse."

"Like how?" I said.

"Like I wanna ask this one girl, only I can't afford no hotel room after—"

"Ho*tel* room?"

"Some kids' parents rent a room for them to party in after prom," Noelle said. "That way they won't drink and drive."

"It's not just that," Ryleigh put in. "My sister said that last year the Labels totally took over the dance floor."

"Labels?" I said.

"The kids wearin' Abercrombie and all that," Kenny said.

"Got it," I said. It was kind of clever, actually. "So go ahead, Ryleigh."

"Anyway, she said she and her friends—she went, like, in a group—couldn't even dance because *they* had it all, like, staked out, and then they'd just stand there locked together practically having—"

"Got that too," I said.

"I don't even want to go."

We all looked at Fred in time to see Noelle sit straight up and untangle herself from him. I expected the arm punch, or at the very least the "shut up," but she just stared at him, eyes filling with tears.

"You never told me that," she said.

"I know—but I'm hearing all this stuff, and it just doesn't even seem worth it."

Ryleigh frosted me with a look. "Thank you," she said.

All of this was stuff I basically already knew from Candace and my research. Time to push it down a different path. "What if it *was* worth it?" I said. "What if it was *your* prom—really yours, the way you wanted it?"

"Not gonna happen," Fred said.

Noelle did give him the "shut up" then. "I'd want to be able to get a really nice dress," she said to me, "and wear it without people going, 'Oh, did you get that at J. C. Penney?'—like there's something *wrong* with that."

"Somebody actually said that to my sister," Ryleigh said. "See, I'd want to get my and my date's picture taken by the professional photographer—"

"A party after, where you didn't have to get wasted to be cool." That was Kenny's input. I wrote it down, wondering what else I didn't know about my cousin who, last time I looked, was an absurd little creep.

"I just don't want all this pressure." We looked at Fred again. This time he didn't get punched. "Isn't it supposed to be, like, fun? Like this big turning point in your life or something?"

"Is that what you want it to be?" I said.

He looked at Noelle, whose eyes were still damp. "I just want it to be nice for her."

"That is so *sweet*," Ryleigh said. "Why are all the good ones taken?"

"I ain't taken," Kenny said.

"I said the good ones." Ryleigh grabbed his arm and shook it, and he messed up the front of her hair. She laughed as it slid neatly back into place. I felt a strange pang.

Noelle nodded at my notebook. "So what are you going to do with all this stuff you're writing down?"

"Come up with a plan."

"For what?"

"For making the prom something anybody can experience however they want to without feeling—"

"Like a loser?" Ryleigh said. "No offense, Taylor—"

"Tyler," Noelle said. "Right?"

"Well, no offense, but like Fred said, I don't see anything changing."

"If it did," I said, "would it matter to you?"

They took a minute to answer, and somehow I was impressed by that. And also nervous. If they said no, I was going to look like more than a moron when that article came out.

"Yeah," Fred said finally. "It would matter. I'm sick of being treated like trailer trash when I'm not—and that's not just about the prom."

The group gave a unanimous nod. I let out the breath I hadn't realized I was holding.

*

Patrick was waiting for me outside the door when the bell rang, and I looked around to see if Alyssa was in the vicinity. She wasn't, but I didn't doubt she'd show up at the exact moment when Patrick said anything that could be misinterpreted as me going after her man. As if.

"Well?" Patrick said.

"Actually," I said, "it's great." I handed him the article. "I marked one little place where you had a subject-verb agreement issue, but other than that ... seriously, I like it."

"Then why do you look like somebody just took away your birthday?"

"It shows, huh?" I said—before I could stop myself. Why did I always end up saying things I had no intention of saying to this boy?

"You just look worried." He nodded me down the hall with him. "I'll walk you to your French class."

"Do you know how disconcerting it is that you know my class schedule?" I said as I fell into step beside him.

"No," he said, "because I don't even know what *disconcerting* means."

"It weirds me out," I said.

"Oh." He grinned again. Still. "Good," he said. "So, what's with the long face?"

I gave up trying to evade the question. He would just ask another one.

"Okay—so I'm announcing my campaign, publicly."

"Yeah."

"And I just interviewed a group of kids who now have a glimmer of hope that something's going to change. Only I still don't know how I'm going to do it."

"Which is why you need a plan."

"I'm working on it."

"You have anybody to help you? Any of your friends?"

I did manage to bite back, *What friends?* I was about to sit across the aisle from Deidre for an hour and a half and I didn't even know if she was speaking to me. She hadn't lied about "staying away."

"I haven't gotten that far," I said.

We stopped outside Madame Upchurch's room. She was about as French as I was, but she insisted on us calling her Madame. We, of course, were Mademoiselle and Monsieur. Monsieur YouTube was my personal favorite.

"You don't have your phone with you, right?" Patrick said. "Okay, write down my number, and if you want—"

"Patrick, you are *not* serious!"

My eyes rolled completely up into my head, I was sure. Was there nowhere I could go without this girl stalking me?

Alyssa stomped up to us and without so much as a glare at me wrapped her talons around Patrick's arm and yanked him to the other side of the hall. *He* looked at me, but I shook my head. I so did not want to get in the middle of *that* situation.

Still I had to wonder, as I went on into the French room, what a maybe-nice and clearly intelligent guy saw in somebody like her. If that was what it took to hook a boyfriend, I wasn't likely to have one. Ever. Not that I was interested right now—but "ever" was a long time. I felt that pang again.

I didn't feel it, however, when I got to my desk and Deidre was no longer sitting next to me. One glance revealed her in the back, where she'd wanted to sit anyway when we first chose seats at the beginning of the year. I always wanted to be closer to the front. So, evidently, did Valleri, who picked up her backpack and moved from the second-to-last seat and slid into Deidre's old one.

"Is this okay?" she said.

"Are you kidding?" I said. "And remind me to work with you on partner assignments. You probably speak French better than 'Madame.' Not that that's the only reason I want you sitting next to me," I added. Had I always been this socially inept?

"So what's up?" she said.

"Am I walking around with a sign on my back that says, 'Ask me what's wrong'?" I shook my head. "Sorry. It's this prom thing."

While Madame Upchurch took roll, during which we each had to answer, "Bonjour, Madame," I filled Valleri in on everything that had happened regarding the prom situation since she did my makeover in the girls' restroom. She never took her blue eyes off me—until Madame told us we could only continue our conversation if we did it entirely in French.

Like that was going to happen.

But the minute class was over and we were headed for the cafeteria, Valleri made me pick up where I'd left off. By the time we turned the corner, I was wrapping up with, "It's bigger than I thought. I'm not sure I can pull it off by myself."

She put her hand on my arm and nodded toward the cafeteria door. The entrance was clogged with bodies, some of them holding others piggyback so they could see in. My stomach took a nosedive. The last time there had been this much interest in something, my entire life had turned upside down.

"Let's go in the back way," I said.

That would mean running into the Fringe—but they were the ones staying away from me, not vice versa. And there was no way I was trying to get through the mob, even though it was eerily quiet. Silent, even.

"What's going on?" Valleri said as we hurried toward the entrance.

"I don't think we want to know. Let's just get our food and go out to the courtyard."

There wasn't a sound in the lunchroom as we pushed through the door. It was as if the entire place had slipped into a coma.

They hadn't. Every single person was merely focused on a scene going down in the middle of the long stretch of freshman and sophomore tables. I couldn't see what it was at first for the wall of people surrounding it. Their silence was explained by YouTube, who was standing on the table, video camera in hand, shooting straight down at whatever was transpiring below. And whatever it was, it was so outrageous that every face in the place was the color of Bob the Tomato.

YouTube motioned to someone beneath him and then watched whoever it was, his own face contorted with the delight of it all. Those in the crowd who had a clear view convulsed anew, and the people behind them elbowed in and then did the same. I, personally, looked around to see where the teacher/monitor of the day was. There wasn't an adult in sight, and with the feeling that charged the air right now, there needed to be.

Matthew, Yuri, and Deidre were sitting at our old table, sharing a plate of generic nachos as if there weren't a silent riot raging around them.

"What's going on?" I whispered.

Somebody told me to *shh*.

The Fringe shrugged at me and went back to their processed cheese.

"Move that over," I said.

Deidre shot me a dark look, but Matthew picked up the nachos and held them out of the way while I climbed up onto the table. Valleri tugged at my hand and I pulled her up with me. And then I froze.

Dead center in the sophomore section, Izzy was slumped over on the tabletop, face slack with sleep, the inevitable drool pooling under his mouth. One of YouTube's cronies was spraying purple dye into Izzy's tumble of hair. Hayley and Joanna were busily painting his nails a hideous shade of magenta. Still another male member of the Ruling Class was holding something up for all to appreciate, which must have accounted for that last spasm of held-back hilarity. I could make out the gold hoop earring in one hand, but what was that thing in the other one?

"They're going to pierce his ear!"

Half the crowd whirled around to look at Valleri, who shouted it again. The other half groaned as Izzy jerked awake and looked up, bewildered. Now that they had permission to laugh it up all they wanted, the whole cafeteria shrieked. The half of Izzy's face that hadn't been turned to the table was a mass of orange blush, scarlet lipstick, and enough garish-blue eye shadow for a whole chorus line.

YouTube brought the camera just inches from Izzy's face and yelled, "You ready for your close-up?"

Izzy shoved the camera away and pushed himself back from the table. He tried to run, but it was hard to do in a pair of gold stilettos.

"That is so horrible!" Valleri cried.

Izzy shot past us, sans the shoes, and Valleri jumped down from the table and went for the door. I climbed down just as Mr. Baumgarten parted the crowd from the other end. *All* I needed was for him to see me standing on a table. I'd probably get the blame for this too.

"She should leave him alone," Yuri said.

"What?" I said.

"Homeschool. She should just leave Izzy alone."

"Like all of you did?" I said.

Deidre sighed. "What do you want us to do—go after him and give him therapy?"

"I'm talking about when it was happening. Why didn't somebody go stop it?"

"What are you, the bully police now too?"

"Just leave it alone!" Yuri snatched up his camera and his backpack and shoved three people out of his path to the door.

"Look out, Matthew," Deidre said in a dead voice. "You'll be the next one she ticks off."

"What is going *on*?" I said. "How did I tick Yuri off?"

Deidre folded her arms and glowered. I turned to Matthew.

He let out a low groan, as if I'd just asked him to open a vein.

"*What?*" I said.

"You weren't here in middle school," he said. "They used to do that kind of stuff to Yuri all the time. He tried to stand up for himself, but like he was going to get anywhere with that. He finally learned how to make himself invisible with his photography and all that, and now they leave him alone."

"And that's the goal — to just be left alone?" I said.

"Works for me," Deidre said to her fingernails. "Worked for you too, until you turned into the ACLU. Matthew — what happened to our nachos?"

"You're against everything," I said. "Even if it's good."

Deidre finally looked at me. "Where did that come from?"

I didn't know. Maybe it was from what I saw when I was standing on the table. Or from what I wasn't seeing down here in my friends' eyes.

"You're against everything," I said again. "But are you *for* anything? Do you *believe* in anything?"

Matthew shook his bangs over his eyes. Deidre leaned into the table. "I believe in getting through this year and getting out of this place. And I'm going to do it by keeping my head down and my mouth shut. I thought we were having a pretty good time doing that together."

"I guess the party's over," I said.

I walked out and left the Fringe table behind.

Valleri met me at the door.

"Did you find him?" I said.

She shook the curls, and tears sparkled in her eyes. "I want to help," she said.

"I know. Izzy might not want help, but — "

"No. I want to help *you* — with the prom campaign."

I looked closer. "You're serious."

"God doesn't want me to sit around and let one group of people make everybody else's life miserable," she said.

I didn't ask her how she knew that. But I didn't doubt that she did.

CHAPTER TEN

That night at the dinner table I escaped going under the maternal microscope, because all lenses were again focused on Sunny.

"I messed up my very first day," she wailed as soon as the amens were said.

My ears perked up. This could be good news.

Mom grunted. "Everybody messes up their first day. My first hour nursing, I dumped a bedpan on a vascular surgeon. A full bedpan."

"No, I really messed up. I didn't know it was Mr. Linkhart's turn to do lunch duty. While I was sitting there in the teacher's lounge eating my salad, evidently all Hades broke loose in the cafeteria." She looked across the table at me. "Did you see what happened?"

That explained the absence of adults on the scene. "I caught the end of it," I said.

"Could I have stopped it?"

I had to say yes. *I* could have stopped it if I'd gotten there soon enough.

"Then I feel terrible," she said.

"Did you get called on the carpet?" Dad said.

Sunny shook her head. "Mr. Baumgarten said not to worry about it. He said nobody was hurt—"

I let my fork drop to my plate, splattering hollandaise sauce. "Nobody was *hurt*? That poor kid was humiliated, and now it's going to be all over the Internet. He'll probably be scarred for the rest of his life."

Sunny put her face in her hands. My mother lowered her chin to look at me.

"I didn't say it was *her* fault," I said. "Those jackals have been at this since middle school, and nobody's stopped them. Not yet, anyway."

Sunny shook her head at me. "It's not going to happen again on *my* watch," she said.

Well. Interesting.

*

I didn't really have time to analyze it, though, because that night and whenever we could grab a minute on Thursday, Valleri and I were trying to come up with a Prom for Everybody Plan.

I went to the Internet and looked up what other schools were doing—everything from canceling the whole thing to replacing it with an elaborate scavenger hunt with a sit-down dinner at the end—but none of it sounded like what Ryleigh and her friends were asking for.

Meanwhile, Valleri was writing questions in different colored markers on a big piece of butcher paper she kept rolled up in her locker—*Where can girls get great dresses at reasonable prices? How can we make the photography awesome AND affordable? What kind of after party would be safe, inexpensive, AND a blast? What do we have to do to keep booze out and fun in? Is there a way-cool way to get to the prom without hiring a limo? Where can you get your hair and nails done without your parents having to take out a second mortgage?*

We thought we'd have time in fourth block—History—to work on some actual answers while people were putting the last-minute touches on their presentations. The Andrew Jackson one was ready; I would be virtually giving it by myself, since Yuri and Matthew weren't returning my calls.

But Sunny—Ms. Bonning as the rest of the class called her—had other plans.

"Anybody whose report is ready," she said to us, "I want you to get a head start on the next unit. These presentations will take care of presidents from Jackson to Coolidge, but I want our study of the Great Depression, World War Two, and the second half of the twentieth century to be a little more in-depth."

Depth? Now there was a novel idea.

"Most American History classes never get much past the Civil War," she went on—eyes sparkling like we were about to leave for the Bahamas. "But what's going to be important to you is what has happened in the last seventy-five years. So those of you who are set for the reports, I want you to read and outline the next five chapters. I'll be fleshing those out in my lecture series."

Egan's hair actually seemed to spike up farther. "You're going to *lecture*?"

"Lecture, challenge you to question, offer you a chance to express your views."

If anybody in there had a view about anything besides how to get out of doing work, it would be a total surprise. Right now everybody's view was of me. They were all glaring like I had personally imported this teacher who was expecting them to get off their rears and be honors students.

"Is there a problem?" I said to YouTube, who was opening and closing his history book and staring me down.

"You need to talk to her," he said.

"*You* talk to her. I have to read the next five chapters."

As much as I hated to admit it, I liked Sunny's approach. But it did mean Valleri and I didn't get to do much more work on our plan that day, and she had some kind of church thing that night. So when I arrived at school the next morning, we still didn't have much more than a list of questions that looked like a work of art. I was just discarding the idea of trying to get a pass to the library to work on it during math—like Mrs. O'Hare would see a connection between geometry and the media center—when Patrick was suddenly there at my locker. I automatically looked for Alyssa.

"I thought you'd want to see this before everybody else got it at lunch," he said.

He wore the same sleepy look he had on Wednesday, but he was losing it fast—like it was Christmas morning or the first day of vacation. He put a folded newspaper in my hand.

"Is this—"

"The *Castle Heights Herald,*" he said.

For a school newspaper, it was pretty impressive. I had seen some lame ones, but this one was almost professional. Ms. Dalloway's staff won awards every year. Right now, however, I was concerned about what they did with the prom queen piece.

I didn't have to look far. Right on the front page was the headline: Prom Queen Finalists Announced.

Below it were two pictures with columns beneath them above the fold, and two under the fold. Mine was on the top right, although I had to stare at it for a few seconds to make sure it was me. I didn't look that gawky up there on the ladder, looking down with an expression of—what could you call it? Amused wisdom? The photo was in color, and the red of Valleri's top popped and made my smile and my eyes sort of rise from the page. It may have been the best picture I'd ever seen of myself.

"Great pic, huh?" Patrick said. He had a whole kick line going in his eyes right then.

"Ms. Dalloway did a good job," I said.

"She had a good subject. And you've read the article—they didn't edit anything out. So are you ready?"

"You mean with a plan?"

He nodded.

"I wish. I have a friend working on it with me, but so far all we have is what *needs* to happen—not how it's *going* to."

"You need more help, then."

I started to agree, but movement at the end of the hall caught my eye. Blonde hair was rounding the corner.

"I've got to go," I said. "And listen, thanks for this. At least it'll raise some awareness, huh?"

I didn't wait for him to answer, because Alyssa was gaining on us. I clutched the newspaper and pretty much ran down the hall until I got to the girls' restroom and darted in.

"Cheated death again," I said to my face in the mirror.

"I wasn't planning on killing you. But don't tempt me."

Alyssa was in the mirror with me, green eyes flashing. She

must have blown right past Patrick without even telling him to "shut up." I decided to do the same thing to her and turned from the sink, but she stepped into my path.

"Oh, come on," I said. "We're not in some cheesy teen movie. Look—I don't want your boyfriend, I don't want your prom queen title, I don't want anything that's yours, so can we just not do this every time we see each other? It's a really small school."

"I didn't *think* you wanted the title." She couldn't seem to help looking past me at her reflection and fluffing her hair. "If you don't want it, why haven't you withdrawn your name?"

"I have my reasons," I said.

"You have one reason." She cut her eyes back to me, and her nostrils flared. How had I ever thought this girl was pretty? "And that's Patrick."

"I just told you I don't want your man."

"He's not *my* man."

"Then why do you care if I have a conversation with him?"

"Let's just say I'm protecting someone else's interests."

"Then you can chill," I said, "because I'm not 'interested' in Patrick that way."

"Huh. Every girl is interested in Patrick. And if she's not, he works at it until she is. Just so you know."

A little piece of me caved somewhere, but I'd have to get back to it later. Right now, I was completely done with this.

"I'll make a note of it," I said.

I tried again to get around her. This time she put the heel of her hand on my shoulder, which I stared at until she moved it.

"Look, you didn't grow up here," she said, "so you don't know how it works."

"Nor do I want to."

"But you need to, or somebody's going to get hurt."

"Enough with the movie script!"

"No—I am dead serious." She got her face so close to mine I could see the veins in her eyes, irritated by those green contacts. "Everybody has their group and nobody's out to bring anybody else's group down. It's always worked fine that way, and the only time we ever have any trouble here is when people come in and start trying to mess with that."

I forgot about trying to get past her as I planted my feet, toes touching hers.

"That is not true on any level I can *think* of," I said. "First of all, your 'group' did everything it could to bring Izzy down yesterday, and not one single person lifted a finger to help him because they were all afraid they would be next. Second of all, your same 'group' had nothing *but* humiliation in mind for me when you nominated me for prom queen. Thirdly—"

"Are you *serious*?" Alyssa's bigger-than-average teeth all showed as she gaped at me. "That thing with Izzy didn't 'bring him down.' He knows we were just messing with him." She raked her hand through her hair. "See, that's what you don't get. We've always done stuff like that—it's like we gave Izzy his fifteen minutes of fame."

"Or infamy," I said.

"Whatever. Nobody even got in trouble for it. If it was a big deal, Mr. Baumgarten would've busted them."

"Oh, well," I said, "then why are we even talking?"

She didn't look the least bit fazed by the sarcasm dripping from my voice. It took me a second to realize she hadn't heard it.

"Exactly," she said. "So, anyway, your little 'thing' with Patrick? It isn't going to last. You might as well give it up and let somebody who really cares about him have a chance."

"Someone from the right 'group,'" I said.

"Yes," she said. "Listen, don't take this the wrong way, but do you even have a group?"

"What way am I supposed to take it?"

She blinked several times and then tossed her hair and let it lead her to the door. "I'm done," she said.

I looked at the newspaper I was still holding. She wasn't going to be done when she saw that. She was just going to get started.

*

I was right. Before Valleri and I even got to the cafeteria at lunchtime, people were passing us saying everything from, "Is that really you in that picture?" to "I didn't think you were actually running for queen. I thought it was a joke." That didn't bother me. What made my stomach juices stir were the people who glanced at me and hurried on, whispering, and the one Kmart Kid who just said, "Good luck with that."

I stopped Valleri before we reached the door. "If you want to bail, this is the time to do it."

"Why would I?"

"You haven't even had a chance to get adjusted here and all of a sudden you're going to be the target of every RC in the school."

"I can't quit," she said, eyes round. "This is a God thing."

"You're going to have to explain that to me." I looked at the doorway. "Later."

The entire Ruling Class was headed toward me, newspapers folded to my picture in angry creases, some held out in front of them like pieces of evidence.

"You'd better start praying," I said to Valleri.

Alyssa was the first one to speak, although I wasn't sure how she could with her lip curled all the way up to her nostrils. "You just don't get it, do you?" she said.

But Egan stepped in front of her, looking like he was ready to spit. "You don't know what we had to go through to even *get* a prom this year. My committee's working their tails off so it won't be lame, or even close to lame." He shook the paper in my face. "You don't even know what you're talking about. This is all—"

He swore and snatched the paper away. I was surprised he *didn't* spit.

"You totally made the rest of us sound shallow or something." That came from Joanna, who was fanning her eyes with her hands. The whine in her voice was enough; she didn't need tears. "I didn't know it was supposed to be like a college interview. I thought we were just talking about prom!"

The fanning didn't help. She cried anyway, and a confused-looking Hayley put an arm around her.

"So what do you want?" I said. "I mean, is there some purpose here?"

"Yeah," YouTube said. "We just wanted to say thanks for ruining prom for us."

"How am I ruining it? I'm just pointing out the inequities in it and encouraging people to get the thing back into perspective."

He looked at the rest of the Ruling Class. "What the—What is she talking about?"

Alyssa drilled her eyes into me. "She's saying we should all feel bad because we can afford limos and the Kmart Kids can't."

"Oh," he said. "Well, I don't."

Egan shook the newspaper again. His eyes were watering. "So is this it? Or are you going to try to have it cancelled or something?"

"I don't want to cancel it." I looked at Valleri, who was still standing next to me, hands folded under her chin. She nodded so slightly I hoped I didn't just imagine it. "I want to give everybody a chance to make it special," I said.

"It already is!" Egan said.

"It won't be for some people if we don't help."

Alyssa clapped her hands over her head. "Y'know what? Why are we wasting our time talking? Nothing is going to happen, because she doesn't even have any friends to help her pull it off."

"Yes, she does."

Every head turned to the door behind them, where Patrick was standing with a rolled-up newspaper, tapping it in the palm of his hand.

"Who?" YouTube said.

"Me," Patrick said.

"She's gonna make the prom lame and tacky and stupid, man!" Egan cried. Literally. With tears in his voice.

"Aw, come on, Egan. Does Tyler look stupid to you?"

Why did he have to ask that question?

But Egan was shrugging, and swallowing so hard it looked painful.

"I think the idea rocks and I'm in," Patrick said. "Anybody else?"

I looked at Joanna and Hayley, fully expecting them to raise their hands and giggle. It *was* Patrick, after all.

But they were looking at Alyssa, who wasn't as subtle as Valleri. She shook her head so many times they would have had to be missing some serious brain cells not to get the message. Their hands stayed down.

So did everybody else's, but Patrick continued to grin as if they'd all jumped right on board.

"I guess it's on, then, Tyler," he said to me over their astonished heads.

"I guess it is," I said.

CHAPTER ELEVEN

I woke up the next morning, Saturday, to find my mother sitting on the edge of my bed. I bolted up, heart pumping. Something major had to have happened, because she hadn't even done this when I was a kid.

"What's wrong?" I said. "Did Dad get in an accident or something?"

"For heaven's sake, no. I just wanted to talk to you about this." She held up a copy of the *Castle Heights Herald.*

"Where did you get that?" I said.

If she'd been digging through my bag, I'd have to assume this woman had tied up my mother somewhere and stolen her face. But even the face didn't look like the Mom I knew. Her lips were all pursed and disapproving, and her forehead was in furrows so deep you could have planted seeds in them.

"Sunny showed it to me," she said.

Somebody remind me to thank her later.

"How long have you known you were a prom queen nominee?"

"About two weeks." I squirmed. "Could I just go to the bathroom?"

"As soon as you explain why you didn't tell us about this."

"Mom, it's not like a suspension or something." I held up my hand before she could remind me about my "tone." "Sorry. You're just making it sound like I did something wrong."

"You didn't do anything 'wrong.' I just want to know why you kept it from us."

I licked my sleep-dry lips. My breath was probably pretty

nasty about now. It occurred to me that I more than likely did not look as cute as Patrick did when he woke up.

"I didn't think you'd be interested," I said. "You were pretty wrapped up in Sunny."

"Try again."

"It was a joke, okay? On me. I just wanted to handle it and move on."

Mom looked at the paper. "It doesn't look like a joke to me. This is a lovely picture, by the way. Where did you get that top?"

"My friend Valleri."

"And she is . . . ?"

"A new girl. Mom—" I dug some crust out of my eyes. "Did you read the article?"

"I did."

"Then you know why I stayed in the contest. It's giving me a chance to speak out on something. You and Dad are always telling me to do that."

"On something significant."

I stared. "This is significant."

"It's the prom, Tyler. I didn't even know you planned to go."

"I didn't. I didn't even want to go through with this until I went shopping with Candace this one day."

"Your dad said something to me about that, but—"

"We had a half day, so she and I took the bus to the mall. Anyway, she's the one who told me how out-of-hand the prom is and how—well, everything you saw in the article."

She nodded. I had to give my mom credit: she was a fair person.

"So," I said, "one thing led to another and Valleri and I decided to do something about it. And now this guy Patrick is helping, which is huge because he's one of them—I mean, he has money, he's popular, all that."

"What do you mean by 'do something about it'?"

"I'm not sure yet. We know what needs to happen but we don't exactly know how to do it, but now that Patrick's behind it, I think we can make a difference."

I stopped, because Mom was no longer nodding.

"It sounds like it's going to take a tremendous amount of energy," she said.

"Yeah ..."

"Are you sure this is where you want to channel it?"

"It's about equality. You and Dad are all about that. This is going to make more of a difference than trying to get more AP classes."

Mom shook her head. "We want you to stand up for what's right, but this—I don't know, I can't wrap my mind around it yet. I need to talk to your dad. *You* need to talk to him."

She stood up.

"Wait," I said. "Are you saying you don't want me to do this?"

"Not saying that at all. I'm saying I want you to really think about it and discuss it with us. We have always let you make your own decisions whenever we can."

"There's a 'but' in there."

"Maybe. I just don't know what it is yet. Your dad had a breakfast meeting, but when he gets home, we should all talk."

"All?" I said.

"You and your father and me."

"Okay," I said. At least she wasn't bringing Sunny into it. I was already prepared to smack my sister the next time I saw her.

I couldn't go back to sleep after Mom left, but I couldn't lie there and try to sort this out, either. Mom was the second-to-last person I'd think would stand in my way on something like this. Dad was the last.

That actually made me feel better. He'd see the principle behind this and tell Mom to relax.

But I still felt sullen when I went downstairs to scavenge for something to eat. Mom had left a note saying she was grocery shopping, so I had the kitchen to myself to pout in. I almost didn't answer the landline when it rang—until I saw *Patrick Sykes* on the caller ID.

"Hey," he said when I picked up. "You ready to get started on this today?"

"Uh, yeah," I said. "When?"

"Now?"

"Oh. I'm still—" I squeezed my eyes shut. Should you mention to a guy that you're in your pajamas? I had no idea.

"Give me an hour," I said. "I need to call Valleri."

"An hour's good. Your house?"

"Sure," I said. "I bet you know where it is."

"I looked you up."

"This *could* be construed as moderately creepy," I said.

"Man—I *love* the way you talk."

"So you've said." In the back of my mind, I heard Alyssa saying, *Every girl is interested in Patrick. And if she's not, he works at it until she is.*

"See ya in an hour," Patrick said, and I knew he grinned his way off the line.

I abandoned the Pop-Tart I'd put in the toaster and ran upstairs to simultaneously find something not Saturday-sloppy to wear and get Valleri on the phone. She answered in a stupor. Evidently not a morning person.

When I finally got through to her why I was calling, she said, in a voice thick as porridge, "Oh, I'm sorry, Tyler. We're going to Albany today. I won't be home until six."

I sagged.

"But you and Patrick go ahead and meet. I'm more of a behind-the-scenes person anyway."

I paused.

"You still there?" she said.

"Yeah. You don't think—I mean, it's okay. Should I meet with him alone, just us?"

"Why not?"

"I don't know," I said.

*

Patrick arrived exactly one hour from the time I hung up the phone. He and my father pulled into the driveway at the same time. In true Dad fashion, my father introduced himself, shook Patrick's hand, and had a good start on Patrick's life story by the time they got to the front door.

"What do you two have planned today?" he said.

"We're working on a project," Patrick said.

"And we thought we'd do it down at Scarnato's Cafe, if that's okay." I widened my eyes at Patrick. Though he looked a little puzzled, he nodded.

"That'll work," Dad said. "You have money, Ty?"

"I'm covered," I said.

We were in Patrick's Jeep before he said, "What was that about?"

"He always asks me if I have money when I go out someplace. He wants me to be independent, take care of myself."

Patrick grinned. "Like he ever has to worry about that. I was talking about the going-to-the-coffee-shop thing. I mean, it's fine — it's great. I just thought you said we were working here."

"We were. But then I thought it would be better ..." I sighed. "Okay, I haven't told him yet what I'm doing, and my mother already interrogated me about it this morning, so — "

"Gotcha," Patrick said. "At least your parents give a rip what you do."

"Yours don't?"

"They do. When they're home."

I just nodded. This was actually a surprise. He seemed like a kid who came from a soccer family that went skiing together every Christmas, that kind of thing. Interesting.

It didn't occur to me until we were staring at the menu board at Scarnato's that I had no idea what to order at a coffee shop. Hot chocolate suddenly seemed unsophisticated, which led me to wonder why I *cared* whether I looked sophisticated to Patrick — so when the guy behind the counter looked at me, all I could say was, "I'll have what he's having." Now *that* was sophistication at its highest.

I didn't have time to decide whether I actually liked it, because we got right to work on the Prom Plan. I went over the questions Valleri and I had come up with, as well as the ideas from other schools that we'd already tossed out. I shook my head at the list, but Patrick was, of course, grinning.

"What?" I said.

"You already did all the hard stuff. No, wait. How would you say it?" He pulled his grin into a face I wouldn't have mistaken for serious in a pitch-black room. "The difficult tasks have been completed at this juncture." The grin reappeared. "How was that?"

"Very impressive," I said dryly. "Do I really sound like that?"

"Nah. It sounds cool when you do it."

My face felt warm. I turned abruptly to the list. "So you're saying figuring out what to do next is the easy part?"

"Piece of quiche. Okay, take the tuxedo rental thing. My dad rents a tux, like, twice a month—I don't know why he doesn't just buy his own—but the guy he does business with? He'd give discounts in a heartbeat if I asked him. Plus, he'd probably do a drawing for a free rental—"

"We'd want it to be a contest, though, like whoever—"

"—comes up with the classiest way of asking his date to the prom gets a free tux for the night."

"Make it the most creative way. Classy sounds like money has to be involved."

"Good call. Okay—done." He put a large check mark next to that item. "What about dresses? Dude—what do you wanna bet Alyssa's got closets full of them?"

"Why?"

"She's all into the beauty pageant thing. She's in, like, three or four a year."

"Has she ever won?"

"I think she's made it to first runner-up. That's why prom queen is such a big deal to her."

I tapped the list. "So she's got fifty designer gowns and most of the girls have zilch. Where are you going with this?"

Patrick talked with his hands. "My mom is like the charity queen, okay? She helps run this thrift shop to raise money for families that have somebody dying and can't afford their medical bills or their rent or whatever."

"Resurrection Thrift Shop."

"Yeah, that's it."

"My mom donates to that. So, what, they have prom gowns for sale? How is that better than J. C. Penney?"

"We get girls like Alyssa, Hayley, all of them to donate their dresses they aren't going to wear again—'cause, like, I've heard them say you can't wear the same one twice."

Which I didn't get.

"And then girls that can't afford to buy stuff like that—or even from J.C. Penney—can come in and pick what they want."

"From things the Ruling Class brings in."

"Who?"

"What?"

"The Ruling Class?"

No—I did not just say that out loud. My face burned, all the way down to my neckline. Even I didn't have the vocabulary to get out of this.

But Patrick's smile was spreading. "You call Egan and those guys the Ruling Class?"

"Not out loud," I said. "Until just now when I opened my big mouth."

"So what qualifies a person for the 'Ruling Class'?"

"Could we just get back to the plan?"

"Yeah, but I wanna hear this."

I pressed my palm to my forehead. "It just seems to me that a certain class of people runs everything at Castle Heights. It's not just the prom and the basketball team and the cheerleading squad—it's what's in and what's not, who's accepted and who's not. That name just came into my head."

Patrick was now nodding soberly, the way he did the day he interviewed me. "Am I considered part of it?"

"You're the student council president," I said, treading carefully. "And you hang out with all of those people. Girls would probably surrender their iPhones to you if you asked them to."

I was starting to sweat.

"What do you think now?"

"I don't have an iPhone."

He blinked. "No, I mean, do you think I'm part of the Ruling Class now?"

"After yesterday, no," I said. "And you were fair in the article, and—" I held out both hands, now sparkling perspiration from every crease. "Here you are. So, I guess I misjudged you. I apologize."

He shook his head, and my entire chest sank. Until he said, "You are so totally different from any person our age that I have ever met. Nobody apologizes when they mess up. They just try to find a way to make it somebody else's fault."

"And you?" I said.

Patrick parked his chin in his hand, elbow on the table, and looked into me. "I'm working on it," he said.

"Hi."

Patrick twisted to see who was behind him. I didn't have to. It wasn't Alyssa, but I could tell by the voice it was one of the aforementioned Ruling Class. Even a "hi" smacked of entitlement.

"Hi, Joanna," Patrick said. "How ya doin', girl?"

Joanna blushed prettily—something I could never pull off—and as she looked down at Patrick, I noticed how long her eyelashes were. There was actually nothing about this girl that wasn't perfect. Alyssa had nothing on her.

"So—what are you doing?" she said, only glancing at me.

"Working on prom," Patrick said.

"Oh." She looked at one of the extra chairs at our table.

"Do you want to sit down?" I said. "I can move my stuff."

"No," she said, as if I'd just asked if she'd like to share my toothbrush. She tugged at Patrick's sleeve. "Could I talk to you privately for a minute?"

"Here's fine," he said. "You can join us."

His smile didn't change, but I could see the dancers disappearing from his eyes. If he was half as uncomfortable as I was, he could hardly stand to be in his own skin right now.

"Y'know, I really need to use the restroom," I said. "You two chat."

I didn't look back at them as I scooted through the café, though I did look thoroughly at myself in the mirror when I had the restroom door safely closed and locked behind me. Bathrooms weren't private places for me lately.

The face that looked back at me was definitely not Joanna Payne material. I'd never cared about that before. I really didn't now, and yet I was thinking about it. This was what we were fighting — Valleri and Patrick and me — this constant comparing and competing and assuring ourselves that we were okay as long as somebody else wasn't.

Did I do that?

No answer came to me, at least not before I'd spent enough time in there to have taken a complete shower. Steeling myself to see Joanna now planning the prom campaign with Patrick too, I opened the door and crossed to the table. But she was gone.

Patrick was doodling on the edge of my notes. He grinned when he looked up, but he didn't look that happy.

"I got you another latte," he said.

"Everything okay?" I said.

"Depends what you mean by okay."

"What do *you* mean by it?"

He frowned into the foam at the top of his cup. "Joanna just informed me that there already *is* a prom committee and that we're making Egan feel like he's not doing a good enough job."

"And that's not okay," I said.

"No. He's a buddy of mine. And he does do a good job — I mean, everything's gonna be, like, first class."

"We're not trying to make it second class. We're just trying to make it so first class doesn't exclude people."

He was watching me the way a little kid looks at your lips when you're telling him something he wants to understand. I suddenly felt like mine were huge.

"Okay," he said, "got it. But we have to make sure he knows exactly what we're doing. We have to put together this plan and then try to get him in on it."

"Do you seriously think he's going to do that?"

"Maybe not. I just said we have to try."

"And if he doesn't?"

"We move on without him."

"What about Joanna?"

"What about her?"

"You're losing friends right and left over this."

"What about you?"

I had to pause. "Yeah," I said. "I have. But I've made one—Valleri."

He pulled both shoulders up to his earlobes. "What am I? Chopped liver?"

"No. What *is* chopped liver, anyway?"

"I'm serious. Do you consider me a friend now?"

I fumbled around in my brain for a snappy little retort, but I didn't find one, and I was glad. He was watching me again through the steam coming off his cup, and his face could only be described as hopeful.

"I haven't had that many friends in my life," I said, "so I'm not good at spotting them when they show up. But, given the information and experience I have to work with, I consider you a friend."

"So was that a yes or what?"

"Yes, it was a yes."

He poked at my notes with his index finger. "Then could we get back to the job here? Dude—you got me off track."

"Like you weren't already halfway there. Okay—so, a 'dress shop'—"

We spent another hour going down the checklist, finishing each other's sentences, embellishing one another's ideas. We had everything covered but the photography; we still couldn't come up with a way for kids to get professional pictures for a low price. Other than that, we couldn't see why every junior and senior at Castle Heights High School couldn't have a great night they'd still be talking about at the ten-year reunion.

"I'm feeling pretty good about this," I said when Patrick dropped me off at my house.

"Oh yeah. We got it goin' on now. I'm gonna call Egan and talk to him. Call me if you come up with any other ideas."

"I don't have your number," I said.

"Yeah, you do." He gave me the day's last grin. "It's on your notes."

Why that made *me* want to grin was a question I avoided as I forced myself not to dance into the house. When I saw my parents standing in the foyer, I was glad I'd opted against breaking into a samba.

"Your mother tells me you were supposed to discuss this project with me," Dad said. Instead of hello.

"I said I would," I said. Yellow caution lights went on in my head.

"Then why didn't you say something before you left?"

"Because I didn't want to get into it in front of my friend."

"What made you think we were going to 'get into it'?"

"That's the way it seemed when Mom brought it up." I hitched up my bag on my shoulder. "I'm trying not to take a 'tone' with you guys, but I don't understand what's going on. I never had to get your approval on every school project before."

Mom leaned on the banister and folded her arms. "You've just never been this evasive about one before."

"I'll tell you anything you want to know."

"We'd love to hear." Dad shoved his hands into his pockets. "Ty, we're not trying to fight you on this. You're just acting a little ..." He looked at my mother.

"Out of character," she said. "It just seems like this goes beyond a 'school project,' and that concerns us."

Dad was nodding. "I read the article and I want you to know I'm proud of you—we both are. But the potential for this to blow up in your face is definitely there."

"You always say effecting change always involves risk," I said.

"Which is admirable if the change you're trying to make is *worth* the risk."

"Raising people's self-esteem isn't worth it?" I said. I had ceased caring what my voice sounded like.

"Does measuring up at the prom raise somebody's self-worth?"

My father's eyes were bright, and he was leaning toward me in that attitude of intensity that signaled he was warming up to the debate. Only I didn't see it as a debate, and I didn't want to argue about it anymore.

"So, bottom line," I said. "Are you saying I'm not allowed to go on with this?"

They looked at each other. Some kind of conversation went on with their eyes, while the skin on the back of my neck prickled.

"We're not going to stop you," Dad said finally. "But we'd like to be kept apprised of your progress."

"And if at any time we think it's not good for you—" Mom said.

"We'll revisit it."

My mother didn't exactly agree with that part, judging from the way she pressed her lips together. They'd be having a *real* conversation about that later, I was sure. Meanwhile, I had to get away from both of them so I could try to make some sense out of what had just gone down. Either that, or I was going to go beyond mere tone.

"May I go, then?" I said.

My father's eyes drooped, but he nodded. I took the stairs two at a time—and I was sure it wasn't from all those shots of espresso I'd just consumed.

And nearly fell over Sunny at the top of the steps.

"Did you hear enough?" I said.

Her face looked genuinely blank. "I didn't 'hear' anything. I was just going down to grab some lunch. You want anything?"

"Yeah," I said. "I want you to let me handle my own business with my parents."

The eyebrows went up. "You're going to have to explain that to me."

"You showed the newspaper article to Mom."

"And that was wrong because ..."

"Because they didn't know about it yet, and now they're

all up in my grillwork because they think what I'm trying to do isn't worth it—and it is. I'm sick of putting up with the way things are and I'm going to do everything I can to change it. So I'd appreciate it if you'd let *me* tell them what's going on with that from now on."

I stopped because I was breathing hard. And because I figured any minute I was going to see tears. All I needed was for Sunny to dip back into depression from me chewing her out.

But she tilted her head, and she smiled the way a person does when she finally gets quadratic equations.

"Well," she said. "The kid that wrote that article was right: you do have passion. I'm glad to see it." She gave me a kiss on the cheek. "I apologize, sis. Won't happen again."

I watched her go down the steps and put my fingers to my cheek. That clinched it, then: everyone I knew had had a personality transplant.

Including me.

Chapter Twelve

Patrick seemed to have made meeting me at my locker his new before-school ritual. Only Monday morning he didn't lazily start a conversation, arm leaning on the bank of lockers. He grabbed my arm and started off down the hall with me in tow.

"What's going on?" I said, running to keep up with him. The boy had some seriously long legs, even longer and lankier than mine.

"We have an appointment," he said.

"With who?"

"Mr. Baumgarten."

I dug in my heels and brought us both to a lurching halt at the corner.

"What's wrong?" he said.

"I'm not exactly Mr. Baumgarten's favorite student," I said. "I've been in his office twice, and both times I made his scalp turn red all the way down to his hair follicles."

I got the morning grin. "Have I told you how much—"

"Yes, about twelve times. I'm serious, Patrick. Why are we meeting with him anyway?"

"Because Egan didn't go for it." Patrick caught my arm again and resumed the towing down the hall. "First he blew off my phone calls. When I finally went to his house, he told me I was a traitor and I had to choose between the campaign or my friends." He slowed us down as we approached the office. "I asked him which 'friends' he meant, and he shut the door in my face."

"Ouch."

"Yeah, it bites, but either he'll get over it or I'll know he wasn't my friend in the first place."

"There's a lot of that going around," I said. "But that doesn't explain why you're dragging me into the principal's office."

"Because we need a way to present our plan to the juniors and seniors. We're going to see if he'll let us speak at an assembly."

He pushed the door open but I yanked him back. "You'll have a lot better luck doing this without me. Trust me. I tried this. He's going to take one look at me and the answer's going to be no before you even open your mouth."

"Not if you follow my lead. Mr. B and I go way back. Just do what I do." He all but licked his chops. "Trust *me*."

The secretary who always viewed me with suspicion was all smiles when she saw Patrick. I wasn't even sure she realized I was with him.

"He's ready for you," she said. "You want some juice or anything?"

Juice? I had never been offered a beverage, unless a metaphorical spit in the eye counted.

"We're good," Patrick said, "unless you're making lattes. That's a cool watch, by the way."

I looked at her wrist. It actually was. But come on—flattery?

"If you're expecting me to compliment Mr. Baumgarten on his tie, forget about it," I muttered to Patrick as she let us into his office.

"Don't say anything unless I scratch my nose," he muttered back. "Hey, Mr. B!"

"How's it going, Patrick?" Mr. Baumgarten beamed at him like a grandfather at the airport.

"I'm good. You know Tyler Bonning."

He nodded and gave me a polite smile. Patrick's hand was nowhere near his nose, so I just nodded too and sat in the same seat I'd occupied before. Patrick took the one across from me, and Mr. Baumgarten pulled up a chair. The last time I'd been there he'd leaned against his desk and looked down on me like a Salem judge. It would only be a matter of minutes before he was there again, unless I kept my mouth shut. If I'd known we were coming here, I'd have brought duct tape.

"Nice job on the article," Mr. Baumgarten said.

Patrick looked at me. "I had good material. That's why we're here."

"Oh?"

Patrick scooted to the edge of his seat and told "Mr. B" everything we'd come up with on Saturday. His hands shaped each idea in the space in front of him, and his eyes sparkled and shone with the nuances. It was like watching somebody create art. I was so fascinated, I almost missed the first nose scratch.

"Tyler can tell you where this is all coming from," Patrick said. "She's done all the background work."

Mr. Baumgarten looked at me. I tried not to focus on the doubt in his eyes.

"I've done some statistical research," I said, "but it's my talks with some of the students that have really spurred me on."

I talked about Candace and Ryleigh and Noelle and Fred and Kenny. My father would have called it "anecdotal," but to my surprise, it seemed to be working. At least Mr. Baumgarten's scalp was still creamy white.

When I was through, Patrick held out a hand as if I'd just flawlessly recited the entire Constitution.

"You can see this is for real, Mr. B. It's not just about the prom." His finger rubbed his nose. "It's about — what did you call it, Tyler?"

"Helping people not only find perspective, but giving them an opportunity to raise their self-worth."

Apparently that made more sense to the principal than it did to my father, because, miraculously, he nodded.

"Now see, Miss Bonning?" he said. "You're so much more effective when you don't come in here telling me how to do my job."

He was lucky Patrick was currently leaving his nostrils alone.

"So what do you need from me?" he said.

Patrick told him about the assembly idea, making it sound like an educational opportunity surpassing entrance into Harvard. By the time he was through, I was sure Mr. Baumgarten thought he himself had come up with the whole thing.

"I'll tell you what," he said. "We have an assembly tomorrow to go over all the end-of-the-year things. We'll just keep the juniors and seniors after and I'll give you ten minutes to talk about your campaign. Does that work for you?"

"Sweet," Patrick said.

He went after his nose, and I said, "That will definitely give us the opportunity we need."

Mr. Baumgarten cocked his head. "How in the world did the two of *you* ever get together?"

"I think it was fate, Mr. B," Patrick said.

He started for the nasal area again. Mr. Baumgarten reached behind him and pulled out a Kleenex.

"Allergies, son?" he said. "It's that time of year, isn't it?"

I managed to contain myself until we got all the way out into the hall, where I stopped and laughed until a juicy sound came out of my nose. Patrick almost doubled over.

"Did you just snort?"

"That was a guffaw," I said. "Could you have been a little more obvious with the nose thing?"

"Did it work or did it work?"

"Uh, you were flawless."

"We. *We* were flawless. We're a team."

He put up a hand to high-five me. When I slapped his palm, he held on and squeezed. I had no idea what to do with that, and I froze. Even with Patrick's eyes inviting mine to dance, all I could do was hang there like an icicle until he let go.

"So — um — tomorrow," I said. "We have a lot of work to do before then."

"See you at lunch?"

"Where?"

"How 'bout the *lunch*room?"

"Aren't you afraid — "

"No. So don't even go there."

As he strode off down the hall he virtually owned, I wondered how I could help "going there." Three girls from the Ruling Class were already staring openly beside the trophy case. One of them was Joanna, who, unless I missed my guess, would be going for the tissues any time now.

But the sight of Valleri in English lifted me again. I gave her my notes to read while Ms. Dalloway took roll, and I brought her up to speed on the meeting with Mr. Baumgarten in bits and pieces between *Red Badge of Courage* assignments and looking up rites of passage in other cultures, which, again, had absolutely nothing to do with us. It wasn't that hard; Ms. Dalloway seemed to be cutting me even more slack since the photo shoot.

By the time third block was over, Valleri was totally filled in, and she'd nodded so many times in agreement I was sure she'd need a chiropractor soon.

"Which part do you want to take in the assembly?" I said as we headed for the lunchroom.

Her blue eyes turned to saucers. "I don't," she said. "I mean, not speaking. Getting up in front of people freaks me out."

"Really," I said. "You seem so confident."

"Until I have more than five people looking at me at the same time. Even that thing about imagining the audience naked doesn't help." She tucked a curl behind her ear; it popped right back out. "What kind of visuals are you using?"

"We haven't gotten that far."

"I could put together a PowerPoint."

"The assembly's tomorrow."

"I know. I do them all the time for our church. By the way, I've been meaning to ask you—"

"Tyler!"

Valleri's eyes graduated to dinner plates as two dark arms came around my neck from behind, and a pair of hands with a ring on every finger squeezed me in.

"Hey, Candace," I said. "Valleri, this is my cousin."

Candace gave her a hug too, which Valleri returned like they were BFFs.

"You two know each other?" I said.

"No," they said in unison.

Candace turned to me and rubbed my forearms. "I was *so* proud of you when I read that thing in the paper. And that picture—you looked *hot*. Didn't she look hot?"

"Oh, yeah," Valleri said.

"You should wear red more often—we need to go shopping again. Ooh, you need a red prom dress. She *needs* one."

"That's what I'm thinking," Valleri said.

"Okay, speaking of dresses," I said. "Did you get yours yet?"

Candace was immediately despondent. "No. I still don't have the money for what I want."

I bit back a warning that a gown wouldn't fit in her purse. "What if there was an almost-free way to get a fabulous dress?"

I described our idea for a "dress shop" and found myself shaping the whole thing with my hands. I didn't have Patrick's finesse—I actually felt a little bit like a robot—but she watched, mouth slightly open in concentration.

"What do you think?" I said.

"I think I'd feel like a charity case."

I turned my head to see Ryleigh standing at Valleri's elbow. Noelle and Fred were right behind her.

"Why don't I just raise my hand and say, 'Hey, I'm poor. How 'bout a dress for me?'"

"Anybody can get one," I said. "It's not just for—"

"The Kmart Kids?"

I took in a sharp breath.

"You think we don't know people call us that?" Ryleigh said.

"Do I look like I shop at Hollister?" Valleri said, voice quiet. "It's not about that."

I actually could have hugged her at that point. "And there's more to it than that," I said. "We're having a contest for a free tux rental, and we're getting restaurants to offer prom specials. It's so you can have everything you said you wanted."

Ryleigh shrugged and shifted her eyes to the wall just beyond my shoulder. I looked at Candace, but she had already closed her face off. Noelle and Fred were whispering to each other. I could feel my spirit sinking.

"It still seems like the Goodwill Prom or something," Ryleigh said.

Valleri nudged me. "I think he's waiting for us."

Ryleigh followed my gaze to Patrick, who was waving from the cafeteria door.

"He's in on it?" she said. "Now I *know* it's going to be the Charity Ball. Thanks, but no thanks."

When we got to the corner table Patrick was saving for us, he pushed two pieces of pizza on grease-soaked paper plates into our places.

"I just lost my appetite," I said.

Valleri and I told him about Ryleigh's reaction.

"Maybe if *you* had explained it, it would have been different," I said to Patrick.

"Or maybe the plan just needs more work."

"We have to present it tomorrow!"

"Then where's the notebook?" he said, nodding and grinning toward my bag.

I pulled out the spiral, but I felt like somebody had stuck a pin in my party balloon. Just when I was starting to see the magic in balloons.

"Uh, here they come again," Valleri whispered.

I expected to see Joanna—Alyssa—Egan—somebody with the proverbial pin, but it was Noelle and Fred, minus Ryleigh.

"Could we talk to you?" Noelle said. She looked like she was asking for an audience with the pope.

"Absolutely," Patrick said. He stood up and motioned for her to take his chair.

There was no way he just did that. The only guy I'd ever seen give up his chair for a female was my father. Noelle didn't seem to know what her next move was supposed to be. Fred jerked his chin at her, a splotch of red forming on each cheekbone. Evidently he'd never done that for her, either.

"We just wanted to talk to you about the prom thing," Fred said.

"I got it," I said. "You don't want to be a charity case."

"See, that was just Ryleigh." Noelle looked at Fred. "We don't think that's what you're trying to do at all. I'm not too proud to take a nice dress if somebody wants to give it away."

"But what about everybody else?" I said.

"We kind of had an idea about that?" Noelle said.

I was still deciding if that was a question or a statement when Patrick leaned on the table and said, "Talk to us." He glanced at me; I touched my nose, and he nodded. Time to shut up and let him do his thing.

"So what if— " Fred said.

"And we're just saying 'what if,'" Noelle put in.

"What if it wasn't totally free? Say you had to, like, earn a coupon by doing something?"

"You mean, to help the whole campaign," Patrick said.

Noelle nodded. "Maybe it wouldn't be anything big, just, like, a bottle of nail polish or a lipstick or whatever somebody else might need. That way, nobody would feel like it was a total handout."

"That idea *rocks*," Patrick said. "What do you guys think?"

Valleri looked up from the sketchpad she'd pulled out at some point and said, "Awesome."

I waited for Patrick to scratch his nose before I said, "I think it has potential. Do you two want to help us flesh it out?"

I could see Fred stiffening. Noelle pulled her shoulders in so far they almost touched each other.

"It was just an idea," Fred said. "You guys can work out the details."

"But you'll support it, right?" Patrick said. "That's what I'm hearing you say."

Valleri touched Noelle's arm. "Would you rather we didn't say anything about this to Ryleigh?"

Noelle nodded. "I'm not as brave as you are. I don't agree with her, but she's still my best friend, and I don't want her to be mad at me."

Patrick grinned at Fred. "Do you understand women?"

"I don't even try," Fred said.

He and Noelle left holding hands, and I stared after them.

"What just happened?" I said.

"They gave us a great idea," Valleri said.

"No, I mean, how did you two just make everything okay for them? How do you do that?"

"I just think it's a God thing," Valleri said.

"That's cool." Patrick dug into his pocket and pulled out a handful of change. "I'm gonna get us drinks. I wish they'd put an espresso machine in here ..."

He didn't get five feet from the table before he was accosted by Hayley. I was watching her put her face right up to his and wondering where girls learned to do that, when Valleri said, "Would you like to come to my church sometime?"

Where had *that* come from?

"No pressure," she said quickly. She looked down at her sketchpad. "Any time you want to come, just let me know."

"Okay," I said. I didn't tell her about me and the bobolinks.

*

By fifth block the next day, when everybody was herded into the auditorium for the assembly, Patrick, Valleri, and I were ready. We'd had to throw everything together so fast, Patrick and I didn't get to look at the PowerPoint beforehand, but I wasn't worried. I wasn't even that concerned about my part. He and I had spent two hours after school over lattes—which I was starting to develop an uncanny taste for—and another hour and a half on the phone later dividing up the speaking. He said that was the best way to do it, so he wouldn't have to be messing with his nose in front of the entire student body. I told him he was very amusing.

The only thing that did give me anxiety—as in dry mouth, jittery knees, and more than my usual flood of sweat, even without caffeine—was wondering what kind of reaction we were going to get. So far the only people we had won over were Mr. Baumgarten, Noelle, and Fred—and Noelle had even made us swear not to tell anybody she was in. As prepared as we were, I still didn't hold out much hope for a standing ovation.

Patrick, on the other hand, was backstage with me, rubbing his hands together and dancing around like he had to go to the bathroom. He told me he was jazzed.

"That makes one of us," I said. "Aren't you even just a little bit nervous that they're going to start throwing stuff at us?" I shook my head. "Of course you're not. It's *you*. I bet you've never been made fun of in your life."

He didn't give me the expected grin. In fact, he sort of squinted at me, like maybe he was experiencing a gas pain.

"Why do you do that?" he said.

"Do what?"

"Put yourself down. You're, like, amazing, but you make it sound like all you do is turn people off."

"I'm starting to think I do."

"You don't turn *me* off. I like it when you get all worked up about this and start talking like Martin Luther King."

"Martin Luther *King*?"

"That was the only passionate person I could think of. You get what I mean, though." He pushed his hair off his forehead and suddenly looked older than seventeen and more serious than Patrick Sykes. "I'm not the only one who can persuade people. You got me to stand up to kids I've been hanging out with since I was five. Just get up there and give them what you gave me." The grin finally showed up. "We'll kick some serious Ruling Class tail."

I didn't know about that. But I did know the minute we went on stage to speak—and people stopped yelling the required things like, "What it is, Pat-*rick*?" so everybody would know they were there—Patrick and I clicked. We kept our spiel going, snapping it back and forth and never missing a beat. And even we were impressed with Valleri's PowerPoint. Most of it was cartoons she'd obviously drawn herself to illustrate every piece of the Plan. They even got some laughs, not the ha-ha-look-at-Izzy kind, but the that-is-so-spot-on kind.

Every time Patrick was talking, though, I checked out the crowd.

The Fringe were incredulous. In spite of everything I'd said to them, Deidre, Matthew, and Yuri still looked at me like they were hearing the concept for the first time and were certain I'd lost my mind.

Graham Fitzwilliam, who had probably climbed out from under his tuba to attend, bordered on hostile. I didn't even see Kenny. Odds were he'd cut to go to the Jiff-E-Mart.

The Ruling Class did a lot of whispering amongst themselves and a lot of trying not to show any emotion, as far as I could see. Alyssa was the exception; she clearly wanted to claw me with her fingernails, which was no surprise. And Joanna, who appeared distraught, the way you do when you've misplaced the paper due next block that's worth 60 percent of your grade. A few of the RC girls, including Hayley, couldn't seem to help gazing, enraptured, at Patrick. Yeah, now was the time to ask for those iPhones if he wanted them.

But it was the kids I really wanted to get through to that I watched the most closely. The ones I, too, used to think of as the Kmart Kids because it was a convenient way to lump them all together. They weren't a lump, though. Every one of them reacted differently.

Noelle and Fred took every opportunity to catch my eye and give me thumbs-ups. Ryleigh sat with her arms folded, but her eyes focused on the PowerPoint, Patrick, and me. Izzy stayed awake, which was a statement in itself. Every kid whose father worked in the dairy or drove a truck or remodeled kitchens gave us a hearing in their own way, faces transparent, reactions real. I realized at one point that they were all a lot like Patrick. And it stirred in me how much I wanted them to know they were somebody, just like he did.

When we were finished, Mr. Baumgarten led the applause, and Patrick grinned all the way to our places at the end of the front row.

"We scored," he whispered.

When he held his palm low for me to slap it—and he held on again—I was almost convinced.

CHAPTER THIRTEEN

My parents went to a dinner at the college that evening, which meant I didn't have to endure the third degree about the prom project. It also let Sunny off the hook, since she now knew about the whole plan but had promised me she would let me be the one to discuss it with them. I actually felt a little guilty about putting her in that position, but not enough to ask what *she* was doing for dinner. I grabbed a Pop-Tart and headed for my room to catch up on the homework I'd ignored the night before while Patrick and I were prepping our presentation.

I found myself longing for a latte. Okay—so I was missing him.

Which was absurd. Also ridiculous. And definitely ludicrous. I was *not* going to turn into a Hayley, making sure she was there every time he walked by, and pouncing on him when he did. Or a Joanna, who cried whenever she looked at him. Fat chance of that happening. Or an Alyssa, who acted like Emma in that Jane Austen novel—like *she* had the perfect partner picked out for Patrick, and it wasn't going to be me.

Well, of *course* it wasn't going to be me. I didn't *want* it to be me. Okay, so there was no doubt he actually kind of got me. But I wasn't forgetting what Alyssa said: if a girl wasn't interested in Patrick, he worked on her until she was.

Enough with that. I grabbed my bag and took it to the window seat, where I planned to finish outlining the five chapters Sunny had assigned to us. Naturally, my phone alerted me to a text message.

"I can't work on the prom tonight, Patrick," I said.

But the message wasn't *from* him. It was *about* him.

STAY AWAY FRM PATRICK U DONT BELONG W HIM

How many different ways did I have to tell these chicks I wasn't after the boy they all claimed like they were part of a harem? Bizarre, too, that half of them weren't speaking to him, and yet they didn't want *me* to speak to him.

Much less squeeze his hand when we high-fived ...

I shook that off and looked for the number on the text. There *was* one way I hadn't tried. I punched the number in and waited for Alyssa or Joanna—who knew, maybe even Egan—to answer. The ringing stopped and a male voice said, "Castle Heights Towing."

"Excuse me?" I said.

"Castle Heights Towing. You need a tow?"

"No."

The guy grunted. "Well I don't deliver pizzas, lady."

"Sorry," I said. "I got a text message from this number, and I—"

"No, you didn't."

"No, seriously, it's—" I rattled off the number. The guy's voice lowered to a growl.

"Then something's messed up, because I ain't never texted in my life. We done?"

"Listen, I'm sorry—"

But he'd already hung up. I looked at the number again; it was definitely the one I'd just called. One thing was for sure: that guy wasn't related to anybody in the Ruling Class. So how ...

I turned my phone off and pressed my hand to my forehead. I was starting to sweat again, and warmth was once more radiating from under the seat cushion. Could this night get any weirder?

I pulled out the RL book, which, just as I expected, nearly melted in my hand. It wasn't even surprising this time that when I opened it only one of the pages was warm. The one that said:

So ... you climbed a tree.

In spite of the heat rising from the paper, I shivered. And yet I had to answer. So few people were talking to me right now.

"I climbed a tree," I said out loud. "How do you figure?"

You got up high. You looked down. You saw things clearly.

Before I could even think *No, I did not*, I had a flash of myself, standing on a table in the cafeteria watching the Ruling Class at work.

Whoa.

You got that story. Ready for another one?

It didn't seem like I had a choice. I propped myself on the avalanche of pillows and let the book warm my propped-up legs.

This is one Yeshua told the same crowd that got ticked off when he invited himself over to Zaccahaeus's place.

So it was a parable.

He said there is a man who has a birthright to run his town, but he has to go to headquarters to get the official okay. There's paperwork for everything, right? Before he leaves, he calls his staff together and gives them each enough money to cover expenses while he's gone and says, "Operate with this until I get back."

I knew this story. He gave them each ten talents. I had to grill my sixth-grade Sunday school teacher on what a "talent" was; I thought he made one a dancer, one a singer, that kind of thing. I even remembered the point of the parable—

Who says there's only one point? Besides, this is a little different version from the one you learned.

By now I wasn't shivering anymore when the thing read my mind. I was actually starting to dig the back-and-forth.

"Okay," I said. "Show me one besides, 'Use what you're given or it's going to be taken away from you.'"

The people in the town basically hate this guy, so they send a commission on ahead to headquarters to protest him taking over.

Really. I never noticed that part in the story.

See? So the guy goes to headquarters and he comes back with the necessary paperwork.

Their petition didn't work either. I could relate to that.

The guy gathers his staff to find out how they did with the money while he was away.

This was the part I knew, but I read on anyway. It couldn't hurt.

The first staff member has doubled the guy's money. The guy likes that. He likes it a lot, so he says to the staff member, "Excellent. For that, I'm putting you in charge of ten departments. Major promotion."

Hence my practice of doing extra credit in every class. Was that biblical, then?

The second staff member says, "Sir, I made a fifty percent profit on your money." And the guy says, "Nice job. That earns you a promotion too. You're now heading up five departments." These guys are thinking, "Sweet."

That sounded so much like Patrick, I laughed out loud.

And then he gets to the third staff member.

If I recalled correctly, this was where it got ugly.

This third person says, "Sir, here's your money, just the way you gave it to me. I kept it in a safe deposit box, because, to be honest, you scare me. I mean, you practically expect perfection out of us, and I've seen you go off on people that act like they don't have a brain in their head."

So — was that like people who only did the bare minimum in class? Kept their heads down so they wouldn't be court-martialed by Zabaski? Or called into Mr. Baumgarten's office to watch his scalp scald?

The guy seems to think so. He gets in the staff member's face and he says, "You got that right. I don't put up with fools. And, dude, you qualify. You couldn't at least have put it in an account so I could earn a little interest on it?"

This was where I remembered getting prickly with this story when I was in sixth grade. The guy didn't say, "Make more money with this money." He said, "Use it to run things while I'm out of town." How were *they* supposed to know he expected a profit when he got back?

Because they knew him. They'd worked with him. He trained

them. These weren't newbies he brought in off the street; he wouldn't expect novices to understand how it worked. These were STAFF members, people who were paid to know what to do.

Why had no one ever told me that? When I asked that same sixth-grade Sunday school teacher, he said that was just the way the story went. When he explained that the guy in the story was Jesus, my opinion of the Lord took its first downward turn. But this — this was different.

So the guy says to the first staff member, "Take the money I gave this airhead." And the other people standing there go, "But he already has double what you gave him!" And the guy says, "My point exactly."

"Wait, don't tell me," I said. To the book. Because my sanity no longer mattered to me. "You take a risk, for something important — not like a ride-your-skateboard-down-the-middle-of-Route-9 kind of risk — and you're going to get more than you put into it. Right?"

And if you play it safe?

"Ya got nothin'. Maybe not even what you started out with." I squirmed. "But I've always understood that."

There's more. The guy knows about the people petitioning against him. Now that he's officially in charge, he says, "Get these jackals out of here."

"No, he did not say 'jackals'!"

He did in YOUR mind ...

He's not in my mind. Is he?

Maybe that's your next step. You climbed a tree, metaphorically speaking, so why not?

Why not what?

Did bucking the guy work? Trying to get him ousted?

No.

And being afraid of him? How'd that turn out?

It was a bust.

What about knowing the master so well that they knew what was expected of them AND had the confidence to go with it?

You're saying get to know ... Jesus.

That's what I'm saying.

The pillows suddenly started to annoy me. I pulled one out and tossed it. That felt so good, I pitched another one.

Problem?

Yes. My whole church life, people were always saying, "Invite Jesus into your heart. Make him Lord and Master of your life." But nobody ever explained exactly *how* you're supposed to do that. I didn't doubt that some people did. I'd seen them speaking in tongues and heard them say how the Lord "put something on their hearts," but when I queried them about the process, they always answered with things like, "Just open yourself up to him in prayer. Seek him in all things." But seriously—what does that *mean*? It's one of the many reasons I stopped going to church. I felt like it was a closed club that I didn't have the right stuff for.

"I don't know *how* to get to know him," I said. "You tell me, and I'm on it. Seriously."

What do you think I'm doing?

I stared at the page. Its warmth eased up my arms and rested in the middle of my chest.

It doesn't get any plainer than this story, it said.

The rest of the page was blank, which I knew meant that was all I was getting for now. The other pages were cold, and this one continued to stare back at me. So ... take a risk? Make a lot out of what I had? Was that it?

The answer didn't appear in the book. But the heat still glowed in my chest. I had to take that as a yes.

*

It was Valleri who met me at my locker the next morning, holding a gorgeous poster that could've been painted by Van Gogh or somebody. She watched, face pensive, as I looked at the girls depicted there, knee deep in a pile of fluffy, pastel gowns.

COME PICK OUT YOUR PROM DRESS! it said at the top. *Saturday, April 30, 10:00 'til 2:00. HAYLEY BARR'S HOUSE*

I stopped before I got to the address.

"Hayley *Barr's* house?"

Valleri nodded her curls over the top of the poster. "Patrick couldn't get ahold of you last night. He said your phone was turned off or something."

"Yeah ..."

"He talked the dress shop up with Hayley and she talked to her mom and ..." She shrugged.

"How does he *do* that?" I said. And then I felt my eyes start into slits. "Is he sure she's for real about this? It could be a setup."

Valleri shook her head at me.

"What?" I said. "Did he make her sign a sworn statement?"

"Sometimes you just have to have faith," she said. "Patrick says this is the perfect way to get the girls with the dresses to participate. It's not us against them, right?"

"It's not supposed to be," I said. "Do you think this is a God thing?"

Something flickered through her eyes — that old look again. "I don't just call everything that goes my way a God thing."

"Then how do you know what is?"

"I feel it," she said. "And I know I've read it."

"Like, in the Bible?"

"I know that sounds hokey to some people."

It couldn't be any hokier than what I was experiencing with a hot book in my window seat.

"Is that the poster?" Patrick said from halfway down the hall.

He came toward us, grinning the wake-up grin and carrying yet another poster. When he turned it around to face us, Valleri read aloud the instructions for getting in on tux rental discounts and the contest for winning a free one for the night.

Turn Your Entries for Most Creative Prom Invite in to the Box in the Office

"Let me guess," I said. "Mr. Baumgarten's secretary."

"Exactly."

"She thinks he's cute," I said to Valleri.

Valleri's face clearly read, *Who doesn't?*

"I'm not hanging this next to yours," Patrick said, looking at Valleri's museum-worthy poster.

"Stop it," she said. "I'm gonna go hang both of them in the cafeteria right now. You coming with?"

I started to nod, but Patrick caught my sleeve. "We'll catch up," he said.

Valleri bounced off with a poster under each arm, and I felt a twinge of envy. I didn't know if I'd ever felt lighthearted enough to "bounce."

"I got Egan to talk to me," Patrick said.

I flipped back to him.

"Here's the deal, and we have to keep this between us."

"Tell me what it is first," I said.

"He's on our side, okay? He's not going to do anything to take down what we do, and he'll do whatever we need him to behind the scenes."

"What's the catch?"

"It's not really a catch. He just can't post any of it on the Facebook Prom Page because all those people are giving him so much grief."

"He's not going to get any more grief than we're already getting!"

"You have no idea. What they're worried about is that what we're doing will make it impossible for them to get alcohol in. That's like some people's main goal in life, I guess. He figures if he—"

"—Keeps his head down, plays it safe, he can still have a prom and not be blamed if people don't have a chance to get plastered."

Patrick nodded, without the grin.

"I hate that there even *are* 'sides,'" I said. "That's so not what this is about."

"Yeah, but you know what, it's something. It's like we have to take baby steps. And Hayley was a *huge* step."

"So how is *she* keeping people from giving her grief?"

He didn't have a chance to answer, because Hayley herself

came around the corner like a cloud of bubbles and floated them around him.

"Is the poster up yet?" she said. She was a veritable soda, for Pete's sake, and she wasn't sharing any of it with me.

"We were going to check it out right now," Patrick said.

"You two go ahead," I said. "I've got to ..."

I trailed off with, "... go defrost my locker." Hayley never did acknowledge that I was there. Patrick may have looked back, but I was already making an exit. I couldn't help wondering if Hayley had had her car towed lately.

*

The announcement in the morning bulletin said that we were collecting not only dresses but jewelry, purses, and shoes, which could either be given away or just loaned. Patrick said Hayley promised him she would get plenty of donations from what he now also referred to as the Ruling Class.

We decided that all the stuff should come to the school and then be transported to Hayley's so we could go through it first, and on Wednesday morning Fred and Noelle brought in a neat rolling rack with hangers to keep the dresses on. His mom, it turned out, worked in retail. Between that and the two heavy cardboard "dressers" with drawers in them that Valleri provided for the smaller items—where did you get stuff like that?—we were set. Our only issue was where to keep them.

"I only have so much clout with Miss Larrimore," Patrick told us.

I assumed she was the secretary who wished she were twenty years younger and would have installed an espresso machine if he'd asked her to.

Valleri and I were going to approach Ms. Dalloway to see if we could use her room, but she was in one of her weary modes, and I didn't want to mess up my status with her. Mr. Zabaski was out of the question, of course. Ditto for Madame, who barely had enough room for the desk, the listening stations, and the replica of the Eiffel Tower that took up one whole corner.

We were standing in the hall before school with our rack and our dressers and our dilemma, discarding the idea of asking Coach Wendover, who couldn't control the class enough to guarantee that everything wouldn't be lifted and sold on the black market before the end of the first day—when Sunny went by on her way to the history room.

"What's all this?" she said.

"It's for the dress shop." Patrick grinned all the way to his earlobes. "Have we met?"

Oh, please.

Sunny's eyes flicked to me and back to him. "I'm Mr. Linkhart's long-term sub. So where's all this going?"

"We don't know yet," Valleri said. "We can't find a teacher who we think will want the responsibility."

"It's for the prom campaign, right?"

You promised me! I wanted to shout at her.

She looked at me as if she'd heard me, and for an awful moment I was sure I *had* yelled it, her eyes looked that stung.

"You should've asked me," she said, gaze right on me. "I'd be happy to help."

"Are you serious?" Patrick said. "It'll be in there 'til, like, Friday, taking up a lot of space."

Valleri giggled. "Don't try to talk her out of it, Patrick!"

Sunny still hadn't taken her eyes off of me. "This okay with you?"

"If it's okay with you," I got out. Because, frankly, I couldn't believe what I was hearing.

"Then it's a done deal. Follow me."

"Sweet," Patrick said. To me he added, as we pushed the rack down the hall, "What did she say her name was?"

"She didn't," I said. And I couldn't believe that either.

*

We didn't get any donations on Wednesday, but Patrick was still optimistic. The word hadn't really gotten out yet, he said.

Still, the what-if-this-totally-bombs thoughts kept me tossing and turning half the night, and I overslept the next morning.

I was barreling down the stairs with my stuff flying out behind me when I saw Sunny at the bottom, car keys in hand.

"You want a lift?" she said.

"You're driving?" I said. "Don't you usually walk?"

She smiled and wiggled her eyebrows. "Can't. I have a backseat full of formal attire to haul."

"Oh," I said. "Wow."

She wasn't kidding. When I slid into her front passenger seat, I had a white sequined number hanging over one shoulder and a blue chiffon something tickling the back of my neck.

"I don't know if anybody's even going to want any of this stuff," Sunny said as she peered over it to back out of the driveway. "But it'll make it look like we have a lot and people will get excited."

"Well, the people in your classes will," I said.

"Actually, I thought I'd put the dress rack out in the hall before and after school and during lunch so they can get a preview. Is that all right with you?"

"I don't know if I can always be there then."

"I'll keep an eye on it. If you don't like the idea—"

"It's great," I said. "Are you sure you want to do this?"

She leaned forward to look at me around a pouf of turquoise tulle. "If I don't do something fun soon, I might implode."

"All right, then," I said. "And—thanks."

Sunny just smiled.

It took us two trips to get all the stuff up to her classroom. When we got back the second time, Joanna and Alyssa were standing in the hallway, each holding a bulging black trash bag.

"Donations?" Sunny said as she breezed past them.

Or this morning's garbage? I couldn't help sniffing the air for traces of rotten fruit.

"We brought a few things," Alyssa said, as usual ignoring me. Joanna wasn't as good at it. My very presence made her eyes water like she was allergic to my aura.

"We'll just leave them," Joanna said as we all followed Sunny into the room.

Sunny dumped her last armful on her desk and turned,

hands on hips. "No, actually, I think—and Tyler, you tell me if you agree—we probably ought to go through everything while you're here and make a list for you to sign so we can get things back to you if they're left over."

Joanna looked at Alyssa, eyes popping like she had a thyroid condition. Alyssa took to scratching at her arm.

"Do we really have to take the time to do that?" she said.

My antennae were already up. "It'll save us from any issues later," I said, nodding at Sunny. I whipped out the loyal spiral notebook and flipped to a new page. "Let's see what you've got."

Joanna appeared to be about to snatch up her bag and run, but Alyssa lifted her trim little chin and removed the twisty from hers. Fixing her eyes defiantly on me, she pulled out a pair of gray silky-looking pants that on closer inspection weren't gray at all but faded black, and riddled with those pills you get on sweaters you've had for ages. That was followed by a short pink sateen-and-net getup that had to have been somebody's Halloween costume. I stopped her when she produced a red velveteen jacket my grandmother *might* wear to a Christmas party in the nursing home.

It was all I could do not to tell *her* to put that stuff on and show herself in public. But I knew it wouldn't work—and this thing was *going* to work if I had to have a complete personality makeover to make it happen.

"Cleaned out Grandma's attic, did you?" I said.

Alyssa sniffed. "I thought somebody could use it."

"Who?" I said. I waited, eyes wide.

"You didn't say it had to be new stuff."

"Yeah, but this hasn't been new since Ms. Dalloway went to the prom. Would *you* wear any of this to a formal dance?"

She tossed the blondeness. "No, but I'm not—"

"Not a Kmart Kid?"

"Exactly. Do you want this stuff or not?"

Joanna was already edging toward the door with her bag.

"What does your dad do for a living, Alyssa?" I said.

"Why?"

"Just work with me here."

"*Dr.* Hampton?" she said, as if I were an imbecile. "He's a dentist."

"What if his practice went out of business tomorrow? Nobody in town had dental insurance anymore, nobody could afford to have their teeth fixed. Decay ran rampant and he was out of a job. No point in moving to another town because it's the same everywhere. Would you get to keep shopping at Hollister?"

"No," Joanna said.

Alyssa gave her the "shut up" look.

"Would you be the same person if six months from now *you* had to buy your clothes at Kmart? Walmart? J. C. Penney?"

"I don't know," Alyssa said.

"I do. You'd still be pretty like you are now. You'd still have every guy wanting to date you. You'd still be you—except you might have to come to our dress shop to get a formal." I tapped her garbage bag with my toe. "And I don't think you'd want anything that's in there. In fact, you'd probably be offended. Then you'd think maybe you were less than the people who had the insensitivity to even offer you ragged pants and an old Halloween costume. And you'd be wrong."

By then, Joanna was already gone. Alyssa snatched up her bag.

"To answer your question," I said, "no, we don't want that stuff. But if you have something that wouldn't insult the people we're trying to help, we'd love to have it. They deserve that respect."

"Thanks for the sermon," Alyssa said.

She flounced out, nearly steamrolling Hayley, who was trying to get in the door with a pile of garments in plastic dry-cleaning bags.

"She didn't bring in a bunch of junk, did she?" Hayley said when Alyssa was gone.

"Pretty much," I said. I had to get my mind around the fact that she was speaking to me.

"She said she was going to and I told her—well, it's not like she listens to me now. Anyway—" Hayley once more did her imitation of a six-pack of open sodas. "I brought some really cute stuff—"

"Is this where we're supposed to drop off the dresses?"

All three of us turned like one person toward the door. Mr. Baumgarten was standing there, up to his chin in silk, satin, and sparkles.

"Let me take that," Sunny said. Of course, in her tiny arms it looked like twice as much. It took everything I had not to envision Mr. Baumgarten in drag.

"My daughter's a freshman at NYU," he said. "They don't do much in the way of fancy dances there. She said you could have these."

I picked up my spiral notebook and my pen. It was working. It was really working.

CHAPTER FOURTEEN

I actually looked forward to giving Mr. Baumgarten's donation for my high at the dinner table that night. I didn't see how my parents wouldn't consider it evidence that what I was doing was a good thing.

I guess my father had never realized the significance of a prom dress.

"This still seems like an awful lot of misspent energy to me," he said. He stopped my protest with a creamy palm. "I'm not saying don't do it. I'm just asking for some hard proof that you're going to achieve anything beyond a bunch of dressed-up girls."

"I'll give you some proof."

My head jerked from Dad to Sunny. She laid her butter knife across her plate and rested her forearms on the table so she could lean toward him.

"You should have heard Tyler talking to some little rich bimbette this morning. She *could* have told that snotty little princess to take her bag of rags and sit on it. That's what *I* wanted to do."

"How did *you* get involved in this?" Dad said. The debate sparkle in his eyes winked out.

"I'm providing the storage space," Sunny said, "because I believe in what Tyler's group is doing. If I could continue?"

"Go on," Mom said. Although she was without dimples, she didn't look angry.

"Tyler was magnificent. She laid it out for that girl in no

uncertain terms, but she did it without putting her down or being condescending. It was impressive."

"How did the girl respond?" Dad said.

"She knew she was wrong. She tried to save face, and Tyler let her." Sunny looked at me. "Me? I'd have made her grovel a little. I tell you, Daddy, I felt like I was watching a master at work."

"Thank you," I said. I couldn't come up with anything more, because I was stunned.

"Good for you, Ty," Dad said. "But is it going to change anything? That's my question."

"I think it already has," I said.

"Tell me how."

"I don't think I know exactly how yet. These are just baby steps."

"Well, we'll see." Dad made a squinty face and returned to his chicken breast.

Sunny stabbed hers with her fork. "For Pete's sake, Dad. Tyler's doing everything you taught us to do and you're giving her absolutely no support." She looked at me again. "I'm sorry—I know I said I'd let you handle it. Just—never mind. If you're planning to keep dogging her, Dad, I'd like to be excused."

I was way ahead of her. We met in the foyer, the suddenly silent dining room behind us.

"You didn't have to do that," I said.

"Yeah, I did," she said. "I'm sorry if I—"

"No. I appreciate it."

She nodded, but I could see the tears in her eyes.

"I've gotta—"

"Go."

We split at the top of the stairs and I went straight to my window seat. I should have felt vindicated, but there was still too much to figure out about this whole parental thing. It was like diagramming a sentence.

Before the heat even got me to the sweaty stage, I was

reaching under the cushion. My phone signaled a text, and I stopped, hand warming on RL.

Another threat from somebody? I'd already decided it wasn't Hayley who'd sent the last one. It just didn't match all her effervescence. Had to be Alyssa, although after me turning down her garbage bag full of rags, wouldn't she know I'd be on to her?

I knew I should just ignore it, but curiosity won out. I grabbed my phone, teeth set for the warning. But it was from Egan.

STILL NEED YOUR ESCORT, it said.

I closed the phone and tapped my fingers on the RL cover. I'd forgotten all about getting a guy to walk me across the stage, and I wasn't any closer to knowing who that could possibly be than I was the last time I remembered.

The prom was now nine days away. Who was I going to ask who wasn't already going with somebody? And who could I ask about who to ask? Valleri was the logical choice, but she didn't know anybody. I even thought of Sunny—how weird was that? But I gave that idea up before I had a chance to warm to it. I'd already caused a split between her and Dad, and I'd seen that it upset her. It upset me too, not being able to spar with him at the dinner table without suddenly being afraid I was going to get stabbed. I had a feeling it went a lot deeper with her. She was, after all, his "baby."

What had happened to my ability to analyze, come up with a plan, implement it, and move on? How long had it been since I'd been able to do that? It was like being nominated for prom queen had erased my rational mind.

I stopped tapping my fingers on the leather cover. Now *there* was somebody I could ask. Did the Bible give dating advice?

Probably not. That even sounded a little sacrilegious. But I opened it anyway, to the first page that felt warm.

You're back. Good.

I closed my eyes. *I need clear instructions. If you give me that, I'll know this is for real.*

And then I swallowed. I *wanted* it to be for real.

Yeshua addresses that very thing in this next story. He was teaching people in the temple, telling them who God is and how they can know Him. They were asking a lot of the same questions you are, actually.

At least I was on the right track.

Of course, the high priests and the religion scholars and the big shots in the temple were all lurking, trying to catch him in a loophole.

That was another thing I'd never understood in Sunday school. What was it about him that they hated so much? Jesus was out there healing people, telling them they were forgiven, that they didn't have to drag their issues around with them anymore. What was to hate?

You digress. But that's okay. It bears explaining.

These guys and their fathers before them had been in charge of the Jewish temple for generations. They'd come to command respect—however grudging it might be—and they got the best seats for dinner, had people coming to them for advice, which was heady stuff for them. And they were in with the political authorities, sort of like lobbyists, to keep the Romans from denying them their rights to practice their religion. So they had two problems with Yeshua. One, if people believed in him, that would sap them of their power, which basically defined them. And two, if there were any problems among the Jews, the Romans would say, "See, you're a bunch of troublemakers," and, zap, they wouldn't be able to worship at all. It'd be like the Babylonian exile all over again. They were too busy protecting the status quo to let any of what Yeshua was really saying get even close to their souls.

So they were the Ruling Class, only on a larger scale.

There is always a "Ruling Class." So this particular day, they were feeling pretty threatened by Yeshua and the way the people were responding to him, so they called him out. They said, "Who authorized you to come in here and speak like this? We want to see some credentials." Yeshua answered them with a question.

Still another thing that had always bugged me. Jesus never seemed to answer the question somebody asked. He just took off on some tangent. Although, now that I thought about it … I tended to do the same thing. Not that I was like Jesus or anything.

We'll get back to that. Do you want to hear the question?

I nodded at the book.

He said, "About the baptism of John—who authorized that? Heaven? Or human beings?" They were trapped, and they knew it. They motioned to him that they'd get back to him, and then they gathered in a knot over in the corner and whispered to each other, all hissy and panicked. "If we say heaven, he'll want to know why we didn't believe John. But if we say human beings, then all these people who were convinced that John was a prophet of God will be on us like white on rice. We'll have a riot on our hands!"

I had to hand it to Jesus. He got them right where he wanted them without a single argument.

They had to tell him they couldn't answer his question. So he said, "Then I'm not answering yours either."

I waited for more, but the space was blank. I actually liked that story, but I still wasn't sure what I was supposed to do with it.

It's what you're *not* ***supposed to do that's important. Like you said, you're not Yeshua. But, then, who*** *are* ***you in the story?***

There weren't a whole lot of choices. I wanted to be one of those people sitting in the temple, absorbing everything Jesus said.

You're getting there.

But?

You're a very smart girl. You can answer that question.

I closed the book and glared at it. Okay, so I was a high priest-y kind of person who asked questions just to get into a debate. Was that it? Or was it just that there was no logical solution to some situations?

That was a scary thought. Was I supposed to *feel* my way to an escort for the prom? Somehow *know* what I was supposed to do about my father arguing with me every baby step of the way? If I could do that, why did I need Jesus?

Because you can't feel your way without me.

I stared at the book. The cover was closed. I hadn't just read that. But, then, where did that thought come from? That thought that didn't sound like me?

I closed my eyes and folded my hands under my chin, the way I'd seen Valleri do. If I couldn't do it without Yeshua, then why didn't he show me what I *was* supposed to do?

Nothing came. Maybe I was asking him wrong.

Actually, was I asking *him*? Or was I still posing some kind of intellectual question?

I picked up the book, hugged it to my chest, and closed my eyes again. "Yeshua?" I whispered. "Will *you* show me what to do? Because thinking this out isn't working. Maybe you don't even care about prom escorts, but parents, that has to be important, right? I want to honor them—but I want to do what's right for the people who are getting tromped on at school. How can I do that and get them on board at the same time? What's it going to take? Asking Kenny to be my escort—the whole family thing? Graham Fitzwilliam? I mean, I'm almost willing to do that ..."

I opened my eyes and held RL out in front of me. "Is that it? Or did I just talk myself into that?"

It didn't answer. And I sure didn't have anything else to go with.

I tucked RL back under the cushion and started the search for Graham's email address. If this wasn't a risk, I didn't know what was.

*

Sunny was in a surprisingly good mood the next morning, and I actually was too, for me. Tomorrow was the dress shop, and that would tell us how much support we could expect for the rest of the plan. When we got to her classroom, two more girls were waiting with dresses and purses and a pair of Pradas I could just see Candace in. If she showed up the next day. I hadn't heard a syllable from her since the assembly, or any of the Kmart Kids for that matter. I was starting to regret emailing Graham. He probably wasn't going to respond anyway.

Wrong.

He appeared outside my math class about two minutes before the bell rang and motioned for me to come out into the hall. I was surprised he didn't have his tuba with him. Although judging from the look on his face, he probably would have hit me with it.

"I can't believe you sent me an *email* to ask me to take you to the prom," he said.

"Hi, Graham, nice to see you," I said.

"Oh, don't even try to take me there." He looked down at me from his giraffe-ish height and scowled until his brows nearly met his lashes. "You act like I have herpes every time I see you and then all of a sudden you're asking me to prom."

"Not as my date," I said. "Just as my escort. For the prom queen thing."

"You are unbelievable." If his voice had gone any higher, only a bloodhound would have been able to hear it. "I'm not good enough to be your date, but I'm okay to walk across the stage with you and get laughed at by those hyenas. Why'd you ask *me*? Because I'm the only brother you know?"

"No. Because it'll make my parents happy."

His mouth came completely open. "Woman?" he said. "Do you have any feelings at *all*?"

All of my blood rushed to my face. All of it. What on earth was I *doing*?

"Graham," I said. "I am so sorry. I'm an idiot."

"You aren't gonna get an argument from me on that."

"Really, I'm sorry. I don't even know what to say. You're totally right."

He relaxed the scowl. "I guess I could sorta see it. My mother's always tryin' to get me to ask you out and I know your mom's on you about it. I just don't wanna be used, you know what I'm sayin'?"

"Yes—I get it."

Mrs. O'Hare came to the doorway. "Bell's about to ring," she said. She looked from me to Graham. "Two minutes," she said and closed the door as the bell sounded.

"I gotta go," Graham said. "But, look—just so you know, I wouldn't have minded taking you—"

"If I hadn't handled it like an insensitive stone," I said.

"No—if you hadn't turned the whole prom into a pity-the-poor-kid thing. I'm not even going."

I groaned. "Not you too."

"Yeah, me more than anybody."

"You're not even poor, Graham. I've been to your house—you live better than we do."

"Yeah, but it's still rich kid reaching down to lend a helping hand to the 'less fortunate.' You don't think that's the way this makes Kenny feel?"

"No!"

"Have you even talked to him since you got up there and did your 'I have a dream' speech at the assembly?"

"My what?"

"You haven't, have you?"

"No."

"Well, he's not goin' either."

"No, he'd rather hang outside the mini-mart. And what's with the 'rich kid' thing?" I said. My face was hot again, but this time it wasn't from embarrassment.

"I'm not gonna argue with you. Like I told you before, you try too much to talk like your do-good parents instead of—"

"You know what?" I said. "I think you don't like this because you just want to keep feeling sorry for yourself, and this doesn't leave you with anything to whine about. I thought the same thing—just be a jerk because nobody understands me, but—"

"Nobody does," Graham said. "Least I don't."

He turned and walked away just as the door opened again. Even after I was at my desk, staring at the Pythagorean theorem, I could still see the anger in his eyes. It was now official: there wasn't a single group in the school I hadn't ticked off.

*

I bewailed that to Valleri when she met me after class.

"I know it doesn't matter what anybody thinks of me," I said. "Except it does, because my face is on this whole project. I should've let you and Patrick be the spokespeople and I should've done the behind-the-scenes. Maybe it would go better if people didn't connect it with me. I can't even ask a guy to the prom without insulting him."

"There's only one thing to do," Valleri said.

"Don't say match dot com," I said.

She shoved curls behind both ears. "No. We need to pray."

"Believe it or not, I did that last night."

She didn't faint like I expected her to. She didn't even blink. She just said, "Let's take a second and get quiet and each give it to God."

I didn't automatically say I didn't know what that even *meant*, because I almost thought I might. I leaned against the hallway wall next to her and gazed down at my feet and silently begged — not for an escort, not even for my parents to give me their blessing, or the Fringe to speak to me, or the Ruling Class to stop sending me threatening text messages. I just prayed that something I was giving would multiply into something good. I didn't even know why I prayed that. It just came to me.

"Hey. Prom Queen. Are you okay?"

My eyes startled open. Ryleigh was standing there, head turned as if she were only looking at me with one eye. It was a something-is-really-weird-here look. And yet the eye I saw was shiny.

"Yeah," I said. "I'm okay."

"I think I'm going to start taking naps in the hallway too," she said. "Hey — I just wanted to tell you."

"Tell me what?" I got ready for the next assault.

"I was thinking about what you said at the assembly about people going to the prom in groups and everybody sharing the expenses instead of taking one date and putting all the burden on a couple." She took a breath. I was needing one myself. "And so a bunch of us got together and decided to form our own, like, prom group?"

"Uh-huh."

"And now we have *twelve* people."

"Seriously?" I said.

Valleri put in a "That's awesome."

"And the guys are like, 'We have a surprise for you women.' I don't know what it is but it's like, I don't know, it feels good to be excited about something for a change. So anyway—" Ryleigh fumbled with the strap on her bag. "I just wanted to say I'm sorry I gave you such a hassle about all this. It's a great idea—and Noelle and I are totally going to be there tomorrow."

"I love it," I said.

She shrugged happily and took off. I felt Valleri looking at me.

"Well," she said. "That was a fast answer."

"Yeah," I said. "Freaky."

And then I looked at her. The blue eyes were waiting, as if they already knew what I was going to say.

"I'm taking you up on your invite to church," I said.

"Sunday?" she said.

"Sure."

"I'll email you the directions," she said. And then she full-out smiled. I was sure she wouldn't have looked that happy if Patrick Sykes had asked her to the prom.

Speaking of Patrick, he emerged from the cafeteria and made a beeline for us. Valleri said, "I have to use the restroom," and melted into the crowd.

"Just the person I wanted to talk to," he said. His grin was kind of soft and mushy, which was different. "Let's go out in the courtyard."

"I wanted to talk to you too," I said, moving just ahead of the hand that hovered at my back. "Wait 'til you hear this."

I told him about Ryleigh and the group thing—and the idea sounded better as I talked. By the time we got to a concrete bench in the courtyard, I'd made a decision.

"I think it's incredible," I said. "And that's what I'm doing. Maybe I'll just grab one of them to be my escort—who knows?" I felt like I, too, must be grinning, not something I could ever have said about myself before. "It's like this huge relief. Egan keeps bugging me, but I think that's just because he figures nobody's going to want to walk with me."

"I don't think—"

"It's okay. There are times when *I* don't even want to walk with me." I nodded at Patrick. "You have no idea how much pressure this takes off. I actually *want* to go to the prom now."

"You didn't before?"

"That's ironic, isn't it?"

"Yeah."

He grinned at me, but it didn't show up in his eyes.

"I'm sorry," I said. "Here I am babbling, and you needed to talk to me about something. Is everything okay?"

"Everything is—yeah, it's okay. I just wanted to ask you …"

His voice faded out. What *was* it I was seeing in his eyes? Now that I looked closer, he seemed—what? Disappointed?

"How many dresses do you think you have?" he said finally. "Hayley's mom wants to know."

I pulled out my notebook, still watching him. Why did I have the feeling that wasn't what he'd brought me out here to talk about? I glanced at the list of items. "We have fifty," I said.

"Ya gotta love that," Patrick said and stood up. "So—lunch?"

"Sure," I said. I didn't point out that it was the only awkward thing I'd ever seen him do.

CHAPTER FIFTEEN

My father used to tell me — when we were actually communicating — that you couldn't always determine success by numbers. That being said, I already considered the dress shop an *outrageous* success when, by 11:30 a.m. on Saturday, we'd outfitted twenty girls for the prom in exchange for offerings none of us — not even Patrick — had thought of.

Ryleigh brought her mom with her — hello, she owned her own beauty shop in Castle Heights — who offered free updos the day of the prom and said if people brought their own polish they could give each other manicures there. We had more nail color than Walgreens, so that wasn't going to be a problem.

Izzy's sister — who knew he had a sister? — brought some expense forms her bookkeeper mom had printed out for keeping track of prom costs. I started helping girls fill those out, calculator in hand, while Hayley, Sunny, and Valleri helped them put together their ensembles. Hayley's mother had juice and fruit and croissants for everyone, and a couple of RC girls walked around with trays. I'd have killed for a latte.

Alyssa and Joanna were conspicuously absent, no surprise there. I *was* surprised when my cousin Candace appeared with a photo album full of pictures of her mother's garden.

"She said anybody wants a corsage, they can pick whatever they want to make one prom morning," Candace told me.

I had totally forgotten that Lana had a major green thumb. What I hadn't forgotten was what Graham told me.

"I didn't think I'd see you here," I said when we were checking out, of all things, the jewelry display.

"Why?" she said.

"You know why. I know Kenny's not going to the prom."

Her eyes flashed. "I ain't Kenny, now, am I?"

"No," I said.

"I been watching you, and I keep saying to myself, if Tyler is in charge of this, I need to get over myself and do it." She lowered her eyes and toyed with a silver serpentine bracelet. "I never will forget what you done for me that day in the mall."

"Don't do it for *me*," I said. "Do it for you. You and Quinn."

She beamed at me. Totally glowed. "We are gon' look *good* in that Camaro, me and him."

"Then you better get over there and pick out a dress," I said.

I was pretty much beaming myself as I watched her dart over to Sunny, arms open. Until I looked and saw Patrick standing there with a very triumphant-looking Joanna on his arm.

She'd finally snagged him. Although, Patrick had never struck me as one to be with anyone he didn't want to be with, especially if she didn't need to be "worked on" to be there.

I didn't like the sadness that settled over me.

I turned to go back to the group poring over their expense sheets in the dining room and almost tripped over Hayley, who shot past and disappeared through a doorway down the hall. It was decidedly slammed.

"Do you know what that's about?" I said to Valleri, who was suddenly there at my elbow.

"She was starting to cry. I think we should go talk to her."

"*You* should go talk to her. This is *not* my core competency."

Valleri grabbed my arm anyway. "She needs a cool head. Let's go."

She half dragged me down the hall to the door Hayley had just slammed. I was all for knocking, but Valleri just pushed it open and tucked herself, and me, inside the room.

Hayley was lying facedown on a bed that had so many pillows it made my window seat look naked. She was beyond "starting to cry." The child was practically convulsing with sobs.

"I'm not good at this," I muttered to Valleri.

She, of course, went straight to Hayley and nodded for me to join her on the other side. I sat down robotically and watched in awe as Valleri stroked Hayley's back until she rolled over and stopped sobbing enough to be able to speak. Personally, I would have just called 911.

"Did you see him with her?" Hayley said to me.

"Patrick and Joanna?" I said.

The sob she gave was a definite yes. "I know he asked her to the prom, the way she was looking, like she's all that."

"Did she tell you that?" I said.

"No! She's not even speaking to me because I'm helping Patrick with this—but she'll speak to *him*!"

"Yeah," I said, "I don't get that either."

I looked helplessly at Valleri, but she gave me a reassuring nod. I had no idea what I was doing.

"So you don't know for a fact that he asked her to prom," I said.

"No." Hayley took the Kleenex Valleri handed her and honked. "Alyssa said he better, or he was going to have to answer to her."

"I'm so sorry your friends have dumped you over this," Valleri said.

"I don't care about them! I just care about Patrick—and I thought he'd ask me if I helped him." She looked miserably at me. "It's been fun and I'm glad I'm doing it—but at first, it really was for him."

"All right," I said, "let's try to be rational about this."

"Okay," she said hopefully.

"Just because Joanna is with Patrick today doesn't mean they're going to prom together. I was in Scarnato's with him one day and she came in, but I don't think she assumed he was taking *me*."

Her hope sagged with her shoulders. "That's different."

"How is it different?"

"Because Patrick wouldn't date you, and he would Joanna. She's in our group, you know?"

The sting went straight through my sternum.

"Yeah," I said. "I know."

Hayley tossed the Kleenex into the white wicker wastebasket and swung her legs over the side of the bed. "I better get out there. I need to wash my face so Joanna won't know she got to me."

Valleri offered to help her, but she shook her head and slipped into the bathroom adjoining her room. I was out the door before Valleri could catch up to me.

"I don't think she realized she insulted you," she said.

"I know. But that's the point. I mean, maybe Alyssa is right. Maybe the whole class system is never going to change."

"Well, not overnight," Valleri said. She turned her head toward the living room, where music was now blasting from a pretty impressive-sounding stereo system. "Sounds like there's a party going on."

I tried not to look for Patrick when we arrived on the scene, but I did, and he and Joanna were gone. Egan had arrived, though, and he looked perfectly at home amid the ruffles and beads and giggles.

"Hey, Tyler," he shouted over the woofers and tweeters. "I thought I'd come by—see how it's going. Chairman of the prom committee and all that."

He didn't need to remind me that *he*—not I—was in charge of the prom. But the back of my neck didn't prickle. He looked way too much like he was enjoying himself to irritate me. Even as I watched, Candace started to walk past him in a sleek cream dress and gold bracelets up both arms. Egan put one hand on her waist and the other in the hand she automatically slipped into his. Everyone had to get their skirts out of the way as the two of them danced in the middle of the room. Candace could definitely move. And Egan—not bad either.

"See?" Valleri said to me.

"Yeah," I said.

Which meant maybe it wasn't the class system that would make it unlikely that Patrick would ever ask me out. Maybe it was just me.

I didn't know until that moment that I even wanted Patrick to ask me, but now I couldn't blot out the vision of *him* escorting me across the stage. A vision of *us* dancing—and greeting the dawn over lattes. A vision that was never going to be real.

I tried to shake it off as I went back to helping with expense forms, but even after we ate the final croissant, counted only ten dresses left, and gave Mrs. Barr the gift of tea and chocolate Valleri had put together for her, the sadness was still there in wisps, like the cobwebs that are left when you think you've totally dusted your room, and then you lie on your bed and see them hiding in the corners of the ceiling.

"You okay?" Sunny said on the way home.

Patrick always asked me that. I guessed his hard work on me had paid off. Now I was like every girl, just the way Alyssa said.

"Tyler?" Sunny said.

I was saved from answering by a text message signal. "I should check this," I said.

But when I looked at it, I wished I'd just gone ahead and confided in my sister instead.

STAY AWAY FROM THE PROM. STAY FAR AWAY.

The phone number wasn't the same as the other message. I had a feeling it belonged to another truck driver or something. Or was it even the same person? I did have somebody in every group in the school wishing I'd never started the Prom for Everybody campaign. For all I knew this could be Graham.

No, not Graham. He'd already told me to my face.

"I hope you're winning that argument," Sunny said.

I snapped the phone closed. "What argument?"

"The one you're having with yourself. Look, I'm not trying to get in your business—"

"Did you ever like a guy and know it was never going to happen?" I blurted out.

The pain on her face was so sharp I felt it in my own chest.

"Oh, Sunny—I am so sorry." My eyes blurred. "Why can't I talk to a single person without sticking my foot down my throat? Do you want to just pull over and I'll get out and walk?"

"No," she said, "I want you to talk to me like my sister. This is one area where I know a lot. More than I want to."

"Talking isn't going to change anything," I said, in a voice I didn't recognize. I sounded like a girl with fragile feelings.

"Maybe not," she said. "But it might make you feel better."

I doubted it, but I just couldn't hold it in any longer. So as Sunny drove up and down the back roads, I told her everything about Patrick — how feelings about him snuck up on me in spite of all my efforts not to be like all the other girls who, as Ms. Dalloway said, drooled over him.

"You're not drooling," Sunny said. "I guarantee you nobody knows how you feel except you."

"And you."

"Nobody's going to hear it from me."

"Do you think that's true? That nobody knows I like him that way?"

"Why?"

I considered telling her about the text message threats but decided against it. She'd feel like she had to tell Mom and Dad, and I couldn't put her in that position. Not now that I was actually starting to like her.

"Is this helping at all?" she said.

"You mean am I over it?"

"No, I mean can you still love yourself even though he doesn't?"

I looked at her sideways. "Are we talking about you or me?"

"When it comes to love, sis, it's all the same. Trust me."

Strangely enough, I did.

And I did feel a little less cobwebby. Enough that when I got up to my room, I could focus on the real problem.

I called the number the text had come from and got a raspy-voiced woman who said she "didn't text nobody today" because she was working a double shift. I could hear pans clattering in the background and somebody yelling about a fat burger.

So the person who texted me to stay away from the prom was probably the same one who informed me I didn't belong with Patrick. Whoever it was seemed to be picking up phones wherever and using them to try to scare me.

It was working. Because saying "leave Patrick alone" was one thing; after the prom was over, we would probably go back to our groups, him to the Ruling Class and me to—

Anyway, that was one thing. But saying I shouldn't even go to the prom ... I couldn't do that. Not now. What was going to happen if I did?

I looked at both of the text messages again, but they were too cryptic to give me any clues. Jackals. They were too cowardly to face me themselves. They wouldn't even let us post on their Facebook page.

My gaze went to my laptop. They wouldn't talk about it on there, would they? Or was that really why Egan said we couldn't be on there?

After seeing Egan dancing with Candace, I didn't want to believe that. But it didn't stop me from logging on and going to the Castle Heights Prom page.

"Do people really hang out on here?" I said to the screen.

Evidently so, because the page was basically a photo album of Alyssa and her friends trying on prom dresses at some boutique—was that really New York City like the caption said?—Alyssa and her friends trying on shoes, Alyssa and her friends having each nail done in a different style so they could decide what manicure to have on prom day. The more I scrolled down the more aghast I was. Especially when I got to the bottom, and found a picture of myself. I was not picking out a prom gown.

It was one of the fifty shots Ms. Dalloway *didn't* use for the article in the school paper. I was trying to get my balance on the ladder, so my arms were going out in what seemed to be five directions. My legs were worse. But my face was the ultimate. The camera had caught me with my eyes at half-mast and my mouth twisted. Anybody who didn't know me would swear I'd just downed a whole bottle of wine.

That hadn't been lost on the creators of the Facebook page. The caption underneath said, *Sorry, Brainiac. No booze allowed at YOUR prom.*

YouTube went on to comment that booze would be readily available at an invitation-only after party. *Show up at the prom. Get your picture taken with your date so your parents'll think you hung out the whole time. Then come to the real party.*

If you get an invitation, Alyssa added in her comment.

My eyes glanced over the rest, all expressing relief that prom night was saved. Only the last one snagged me.

Don't bother sending me an invite, it said. *I think this is juvenile.*

It was posted by Patrick.

Somebody else responded: *You've been hanging out with Brainiac too much.*

There were no more comments from Patrick.

At least not that I could see through the fog of tears. I didn't like Patrick for what "every girl" saw in him. I liked him because he would say that on Facebook. And because that was all he would say.

I turned off my laptop and let myself hurt.

*

The first thing I thought when I woke up the next morning was that it still hurt. The second thing I thought was that I'd promised to go to Valleri's church today. It had to be better than staying home with myself. I was sure no bobolinks were going to show up.

Once I was showered and dressed, though, my parents had already left for their own church. Walking there was out of the question in the rain that was now pelting my mother's pansies to a pulp.

I was staring dismally at the drips running down the kitchen window when Sunny came in.

"Where are you going all dressed up?" she said. "By the way, have I mentioned that I like the way you're putting yourself together these days?"

"No," I said. "I was supposed to go to Valleri's church but—" I gestured toward the storm.

Sunny finished pouring herself a cup of coffee. "I can take you. How long do I have?"

"Thirty minutes."

"Let me get dressed. Um—" She stopped in the doorway. "Do you mind if I stay for the service?"

"No," I said. In fact, it would feel better to have a cohort.

Interesting how I thought of Sunny that way now.

*

We followed Valleri's directions, but after driving through the downpour past the address five or six times until Sunny was giggling hysterically, we were satisfied there was no church on Sunnyvale Drive. Fifteen fifty-six was somebody's two-story stone house.

"There are a lot of cars," Sunny said, still gurgling. "Do you think they meet here?"

"What—like in somebody's living room?"

"I've heard of that." She shrugged. "All we can do is knock on the door."

I just hoped nobody was going to greet us in their pajamas and look at us like we were nuts. As we ran up the walkway, bumping against each other under Sunny's umbrella, I imagined somebody poking their head out and saying, "Does this look like a church to you?"

Actually, it sounded like one. When we got to the front porch, guitar music and singing wafted from an open front window—along with the aroma of fresh bread.

"I don't care if it's a church or not," Sunny said. "I'm staying for breakfast."

She started to knock but the red door flew open and so did Valleri's arms.

"You *both* came! I love this!"

I wouldn't have thought Valleri could be any more bouncy than she was at school, but she virtually had a built-in pogo stick here. She hugged us both multiple times and kissed us each on the cheek and repeated, and repeated, how thrilled she was that we were there, all as she ushered us into a sunny room filled with music and people.

As it turned out, there were only about twelve, but I still hoped while Valleri was introducing them all that there wasn't going to be a test. The only names I remembered for more than two seconds were Mr. and Mrs. Clare, Valleri's parents. Her mother was creamy skinned and had a French accent and the blue eyes Valleri had inherited from her. Her father was, to my surprise, a stocky African American with the I-like-you-immediately face she'd gotten from *him*. She was the two of them put together, and then some.

Somehow we were seated with Valleri between us, and the service started. Valleri clutched my hand through a lot of it. It was the most I'd been touched since I stopped climbing into my father's lap, and that thought almost made me cry.

Sunny *did* cry, almost from the opening, "The Lord is risen. The Lord is risen indeed, alleluia." Through the singing, the round-robin of prayers, even the lively talk-and-discussion on the Bible reading about giving Caesar what's his and God what's His, Sunny wept quietly. I could feel the sorrow seeping out of her. I could feel it.

Toward the end, they passed around that bread I'd been smelling and a heavy pottery chalice of watered-down wine. Each person looked into the eyes of the next and said their name and, "The body of Christ is given for you. The blood of Christ is the cup of salvation." I'd heard those words before countless times and had yet to really understand them. But when Valleri turned to me and dipped a torn-off piece of the bread into the cup and said, "Tyler, this is for you, from Jesus," the tears came. The ones I'd been holding back. The ones that washed over the hurt in my chest.

The rain had stopped when Valleri walked Sunny and me to the car, her arms looped through ours. It was slow going, walking attached, and I didn't know exactly how to do it. I stepped on Valleri's toe more than once before we got to the end of the driveway.

"I want to come back," Sunny said.

"And we *want* you to."

Valleri squeezed her arm and let go, and Sunny went to the car to unlock it.

"I don't know," I said to Valleri.

"Don't know what?"

"Whether I'll come back."

Valleri's eyes clouded, but she said, "That's up to you."

"I keep telling you—I am so *bad* at this."

"At ..."

"At feelings. I feel something and I blubber all over the place. I try to talk about it and I make *other* people cry—or tick them off, or stir up trouble."

"Well, yeah," Valleri said.

"I liked the service—I loved it, in fact. It was the first time communion ever made sense to me, and nobody even explained it—it was just there." I blew out a frustrated breath. "But I'm too much of a mess right now to be in a room with people who get all of it, everything. I have too many questions."

The big blue eyes blinked. "That's all we do is ask questions," she said. "We hardly ever have any answers, except just keep loving."

"How do you do that?" I said.

"That's what everybody's trying to figure out."

I folded my arms. "Okay, that is just impossible to fathom. There's a room full of people hugging you at ten-second intervals and *feeding* each other by *hand*—and you're saying they're still trying to figure out how to love? They look like they invented the concept."

Valleri's face burst into a smile, and she threw her arms around my neck. "I love you, Tyler," she said.

"Why?" I said.

"Because you're so you."

When I'd disentangled myself and got into the car, Sunny nodded at me.

"You're going back too," she said.

"Yeah," I said, "I am."

CHAPTER SIXTEEN

I was surprised to find Mom alone in the sunroom nursing a lemonade when we got home. I was even more surprised that the dimples weren't in evidence. Usually she loved a few hours to herself, "to think what I want to think when I want to think it," she always said. That was definitely a gene I'd inherited. So the biggest surprise was when she said, "Come out and join me. I want to talk to you girls."

I gave Sunny a what-did-we-do-now look. She gave me one back. Not very reassuring.

"Where's Dad?" I said as I dropped into a flowered chair across from Mom.

"He had a board meeting at church. I escaped. Where were you two?"

Oh. So that was it. I'd forgotten to leave a note.

"We went to church," Sunny said. "A friend of Tyler's invited us — it was kind of spontaneous."

Mom waved a hand at her. "You can stop defending her. It's fine. A little unexpected, but fine."

She took an interminable drink from the lemonade, while Sunny and I again exchanged glances. This was about *something*. Could we not just get to it?

"All right, here's the thing," Mom said finally. "I've been thinking about your prom project."

I worked hard not to groan.

"And I would like to offer the house for a preprom party."

Okay — *that* was the biggest surprise. If *I* had been drinking a lemonade, I'd have choked on it.

"We'd have hors d'oeuvres and whatever drinks you think — maybe some music — just a chance for your friends to gather and appreciate each other before they get to the prom and it all gets crazy." She ran a finger through the condensation on the glass. "People could do this instead of feeling like they have to spend a lot going out to dinner. Isn't that what you're trying to accomplish?"

It was. And I liked the idea. But there were so many questions.

The first one was, "What does Dad say?"

Mom grunted.

"No, seriously. What does he say?"

"That's what he says. We still haven't won him over on this, but he'll come around."

"So *you're* won over?"

Mom set the glass aside and slanted toward me. "Tyler, I have seen a huge change in you since you started this. I admit I didn't like it at first, but most of that was my own stuff."

I didn't even know my mother *had* stuff.

"But I think this is good for you, and for the community, which is what we're always preaching at you. So I'd like to support you. I really would."

Which was why I didn't ask my next question: Who is actually going to come to *my* house for this?

"We don't have to do it if you don't want to," Mom said.

Sunny put her hand on my arm. "Maybe you need to think about it?"

"No," I said. "Let's do it."

Because I couldn't hurt another person I cared about. I knew what that felt like now, and I just couldn't do it.

*

Mom said to make up a list of people I wanted to invite, which was still one person long when, after going to my locker, I sat in the school courtyard the next morning before school. Sunny and I had gotten in early so she could prep for our exam in fourth block, which gave me plenty of time to continue agonizing.

Joanna found me there.

She sat at the concrete table across from me and bit at her pretty lip—for so long I finally said, "Was there something you wanted to say?"

"Yes," she said. And then burst into tears.

Could any of us girls do anything but cry these days?

I produced a tissue from my bag and handed it to her.

"You're going to have to give me more information," I said.

"You're the whole reason Patrick hasn't asked me to prom!"

My chin dropped directly to my chest.

"It's true!"

"Uh, no," I said. "First of all, I thought he did ask you. You were wearing it all over your face Saturday."

"I was sure he was *going* to, especially since I let him drag me to that dress thing at Hayley's. I thought for sure that would do it."

That seemed to be the consensus among the Ruling Class.

"I don't know what else to do," she said, eyes filling again. "It's all about *you* now with him."

"Yeah, well, if it's any consolation, he hasn't asked me either, and I don't know why you think he would. I've already been told that's not an option for him since I'm not in your 'group.'"

She looked at me blankly for a moment.

"I'm sorry," I said. "I don't know any other way to talk."

"No, it's not that. Patrick's different around you. Maybe it's the Help the Kmart Kids thing or whatever, but he's nicer since he's been hanging out with you, and he thinks different or something. I don't know, but I *do* know he would do just about anything you asked him to, so ..." She swallowed as if she were trying to get a wad of bubble gum down. "Could you maybe just tell him he should take me to prom?"

I didn't know where to start answering that, and even if I had, my mouth was no longer working. First of all, she was confronting me head on—so not the Ruling Class approach. Second of all—*what*? Patrick would do anything I asked him to? This child was clearly delusional.

However, right now *she* might do anything I asked her to.

"Okay," I said. "I'll talk to him."

She almost came out of the chair.

"But on one condition."

"Anything."

"You have to tell me if you sent me this text message."

I pulled out my phone and showed it to her, my eyes glued to her reaction. She frowned in that delicate way only she could pull off, but when she shook her head, I believed her.

"This one either?" I said as I clicked to the second text.

She shook her head even harder.

"Do you know who did? I have to know, Joanna, just for my own peace of mind." I swallowed some bubble gum of my own. "If you tell me, I'll even promise not to accept if Patrick does ask me."

It was an easy thing to offer, since it was obvious he wasn't going to, but her eyes widened as if I'd just said I'd sever an arm for the cause.

"I swear to you I have no idea," she said. "And you *know* I would tell you for that."

"So ... a date with Patrick trumps loyalty to the group. Is that what you're saying?"

"I don't even know what that means."

"You'd rat on your friends if it meant going to the prom with Patrick."

"Well, yeah," she said. "Wouldn't you?"

"No," I said. "If I had a group of friends I really loved, I wouldn't just automatically ditch them for a guy, no matter who he was."

Joanna looked at me as if she'd just realized I was there. "You are so—different than I thought," she said. "I can totally see why Patrick likes you."

That seemed to stun her so deeply, she walked away without making me promise again to follow through. I was a little stunned myself.

My invitation list still read only *Valleri Clare*, but I needed to get to my locker and grab my stuff for class. When I got there, I wasn't sure whether to be relieved or disappointed that Patrick wasn't waiting for me. No wonder I'd always steered clear of this kind of drama.

I had to yank to get the locker door open, and when I did, the reason why dropped to the floor. Someone had stuck a folded piece of paper in on the hinged side. Had to be Valleri; she was the only one I knew who didn't text everything she wanted to say.

The minute I unfolded it, however, I could tell it wasn't from her. The letters had been cut from a magazine and pasted on in haphazard fashion. And Valleri would never have written what this note said:

IF YOU GO TO THE PROM, YOU WILL REGRET IT. IT'S GOING TO BE LIKE A SCENE FROM CARRIE.

Carrie? The movie where they dumped blood on the girl who was elected prom queen?

"What's happenin', girl?"

I jerked so hard the paper fell out of my hand and my elbow connected with my locker.

"Sorry," Patrick said. "Didn't mean to freak you out."

Before I could stop him, he leaned over and picked up the note. I watched his face go white.

"What is *this*?" he said.

I started to shake. "It was stuck in my locker. And I know it wasn't Joanna, because I was just talking to her, and this wasn't here the first time I came."

Patrick was following my babbling lips with his eyes. "Joanna?" he said. "Nah—this has Alyssa all over it."

His voice alone stopped the jitter in my head. I took a breath.

"Alyssa would never risk getting glue on her manicure," I said.

Patrick shook his head. "You don't understand—she wants prom queen *bad*. She's, like, obsessed with it."

"And she's probably going to get it, so why would she do this?"

"Because she knows *you* are probably going to get it."

"In whose world? Are you kidding me?"

He stuck the note into his pocket and put his face close to mine. I couldn't move. Or breathe.

"You, like, symbolize the prom this year. People respect you. Even people who would never admit it. And Alyssa knows it."

I wanted to come back with a quip, but I couldn't think of one. I still wasn't breathing when he pulled his face away.

"I'll take care of this," he said. "Don't worry about it, okay?"

"Okay," I said.

When he left, I let out all the air and sagged against the locker. I realized I hadn't told him he should ask Joanna to the prom. I would do it, of course. But there was suddenly nothing I wanted to do less.

*

I didn't see Patrick again until after lunch. Valleri and I watched him from across the cafeteria while he sat in a corner with Alyssa, shaping the conversation with his hands.

Valleri slowly shook the curls. "He even makes chewing somebody out look like, hey, would you chew *me* out now?"

I looked at her in surprise. "Valleri Clare," I said, "do you have a crush on Patrick?"

She laughed. "No. But I appreciate a nice guy. There aren't that many of them. I met one in France and—I know we're too young and all that, but we email every day, and who knows about someday? But I'm not going to date just to be dating, you know?"

"I never thought about it. It's not like I've ever been asked out."

"You will be," she said. "Trust me."

"Did you talk to him?"

I looked up from my sandwich at Joanna. Her lip was quivering. Actually, her entire body was quivering.

"Sit down before you *fall* down," I said.

I could feel Valleri staring at me as Joanna dropped into the chair beside mine.

"So did you?" Joanna said.

"I haven't had a chance."

"You waited too long! Look at that—he's asking Alyssa right now."

"No, he's not," I said. "He's interrogating her."

"Huh?"

I looked hopelessly at Valleri.

"He's just asking her some questions about something," Valleri said.

"She didn't send those text messages either," Joanna said. "I asked her."

I felt my eyebrow go up. "Excuse me if I don't automatically believe everything Alyssa says."

"No, it's true. She *wants* you to go to prom."

"Because ..."

Joanna shifted in the chair. "Okay, no offense, but she totally thinks you're going to lose prom queen and she wants to see you suffer. *I* don't think that. And I don't even care about winning, if I can just go with Patrick."

"Well, if you want to do that, you better get lost," I said, "because here he comes. I can't ask him if you're sitting here."

She bolted from the chair and then stopped. "Just one more thing," she said.

"What?"

"You can't tell him that I asked you to talk to him."

I wasn't sure I followed that, but I nodded.

"I'm going to leave too," Valleri said.

"Don't!" I said.

She squeezed my hand. "Just trust me."

So it was just me at the table when Patrick joined me, already shaking his head.

"Alyssa didn't do it," he said.

"How do you know?"

"Because I tried everything except waterboarding. I've known Alyssa since kindergarten. I've always been able to get her to fess up to a lie, but she's not cracking. Too bad too. I wanted it to be her."

"Why?"

"Because if she was the one, we'd know what we were dealing with. Now we don't, and I hate that."

"Okay," I said, "now that I'm thinking about it, I seriously don't think anybody is going to dump a pail of O negative on my head at the prom. They're all about it being first class. They wouldn't mess it up."

"So, what, it's an empty threat? Why go to all the trouble of pasting words on a piece of paper?"

I looked around the cafeteria. Nobody looked like they had that much energy. Izzy was asleep with his head on the table as usual—though how he could still do that after the YouTube fiasco . . .

"What?" Patrick said. "You just thought of something."

"Maybe it was YouTube. Maybe he was hiding with his camera while I was reading it. It's probably on the Internet already."

Patrick's brown eyes narrowed. "Are you just trying to get me to let this go? Because I'm just about to go to Mr. Baumgarten—"

"No!" I said.

Izzy actually stirred two tables over. I lowered my voice.

"He'll cancel the whole prom," I said. "We've worked too hard for that to happen."

"But we can't just ignore it."

I chewed at my thumbnail. "Okay, what if we both keep investigating? Somebody's going to say something sooner or later. You could keep an eye on the Facebook page—"

"I'm not going on there—I hate that thing."

The heat in his voice was so un-Patrick, I blinked. "Okay. But see what you can get out of YouTube."

He nodded, face still doubtful. "But I'm not saying anything to Egan."

"Good call."

"Man, I am so bummed about this. Everything was going great."

"Okay, here's something that'll cheer you up. Or not."

"Talk to me. I'm dyin' here."

I told him about the pre-prom party at my place, and to my relief the grin returned.

"I was trying to come up with a guest list," I said. "And then you just said how much you hated that Facebook page, with the invitation-only party, and I just realized—"

"You saw that?" Patrick said.

"I went on there one night—"

"Man, why did you do that, Tyler? I *hate* that you saw that."

"The picture of me looking like I'm stoned?"

I tried a laugh, but he didn't join me.

"I'm really sorry," he said.

"You didn't do it."

"People I used to think were cool did. I'm sorry I ever thought they were."

That look was back in his eyes, the one I couldn't name before. I knew now that it *was* disappointment, and I didn't like seeing it there.

"So, do you want to know what I was thinking?" I said.

"Sure."

"I think since having an exclusive, closed party after the prom goes against everything we're trying to do, an invitation-only pre-prom party would do the same thing."

"Go on."

"So what if I opened it up to everybody who's going to the prom? I still don't know who would come—"

"I'll be there," he said. "That idea *rocks*."

That, and the dance in his eyes, was all I needed.

But for Joanna, I remembered, it was a different story.

"You can bring your date, of course," I said.

"I don't have a date."

So far so good.

"Then you want to know what I think?" I said.

He grinned. "Do I have a choice?"

"I think you should ask Joanna."

The grin froze, right there on his face, like I'd blasted it with liquid nitrogen.

"I'm not asking Joanna," he said.

The look in his eyes warned me not to ask why.

"Oh," I said. "Just thought I'd throw that out there."

"Because she told you to?"

Ew.

"She did," he said.

"You didn't hear it from me," I said.

Patrick worked his shoulders. "Could we change the subject?"

"The party."

"Valleri could make up, like, a huge invitation—"

"—and fliers—"

"We could do a group picture at the party and print it in the *Herald*—okay, we totally need to go to Scarnato's after school and plan this out."

I smiled and he smiled and we were okay again. I could settle for "okay" and a latte, couldn't I?

*

That was Monday. With the prom on Saturday, that gave us five days to find out who made the threat. The good news was that there weren't any more messages. The bad news: we still didn't have a clue by Thursday.

That wasn't the only thing bothering me. Mom was all about the pre-prom party, and she and Sunny had already made two trips to Albany for supplies—none of which I was privy to, because they said I was the hostess and needed to save myself. That was all fabulous, except that my father never missed a chance at the dinner table to try to lure me into a debate about the practical applications of the prom to future life. He would only stop when Sunny threatened to leave the table. I was really beginning to love my sister.

Then there was the issue of the photographer. The studio Egan's committee had hired was charging some exorbitant fee for just one shot, and he was charging extra for groups larger than a couple. Egan kept telling us they couldn't find anyone cheaper, but he promised to keep trying. With only a few days left, I didn't hold out much hope for that. We just told people to bring their own cameras to my house and we'd do something nice.

And then there was the matter of Joanna. I couldn't go on letting her think Patrick was going to pop the question any minute, so Monday after school I'd tracked her down in the library, where the prom committee was having their final meeting. When she saw me come in, she all but leaped over two tables and a dictionary stand and dragged me out into the hall. I heard YouTube behind us, saying, "What the—"

"Did you talk to him?" she said.

"Yeah," I said.

"And?"

"Look, Joanna, I—"

"He said he wasn't going to, didn't he?"

I nodded.

"Did you tell him he *should*? Did you try to talk him into it?"

"Actually, I started to and he just wouldn't listen to me. Look, maybe you should just talk to him yourself and find out why."

"I don't want to know why!"

She put her face in her hands and leaned against me. I didn't have much choice but to put my arms around her.

"Did he ask you?" she said. "He did, didn't he?"

"Uh, no, he did not."

"I'm so sorry, Tyler," she said through her tears. "I'm so sorry for both of us."

Alyssa chose that moment to pass by. Her eyes enlarged; she clearly couldn't believe what she was seeing.

That made two of us.

At least Candace, Ryleigh, Izzy, and Noelle and Fred and the rest of the twelve who were going as a group were happy. They gathered at the lunch table with Patrick and Valleri and me daily and made up for the Fringe averting their eyes every time I got within ten feet, and Kenny and Graham acting like I was carrying the plague.

Still, I felt unsettled. I'd tried so hard to do this good thing, and there was still so much of it that wouldn't fall into place.

No amount of extra credit was enough. It wasn't until I was sitting on my window seat Wednesday night that I realized — in a sudden sweat — what I needed to do.

I pulled out RL.

Thought you'd never ask,

the first warm page said.

I have a story for you.

Thank God. Literally.

Yeshua was getting sick of the religion scholars and the big kahunas we talked about last time trying to catch him in all these technicalities, like having a logical explanation for everything was what mattered.

I used to think it was. Now I'm not sure.

Not sure is good in this instance. He said to his disciples, "Watch out for those guys. They love to walk around in their robes and hoods that tell you how much education they have, and bask in the flattery, and assume they're going to win every election because, well, because they're them." He said, "Don't be drawn in by that, because the whole time they're being all that, they're exploiting the poor and making it hard for people who can't help themselves." He said they'd get theirs in the end.

I knew all this. And I wasn't doing that, so how was this supposed to help me?

We're getting to that. Just then he looked over and saw the rich people dropping bags of money into the collection plate and making a huge production out of it, like "Do you see this? Do you see how much I'm giving?"

I knew that too. I'd seen it firsthand.

This is the part I want you to get. Then Yeshua saw a widow that was pretty much destitute drop in two pennies. And he looked at his disciples, and he said, "That's the biggest offering that's been given today. All these wealthy types? They're never going to miss a cent of what they brought in here. But that woman gave what she couldn't afford. She gave everything."

The book was quiet. It had yet again told me a story I already knew. Only this time, I also knew enough to ask —

"What do you want me to do with that?"

What do you think?

"Give everything I have."

Have you done that?

"I didn't have any dresses to donate, but—"

Are you serious? Go deeper. Did you give what you couldn't afford?

I pondered that. The book waited.

I gave up my so-called friends. But then I got more.

More waiting.

I gave up my easy relationship with my father. But I gained a sister. I guess I gave up being sure about everything. But I got feelings. I still don't know if I even like that.

So what's left to give?

"I don't know. I'm feeling pretty naked right now."

She gave everything she had.

I looked around the room, puffing frustration.

You'll know it when you see it. If you stick with Yeshua.

I was startled. Wasn't that what Valleri said—she just knew it was a God thing when it happened? But I was no Valleri.

No, but you're some Tyler.

There it was again: the voice that wasn't mine but didn't come from anywhere else. It was there, though. And I liked that it was there.

I looked down at the page and nodded at it.

"Okay," I whispered. "I'll keep my eyes open."

And your heart, the voice whispered back. *It will be in your heart.*

CHAPTER SEVENTEEN

Thursday. Two days before prom, and the excitement was so real you could feel it on your skin. All that *we* could do had been done, and now *I* had to take care of a few things.

Like, oh, what I was going to wear. I brought that up to Sunny Thursday morning on the way to school.

"I was wondering when you were going to get around to that," she said. "If you hadn't said something by tonight I was going to."

"I guess I should have picked something out at the dress shop."

Sunny shook her head. "There was nothing there for you. I do have a dress I held back, if you're interested."

I gave her a look. "I could so not get my big toe into anything that fits you."

"Get outta town, girl. Come to my room tonight and we will just *see*."

I was still sure I would look as if I'd been poured into any dress of hers, but I felt happier anyway. Now I just had to ask one of the boys in the Twelve if he would escort me on stage. I would actually ask Izzy if I thought he could stay awake long enough.

I was headed for the table at lunch, still pretty much playing eeny, meeny, miny, mo, when a hulking figure with shaggy black hair cut into my path.

"Hey, Tyler," Matthew said.

"Well, hey yourself."

"I thought maybe you'd want to go to lunch."

I looked behind him.

"It's just me," he said.

"And you want to go to lunch. Why, all of a sudden?"

I hoped I didn't sound rude, but this *was* out of left field. Actually it was from way out of the park. Nobody in the Fringe had spoken to me since the YouTube/Izzy incident.

"I know it's kind of random," Matthew said. "But I need to talk to you. I'll buy."

"I'll eat lunch with you," I said. "But I'll buy my own food, and I am not getting in a car with you. How about the courtyard?"

"Fine with me. I'm not that hungry anyway."

I started toward the outside door. "As I recall, you always mooched off my lunch. Come on."

I may have appeared casual as I led the way to the courtyard, but my mind was reviewing the possible topics. He wanted to apologize for leaving me to do the whole Andrew Jackson presentation. He wanted to tell me something about Yuri or Deidre. He wanted to announce that he was becoming a priest. Okay, ridiculous, but it was about as plausible as the other two. Matthew just didn't "talk" about things.

We sat at the only concrete table that wasn't occupied by an RC. Matthew surveyed them from under his bushy eyebrows, but I shook my head at him.

"They're all harmless," I whispered. "Just don't tell them that, because they don't know."

He gave them one last scowl and turned to me. "I know this is going to sound really weird, but I heard you need an escort for the prom queen—thing—and if you want, I'll do it."

I froze with my sandwich midway to my mouth.

"Like I said, I know it's weird, random, whatever—but I want to do it."

I put the sandwich down. "Why?"

"Because ..." He looked warily at YouTube and the crowd around him at the other end of the courtyard. "You know they're going to try to humiliate you again, especially now that a lot of people are looking up to you. I could protect you, maybe."

"How are you going to do that, Matthew? All you've ever done up until now is hide from them."

"I can come out for one night."

I laughed. "And then you'll climb back into the crypt?"

"I want to do it, okay? You need somebody and I want it to be me." He rubbed the concrete with his finger. "Unless you don't think I can clean up my act or something. I guess I might not be what they have in mind."

Everything I'd said about Prom for Everybody flashed through my mind. Right along with RL saying *Did you give everything you had?*

"I would love to have you as my escort, Matthew," I said. "We will be stunning on that stage."

He closed his eyes, and for the first time I saw the under-the-skin tremble around his mouth. "I swear I'll drive safe."

"Yeah, well, it's a good thing my house is only four blocks from here."

"Dude, that's harsh."

"You'll come to the party before, right?"

He shook his bangs over his eyes.

"You can still back out," I said.

"No. I'm there." He actually smiled at me. "This is me being there."

And this was me, still trying to keep my teeth from dropping out of my mouth.

*

Seventeen days of full-out preparation, and suddenly, prom night was just—there. The last day was the fullest.

Do's at Ryleigh's mom's shop, although I just went to watch. Sunny did mine and Candace's, because African American hair is a whole other thing. I had never seen Candace's hair look so ... sane.

Manicures à la each other. Hayley did mine, in red to match the dress Sunny gave me. By some miracle it fit as if it were made for me, with a trumpet skirt and a long, fitted waist that made me feel like somebody glamorous.

"You *are* somebody glamorous," my mother told me. Her eyes were actually misty when she loaned me the perfect lipstick and her diamond tennis bracelet. For the first time ever, I wanted to be me when I grew up.

The last half hour before the party was supposed to start, I had a major attack of the doubts. I paced them out in the foyer. No one was going to come. There were going to be all these Swedish meatballs and cheese puffs and white roses waiting in an empty house until midnight, when I would turn back into a pumpkin. What *was* I going to do when the prom was over?

"Well now. Who is this?"

I looked up at my father, who was standing halfway down the stairs, wearing a suit and a wobbly smile.

"It's just me," I said.

He took the rest of the steps down shaking his head. "No, no, this is not 'just' anybody. This is my beautiful daughter."

Dad held out his hand, and when I took it, he twirled me around so that the trumpet skirt sailed at my calves. He stopped and took both of my hands in his—not something the father I knew would ever do.

"I still have my misgivings about all this," he said. "But I have to say this: I think it has turned you into a young woman."

"It's the dress," I said.

"Dresses don't make young women. Integrity makes young women. And character. Now, stubbornness"—he gave me his boy grin—"that just makes me remember you're still my kid."

"That and my big feet. I couldn't wear Sunny's shoes."

"Some of the most beautiful women in the world have worn size nine or over. Jacqueline Kennedy—"

"How do you even *know* that?"

I didn't get to hear, because there was a commotion out front. I went to the window in the door and felt a guffaw burst right up out of the neckline of that red dress.

A large farm wagon was stopping at the curb, lined with seats and festooned with garlands of ivy and daisies and white fluff. The Twelve filled the seats, a profusion of color and laughter and joy. The whole thing was pulled by four horses.

The prom was now officially for everybody.

It only got better after that. Candace arrived in the Camaro with the much-anticipated Quinn. He was everything she said he was and more. I couldn't take my eyes off the gold tooth. Hayley showed up in a limo with a date someone told me was her cousin, along with Joanna and a sophomore boy she must have corralled at the last minute. He looked pretty much ecstatic to be there. She was keeping up a brave front. I secretly hoped she'd be crowned queen.

Valleri was my personal favorite guest. When she walked in wearing a coral party dress that screamed Paris, everyone stopped in awe.

"Who *is* that?" Joanna's date whispered to me. "I never even saw her before."

"Pretend you don't see her now," I said. "If you get my drift."

He evidently did, because he scurried back to Joanna.

When I got Valleri alone at the hors d'oeuvres table, I told her how fabulous she looked, and then I asked her something I never thought to even bring up before.

"Are you going to prom alone?"

"Oh, no. My date's meeting me here and we're going to walk over."

"I feel like a totally heinous friend for not already knowing this," I said. "Who is it?"

She smiled and nodded toward the door, which Sunny was opening with one hand while she balanced a tray of drinks with the other. I hoped it wasn't Matthew she was letting in or she was going to be wearing those drinks.

But it was Patrick who walked into the foyer, looking far hotter than any seventeen-year-old boy should be allowed to look. White dinner jacket. Blond hair shiny and falling into all the right places. And even from where I was standing, I could see the brown eyes dancing.

My heart stopped... Valleri was going to the prom with Patrick? I whipped around to face her, but she was already headed for the door. With a quick wave to him, she greeted the next person who stepped in—with a hug and a huge smile. I stared for a full five seconds before I realized it was Izzy.

"He sure cleans up nice," Sunny murmured behind me.

"Yeah," I said. "Who'd have thought?"

Nobody, except Valleri, who brought out the hidden self in everybody, it seemed. Izzy was combed and shined up and fitted nicely into a gray tux. Best of all, he was wide awake.

"I knew you'd look this way."

I closed my eyes for a moment before I turned to Patrick. He looked—and smelled—even better close up. I should have kept my eyes shut longer.

"You're fabulous," he said.

"So are you," I said.

"We did it, didn't we?"

"I think we did."

He put up his hand and I touched my palm to it. This time when he squeezed, I squeezed back. His date probably wasn't going to like it. I should probably let go ...

I looked around. "Did you come with someone?" I said.

"No, it's just me."

A stab of something went straight through my heart. He'd rather go to the prom alone than ask me?

"Tyler?"

That was Sunny, singing out to me from the front door. Matthew was standing next to her, all in black, hair combed back, looking almost handsome in a haunted sort of way. Haunted and out of place.

"Excuse me," I said to Patrick.

Somehow I pulled Matthew into the dining room—I was in need of that guy from Castle Heights Towing—and got him focused on the food. Fortunately, any food was comfort food to Matthew, including cheese puffs. Then I turned around to find Patrick again, but Noelle and Fred cornered me.

"Do you like the tux?" she said, eyes alive and shiny.

"I do," I said. Fred too "cleaned up nice" in tails and a top hat.

"He won it," she said. "In the contest."

"You mean the Most Creative Invite contest?"

She nodded proudly and wrung out his arm. "Tell her what you did."

Fred shrugged. "I'd already asked her before and it was lame, like, 'You don't really want to go, do you?' So I decided to ask her again, for real—"

"—And he *sang* it! In the middle of the night, under my window. It was so romantic!"

"The neighbors weren't that happy about it," Fred said with another shrug. "But who cares? This only happens once in our whole life."

I followed his gaze around the room. People I saw every day in their jeans and their T-shirts and their I'm-so-over-this expressions had been transformed, not only by their heels and bow ties and Lana-made corsages, but by the poise in their shoulders and the softness in their manners and the self-respect in their voices. It was like a peek into the future, at the adults we would all be if we treated each other well: Joanna was exclaiming over Candace's bracelets, and Hayley was chatting Izzy up about the lobster rolls, and Egan, sweet Egan, was telling Ryleigh she was beauty pageant material. We could all be ladies and gentlemen, no matter how much money we ever made, and this was our rite of passage into that.

I was going to have to explain that to my father. Because this was why a prom was significant.

"We have to go," Ryleigh said to me. "We're going for a ride around the lake before we go to the school. You're coming, aren't you?"

I shook my head and glanced around for Matthew, who was currently trying to become one with the wainscoting in the foyer.

"I wish I was," I said. "But I'll see you all there."

She hugged me and flew off, taking the rest of the Twelve with her.

"You're not going with the group?" Patrick said at my elbow.

"No," I said. "I'm going with Matthew."

He looked as if I had just slapped him across the face. There was more than disappointment in his eyes.

"I thought you were all about the group thing," he said.

"I am. But Matthew volunteered to be my escort—and the prom *is* for everybody." I finished off with a dry, "Even him."

"So if somebody else had asked you sooner, you'd have gone with him."

I opened my mouth to answer with who knew what, but he shook his head. "Doesn't matter. Look, I just wanted to tell you a couple things."

"Okay."

His voice was chilly. Or maybe I was imagining that. Or maybe I wasn't.

"Egan," he was saying. "He said at the last minute they got a cheaper photographer, so even that got done. Cool, yeah?"

"Yeah," I said.

"And the other thing? YouTube and, like, four other people already got busted with alcohol in their limo."

"The prom hasn't even started yet!"

"Yeah, well, now it'll be even better. We never found out for sure who sent those threats, but without them there, I don't think you have anything to worry about."

"Maybe not." I was trying to swallow that bubble gum again. "Patrick," I said, "are you okay?"

"Fine. I'm going to go tell your parents thanks."

I nodded numbly and watched him go toward the kitchen. If he'd turned around and said, "Forget this whole thing. Let's you and me go to Scarnato's," I'd have done it.

But he didn't.

"You ready?" Matthew said.

He was there beside me, jangling his car keys.

"Yeah," I said. "We might as well go."

I didn't feel much like talking when we got in the car, not even to comment on the fact that Matthew had cleaned it out. At least I didn't have to contend with a liter of Mountain Dew. That day seemed like a lifetime ago now. That was the day I'd first suspected that Patrick was a decent human being.

Okay—I had to stop thinking about Patrick. He was

obviously already pulling away now that the prom was here. I needed to focus on Matthew. It was the least I could do.

"Thanks for not driving like we're in a NASCAR race," I said.

"Uh-huh," he said.

I looked ahead of us. "Of course, you still have about as much sense of direction as — Matthew, this is not the way to the school."

"I know."

"Where are we going?"

I watched him squeeze the steering wheel. "I'll tell you where we're not going."

"What?"

He took his eyes off the road and turned them on me.

"Sorry, Tyler," he said. "We're not going to the prom."

CHAPTER EIGHTEEN

I don't see the humor in that, Matthew," I said.

"That's because there isn't any."

The car lunged forward, and he took a corner on what felt like two tires.

"Matthew — stop."

"I can't do that."

"Then slow down — unless your plan is to try to kill me. I'm serious. Slow down or I'm calling 911."

"That's going to be kind of difficult," he said.

But he eased back on the speed and took the next curve on all four tires. I wasn't reassured. Matthew was pulling his hair back over his eyebrows, and his black tie was already flopping where he'd loosened it. We really weren't going to the prom.

"Look," I said, "if you don't want to escort me, I totally get that, but I have to be there. Just take me back to the school and drop me off. No hard feelings."

"I can't," he said.

"Would you stop saying that!"

"How about, 'I am not able to accommodate you at this time'? Does that work for you?"

I pressed my fingers to my temples. "Okay. Tell me what's going on — and don't say you can't, or I *will* call 911."

"No, you won't."

"Bet me." I fumbled with the clasp on my purse — and hoped I *could* call 911 with my fingers shaking like I had some kind of palsy. When I finally got the thing open, my phone wasn't in there.

"I took it out when you were talking to Patrick Sykes," Matthew said.

I went cold. But I forced myself to roll my eyes at him. I had to pretend until I got my brain around this. I wished I were better at it.

"The prom wasn't exciting enough so you thought you'd throw a kidnapping in?" I said.

"The kidnapping part is right."

"And you're doing it because ..."

"Because you didn't get the message."

"What mess—" I stopped and stared. The pretend game was already over. "You sent those text messages?" I said.

"No, Deidre did. It was actually kind of slick the way she—"

"Picked up somebody's cell phone wherever she happened to be," I said.

She was always having her car worked on. Castle Heights Towing. And she ate at Five Guys at least twice a week. She loved their Fat Burgers.

Why hadn't I put that together before?

Because it didn't make any sense then. It still didn't. And that broke me out in an icy sweat. I coaxed myself back to pretending.

"Are you going to tell me why?" I said. "Or do I have to deduce it for myself?"

Matthew swore under his breath and jerked the steering wheel, sending us at a squealing angle as we made another corner. Barely.

"Where are you taking me?" I said. "Just curious—you know, in case I'm dressed wrong."

"This isn't the way I wanted it to go."

I glanced out the window and felt an iota of relief. We were coming up on the Jiff-E-Mart, which meant there would be people around. There were always people. Ahead the light was red, and Matthew showed no signs of stopping. I planted my hands on the dashboard and glared at him, hard.

"If you don't stop," I said, "I will jump out of this car."

"Yeah? If I do stop, you'll definitely jump out and run."

"I swear I won't—just don't get us killed!"

As he braked and sent the car into another slide, I looked frantically out the window toward the Jiff-E-Mart. As I'd hoped, several guys were hanging out in the parking lot, and they all jerked their faces toward us at the sound of Matthew's tires screaming on the pavement. One of them was my cousin Kenny.

Not that it would do me much good. Matthew was gunning the engine at the light, one hand on the steering wheel, the other holding onto my arm. His grip was like an iron claw, and it sent spasms of fear straight through my chest.

By then the guys were all standing up, and Kenny was squinting through the dusk like he was seeing something familiar. I waved and mouthed HELP.

Matthew tightened his man hold on my arm. "What are you doing?"

"I'm waving to my cousin. He saw me, and if I don't wave he'll think something's wrong."

Matthew swore again and peeled out of the intersection to the screeching protest of two cars braking on either side of us. He missed them both, somehow, and jammed his foot on the accelerator. I was plastered to the back of the seat.

"Stop it, Matthew! Just stop it—please!"

He slowed down again and swerved onto a back street that led down to the river. My fear spasmed to a new dimension.

"Can't you just park somewhere and we'll talk?" I said.

"I—"

"I know, you can't. Then can you just not kill me tonight? Please."

He eased off on the gas and turned onto the road that ran parallel to the water. I let myself breathe.

"We'll just drive," he said. "I'll go slow."

I didn't consider houses whipping past me "slow," but it was better than clinging to the door handle and fearing for my life. Without all the tire squealing and the heart pounding I could think again, and the first thing I thought was that nobody in the Fringe was violent. They didn't care enough about anything to get worked up about it.

And suddenly, that made me mad.

"So—you hate the prom so everybody else has to?" I said.

Matthew glanced at me, eyes startled.

"Watch the road, Earnhardt Junior," I said.

He whipped his gaze back to the windshield and brought the car off the shoulder.

I sat up straight in the seat and folded my arms. I could feel my heart beating, as much from anger now as fear. "I don't get it," I said. "You and Deidre and Yuri don't care about anything. Why did you suddenly get a case of conviction over *this*? Something that means something to *me*? I just never thought you were mean."

"I'm not mean." His cheek muscles twitched. "You're the only girl who ever treated me like I don't have the plague. Even Deidre doesn't get me half the time."

"So that's your argument for—"

"I'm protecting you, okay? Something's going to go down when you do that prom queen walk thing, or whatever it is, and this was the only way we could think of to keep you from getting hurt."

"Why couldn't you just come to me and tell me, instead of sending me a note with cut out letters like some serial killer?"

Matthew slammed on the brakes and took the car off the road onto the gravel. The mirror on my side grazed a sign pole before we skidded to a stop. He had both hands on my arms before the car even stopped rocking.

"What note?" he said.

"You know what I'm talking about."

"I don't!" He shook me, hard enough to clack my teeth together.

"Okay, stop," I said. "You're freaking me out, Matthew."

His grip tightened. "What note?"

"The note *you* evidently sent, telling me if I went to the prom it was going to be like a scene from *Carrie*. *That* note."

"I didn't send that note," he said. "I don't even know who Carrie is."

"Whatever. Matthew, the RC's aren't going to ruin their own prom just to humiliate me. YouTube and his little minions aren't even going to be there. They already got picked up for drinking."

Matthew shook his head and pulled me closer to his face. His breath had the odor of dry-mouthed anxiety. "It's not them I'm protecting you from," he said. "It's Yuri."

"What?"

"He hated the way they were treating you over this prom queen thing, so he had Deidre set up the explosion in Chemistry to scare them."

"How did Deidre—"

"But then you started hanging out with those people—the same ones that made his life a total nightmare in middle school."

"I wasn't 'hanging out' with them—"

"In Yuri's eyes you were. And he just wants to make you pay for turning into one of them."

"That is the most inane, stupid—Matthew, that doesn't even make any sense."

Matthew let go of one arm to wipe the sweat off his forehead with his sleeve. I was sure we were both giving Mr. Linkhart a run for his money at that point. "I tried to tell him that, but it's like he's lost it or something. The only thing I could think of to do was to tell him I was taking you to the prom, and then *not* take you."

"I don't even want to know what you were planning to do with me for four hours."

He started to answer, but I put my free hand on his mouth. A thought seared right in front of everything else.

"He's there?" I said. "Yuri's at the prom right now?"

Matthew nodded.

"You have to take me there."

"I can't."

"Enough with that! Don't you see? If he's losing it like you say he is, he's going to be *livid* when he doesn't see me on that stage. Other people besides me are going to get hurt, Matthew. What about all the kids like, like, okay, Izzy?" I felt the panic rise. "What about *Valleri*?"

I clawed my fingers into the front of his shirt and pulled him even closer into my face.

"You have to take me to the school," I said. "Now. And so help me, if you say you can't, I will lay on that horn—"

"Okay, okay, chill."

"No, Matthew," I said. "I can't."

He swallowed, licked his lips, did everything but open the window and throw up.

"Come on," I said. "There's still time before they make the announcement."

Finally he nodded. I closed my eyes, and I prayed.

*

The drive to the school was never ending. I alternated between silently talking to God and talking to Matthew in the calmest voice I could manage, telling the kid he was doing the right thing, assuring him that he wouldn't regret it.

"This might even be a God thing," I said. "Now that we know this about Yuri, he can get help."

Matthew went over the center line on that one. Okay, so maybe God and I should keep our conversation private.

At least it was working. Matthew was driving at less than through-the-windshield speed and was nodding at most of what I was saying.

Until we made the last turn onto the school street. Two police cars were parked in the circular driveway. The four officers leaning against them looked up in unison as we careened around the corner. One of them was already charging toward us when Matthew floored the gas and shot past the driveway toward the gymnasium wing.

Cars were parked on both sides of the road, barely leaving room for Matthew's car to screech through. The engine was whining almost as high as I was screaming, but he didn't stop.

Not even when a figure stepped out from behind the last parked car. There was no time. I heard the sickening thud before I could even yell for Matthew to stop.

"You hit someone!" I cried.

Matthew pawed for the brake, and I found the door handle. But with my door halfway open, he hit the accelerator again and the car leaped forward.

Still screaming, I pushed the door all the way and jumped. The road came up to meet me and I slid on my side until I hit something. It moaned under me.

"Oh my *gosh*—are you all right?"

I turned over and pushed myself up with my arms. I was up against a crumpled heap of coral fabric that oozed blood as I stared in horror.

"No," I said. "No, no, no, no—"

But before I even uncovered her face, I knew it was Valleri.

Chapter Nineteen

I screamed for help, even though footsteps already pounded toward me. But when they reached me, I couldn't let go of Valleri.

"Let me stay with her," I begged the officer who crouched beside me. "Don't make me leave her."

"I need to find out if she's breathing, hon, and stabilize her head," he said.

I didn't let go of her hand, and when he pressed his fingers to her throat and her eyes fluttered open, I held her hand tighter to my chest.

"It's okay," I said. "It's okay, it's okay."

"You stay right here with her," the officer said. "I'm going to clear a path for the ambulance."

"Tyler."

I turned my ear to Valleri's lips.

"Pray," she whispered.

I did. Through the tears and the panic and the faraway whine of the ambulance, I prayed. Valleri breathed on; I could hear the wheeze against my cheek and it terrified me. Between prayers I just kept saying, "It's okay—you're going to be okay." And then I prayed again for it to please be true.

She stayed with me, moving her lips even when no sound slipped through, until the EMTs came. Then she went limp in my arms.

"We're going to have you wait right over here," one of them said to me. "We'll get to you in just a sec."

I would have protested if other hands hadn't found their

way to me and pulled me off the sidewalk and onto the grass. Even then I tried to get away, but a sharp pain in my side and the sound of Kenny's voice stopped me.

"I seen you by the Jiff-E-Mart—"

I turned and reached for my cousin, hands groping. Someone else grabbed me and kept me from pitching face forward.

"*You* need an ambulance," Graham said.

"No—you have to help me," I said.

Thoughts scrambled to get a footing. Yuri was still in there—in there at the prom. I had to get him out—and I had to get him out myself.

"Help me get inside," I said to Graham.

"Are you nuts? You can't even hardly stand up—"

"Then *hold* me up. I have to find Yuri."

"You have to get to a hospital—"

"You ain't gonna stop her now, I know that thing." Kenny buried his shoulder under my armpit. "You get the other side."

"This is crazy," Graham said.

I took in a ragged breath. "You can have me locked up after I find Yuri. Just get me inside."

"I don't believe I'm doing this."

Graham got on the other side of me and held me up with an arm that was unexpectedly strong. For some reason my head swayed, but I put one unsteady foot forward and then the other one. Without both of them hanging on to me, I wouldn't have stayed vertical.

"Pretend you're my dates," I said as we got near the door.

"Yeah, we look it," Graham said.

"It'll be dark," I said. "Just get me inside and you can wait out here if you want."

"Not happenin'," Kenny said.

Graham stopped us. "I'm not taking you any farther 'til you tell me what's going on."

My face wanted to collapse. I couldn't fold now.

"He's going to ruin the whole thing," I said in chokes and sobs. "All I want to do is get him out of there before he does."

"It's just a freakin' prom," Graham said.

"It's not about that! You don't understand. People deserve—"

"I'll explain it to you later, dude," Kenny said. "Let's just go 'fore she falls out right here."

Graham sucked in air and nodded. In one final lift, they got me to the door. The only adult there was Ms. Dalloway, who looked at us with her usual weariness. I almost cried again I was so thankful for that. The news of the accident hadn't gotten this far yet. I still had time.

"I was wondering where you were," she said over the din from inside.

"I'm here," I said. "I left my ticket in the car—"

"Oh, for Pete's sake," she said. "Get in there and enjoy yourself. You deserve it."

She returned to her post. I peeled my arms away from Graham and Kenny.

"Can you just watch for him outside?" I whispered in Graham's ear.

"Five minutes and then I'm getting the paramedics."

"Do whatever you have to," I said. "Just stop him."

They both let go of me, and I stood for a moment until the room stopped moving. With one hand on a wall of flowers, I got myself down the tunnel of blossoms and through an archway dripping in vines. It was probably beautiful. All I wanted it to be was strong enough to hold me up.

I finally reached the gym-turned-Wonderland and leaned against a column wound 'round with more blooms. A slow song was playing and the lights were lowered to a sultry blue. Everyone was a shadow, clinging to another shadow. I couldn't see who anybody was, and I started to panic again. How was I going to find Yuri in this?

My knees were weakening, and I had to put my arm around the column to keep from going down while I tried to think. My side was starting to hurt. I pressed my hand there, and felt another hand slip around my waist.

"You got my message," someone said.

I gasped and turned my face up—to see Patrick grinning down at me.

"You wanna dance?" he said.

I flung my arms around his neck and held on. And shook.

Patrick started to sway, but I held on harder.

"Tyler?" he said. "Tyler, what's wrong?"

Still clinging to him, still forcing myself not to give in to the pain that was now throbbing in my side, I rattled off the basics into his ear. I didn't even tell him about Valleri or Matthew. I finished with, "We have to find Yuri before they announce—"

"I know where he is," Patrick said. "He's taking pictures."

I tried to pull away to look, but it was now Patrick who held on.

"What happened to you?" He pushed my face into the beam of light that escaped from behind the column. "Oh my—"

"We have to get him out of here!" I said.

The song shifted into something faster, and voices squealed and bodies pulled apart and formed more shadows.

"One more dance!" Egan's voice cried through the speakers. "And then we'll announce the queen of the prom!"

"Now!" I said. "Hurry!"

Patrick nodded and scooped me into his arms. Someone yelled, "All right, Sykes!" as he carried me through the gyrating crowd over to the corner where Noelle and Fred were smiling into the camera. Yuri held up three fingers, counted them down, and flashed. Patrick set me down and had Yuri by the shoulders from behind before the smiles faded from their faces.

I didn't know what Patrick was saying to Yuri, but I could see him struggling under Patrick's hands.

"Patrick, wait!" I said. "Let me—"

In the instant that Patrick turned from him to me, Yuri wriggled himself free and ran straight for the Exit sign that jarred through the misty lights of Wonderland.

Patrick took off after him, with me groping through the pain and the dark patches.

"Let me talk to him!" I cried again.

This time Patrick didn't turn to me. If he had, he would have run into the steel door Yuri flung open.

And then it all stopped—me, Patrick, even Yuri. Because the doorway was blocked by something huge and brassy.

A tuba.

Patrick wrapped his arms around Yuri from behind and lifted him off the ground. The tuba backed up, and Kenny caught me just as I toppled forward and out into the dark. The door closed behind us. The music never stopped playing.

"All right, everybody just stay where you are."

I didn't have to look to know it was one of the policemen.

"Tell him he doesn't have to break up the prom," I said to Kenny. "Tell him!"

And then the dark places became one hole, and I fell into it.

*

No one told me until the next morning that Valleri was in a coma. Mom told me other things too as she fiddled with my IV and rearranged my covers and fed me ice chips and monitored my pain meds—all under the exasperated looks coming from the nurses.

She told me that I'd ruptured my spleen when I jumped out of Matthew's car. That they'd had to do surgery. That I was a complete idiot for doing what I'd done. And that she loved me.

My father was in and out. Whenever he was in, I pretended to be asleep so I wouldn't have to hear him say he told me so. He still talked to me—told me it was going to be all right, that I had the best doctors, that he'd get me anything I needed.

But all I really took in was that Valleri was alive. It didn't hit me until early afternoon, when the anesthetic fog had lifted, that a coma was not a good thing. That Valleri, my Valleri, could die.

I drifted through tears and pain-drug sleep until almost sunset, when Sunny rubbed my arm.

"Where are Mom and Dad?" I said.

"I chased them out of here—they're getting something to eat downstairs. They were driving everybody nuts." She smiled close to my face. "You have some visitors."

I turned my head. "I don't really want to see anybody."

"You're not going to want to miss this," she said. "Just for a minute?"

I nodded. Maybe it would be Patrick. I did want to talk to Patrick.

But it was Joanna. And Hayley. And Alyssa. They looked nothing like prom queen candidates and everything like white-faced, frightened little refugees cut off from their old reality.

Joanna said nothing but crossed the room and found space among the IV tubes to get her arms around me. She cried, of course.

Hayley leaned over me, not a bubble in sight. "You don't look as bad as I thought you would," she said.

"Very nice, Hayley." Alyssa licked her lips, which seemed naked and young without their gloss. "We brought you something."

Joanna pulled herself off me, just as I was about to tell her she was pressing on my incision. "You won," she said.

"I'm sorry?"

"You're prom queen," Hayley said. "They called your name and everybody went nuts—but there was no you."

She looked so desperate for everything to be okay I forced myself to smile. "So who accepted for me?"

"I did."

Alyssa took a stiff step forward and held out a tiara that would have outshone Candace's entire jewelry collection. The effect was dulled by the hospital lights, but once again I made up a smile.

"Who'd have thought, huh?" I said.

"Evidently a lot of people." Her voice was dry and crackly. "Look—I'm sorry for setting you up. I never thought you'd actually go for it."

"I don't think this is coming out right," Joanna said. Her hand on my arm was clammy.

Hayley rolled her eyes. "Just say it, Lyssa."

That was apparently the most arduous task Alyssa could endure; she would obviously rather be donating a lobe of her liver right now. Any other time I might have enjoyed it. But this was no other time.

"Apology accepted," I said. I closed my eyes and hoped they'd take the hint.

"We wanted to take you down because you always acted like you were better than we were."

The eyes came open. Alyssa swallowed that same wad of bubble gum we all seemed to be sharing.

"It turns out you are," she said.

I was still staring at her when Hayley turned her head halfway, her gaze on my IV bag.

"It was only 'we' at *first*, Lyssa," she said. "I told you two weeks ago she was all right, but you wouldn't stop."

Alyssa's face tightened. "I thought it was always 'we,' no matter what."

"Not when we're wrong." Joanna looked straight at her. "Then we each have to figure it out for ourselves. And I already did."

She leaned across me and kissed my cheek. Face crumpling, she turned to go.

"Wait," I said.

She stopped.

"You take this." I nodded at the crown, stuck like a lost princess between the plastic pitcher and the box of Kleenex on the rolling tray.

"It's yours," Joanna said.

"No," I said. "You're the real queen."

When they had filed out, a sob escaped from somewhere in my gut. It felt as if it were ripping through my incision but I let another one come, and another one, until Sunny was there, with her warm hands holding my face.

"Tyler, what is it, baby?"

"I'm not a queen."

"Yes, you are—"

"No!" I shook my head, and that hurt too. "It's my fault Valleri is in there trying to die."

"No—baby girl, it was Matthew's fault. And they caught

up with him two blocks away from the school." Sunny sat on the edge of the bed. "He's been charged with vehicular assault and leaving the scene of an accident."

"I should be charged," I said.

"Tyler, you didn't do anything wrong."

"The whole thing was wrong. If I hadn't tried to change everything, none of this would've happened."

"That's right."

I jerked.

"For openers, Yuri wouldn't be getting the help he needs."

I held back the next sob. "What happened with him? The girls didn't say anything."

Sunny smiled. "Nobody saw him run out the back door except Noelle and Fred. Noelle went and got her dad—"

"Her dad was there?"

"Yeah. He was one of the cops."

"No way."

"Way. Between you and Noelle—and ol' Graham—he didn't have a chance. The police took care of it quietly and nobody in the prom ever knew a thing."

"I don't understand. Weren't they afraid he'd planted a bomb or something?"

Sunny shook her head. "This is the really sad part of the whole thing. When they searched his camera bag, they found a paint gun in there, loaded with red ammunition."

The sobs started again.

"What, Tyler? What, baby?"

"Valleri could've been killed over a *paint gun*." I dropped my hand over my eyes. "She might die because—"

"Because Yuri was headed for a breakdown. Matthew and Deidre didn't know what to do with that." Sunny pulled my hand from my face. "Yuri's upstairs in the psych ward. He's getting help."

"But what about Valleri? She never did anything to anybody. Why was she even out there?"

"I don't know," Sunny said. "When she wakes up, you can ask her."

"What if she doesn't? You can't say she will, because you don't know."

"No," she said, "I don't."

"I just need to cry," I said. "But it hurts too much."

Sunny's eyes filled. "I could cry for you."

"Valleri would pray."

"We can do that too."

"Hey now, what's this?"

My father crossed from the door to the bed and stood behind Sunny. He put his hands on her shoulders as he searched my face. There was no avoiding him this time.

"You should go down and get yourself something to eat, baby," he said to Sunny.

Mom grunted from her resumed post at the IV stand. "Don't get the tofu thing. It tastes like a makeup sponge."

Sunny kissed my forehead and left me at the hands of my father. If I hadn't loved her so much, I would have called her a jackal.

I looked at Dad and decided to get it over with. "You don't have to say you warned me," I said. "I already know."

"Did you think that was what I came in here to say?"

"Didn't you?"

"I don't think a debate is on her chart," Mom said to him. "Let's cut to the chase for once."

Dad nodded and pulled a chair up to the bedside. My heart headed straight to my throat.

"Is it Valleri?" I said. "Is she gone?"

"She's still the same," Mom said. "No worse."

"But the longer she stays in a coma, her chances of coming out of it decrease. I read that."

"I think you read too much, Ty." Dad gave me a half smile. "Bet you never thought you'd hear me say that."

I plucked at the sheet. "What *are* you going to say? Would you please just tell me?"

"All right. First, just let me say that going into the school when you were bleeding internally wasn't one of your best choices. You could be charged with leaving the scene of an accident too, but they're cutting you slack. There were enough other witnesses—although the police still want to question you at some point."

I didn't bother to explain *why* I had to go into the school. I wasn't sure I would have bought it myself right now.

"In terms of the prom," Dad went on, "it did turn out for the best. But not knowing what this Yuri kid had in mind, you should have gone to the police instead of charging in there yourself."

"I know," I said. So far he wasn't telling me anything I hadn't already figured out.

"That being said, I know now that you were right about one thing."

Right now, I couldn't even imagine what that might be.

"You do need to be in a private school."

My hand startled, and Mom put hers over it. "Easy. You're going to pull out your IV."

"You'll be more focused on your courses, be more challenged," Dad said. "I know there's drama in any high school, but I don't think you'll have to deal with it at this level." He patted the mattress. "As soon as you're up to it, we'll go over some options. It's hard getting in for a senior year, but I've made some phone calls. Your academic record speaks for itself."

Mom smoothed her hand down my arm. "This *is* what you wanted, isn't it?"

"It *was*." I closed my eyes and felt myself sink. "I'm really tired. Can I sleep now?"

But I didn't drift off. I just waited until Dad left for home and Mom was breathing evenly in the recliner in the corner. Then I turned my face as far as I could into the pillow, and I cried.

CHAPTER TWENTY

Early Monday morning, I had three more visitors. One was the doctor, saying I had a slight fever and couldn't go home until it came down. That it could indicate an infection and they weren't taking any chances.

The other two came out of one of my blurred naps — a dark face and a creamy-white one. It took me a minute to realize they were Valleri's parents, heads bowed, hands clutching each others', lips moving. I didn't know if it was okay to interrupt praying. But I had to know.

"Is she still …"

Mrs. Clare raised her head and moved her hand from her husband's to mine. "She is still with us," she said in her soft Frenchness. "We have friends praying around the clock."

"Were you just praying for *me?*" I said.

"We were," Mr. Clare said.

"Why?"

His face puzzled. "Why wouldn't we, my dear?"

No one had ever called me "my dear." I felt myself caving again.

"You are Valleri's good friend," her mother said. "Her best friend. She loves you."

"But if she hadn't loved me — she wouldn't be where she is right now. Why don't you hate me for that?"

"Oh, no, no, no, no, no." Mrs. Clare put her hands to my face and rubbed my cheekbones with her thumbs. Her mouth was like a rosebud, murmuring the no's between presses on my forehead.

"We have no idea why this thing happened," Mr. Clare said. "We don't say 'it was God's will' or 'it was Satan having his way' or 'it was planned to teach somebody a lesson'—nothing like that. And my dear"—his voice caught—"we are certainly not blaming you. We're just praying that God will show us what to do next and give us the comfort and strength to do it. That's all."

"I want to hear it," I said.

Mrs. Clare stopped kissing my face. "What do you want to hear?"

I begged her with my eyes. "I want to hear you pray."

*

By noon, I was fidgeting in the bed, so they let me get up and walk down the hall, trailing my IV behind me like a reluctant dog on a leash. One trip to the nurse's station and back and I was wiped out, but I couldn't sleep anymore. My soul knew what it wanted, and my mind wouldn't rest until I got it. When Sunny came in right after school, I was on her.

"I need you to get me something from my room at home," I said. "Would you?"

"Not if it's schoolwork," she said. "You're supposed to rest."

"No. It's just my—it's a—okay, it's a leather book under the cushion on my window seat. It says RL on the cover."

"Okay."

"Could you bring it to me? I really need it."

"Absolutely." She squeezed my hand. "Everybody and their brother was asking about you. We spent the whole fourth block talking about it." She grimaced. "Most of the kids are really down. They think Valleri's accident negates everything else, everything good."

Yeah. I heard that.

I slid my gaze down to my lap. "Did you see Patrick?"

"I didn't. In fact, Hayley told me he wasn't even in school today."

"Is he sick?"

"Don't know. I can see what I can find out."

I shook my head. "If he wants to get in touch, he will."

"Uh-huh."

I looked at her.

"You sure that's the way you want to handle this?" she said.

"Handle what?"

"Uh-huh," she said again and stood up. "I'll go get your book for you."

*

I could feel RL's warmth even before Sunny handed it to me. I watched her as I took it from her, but I didn't see any tiny beads of perspiration on her upper lip.

"Did you read any of it?" I said.

"Uh, no. It looked private—of course I didn't read it."

I opened it and turned it toward her. "What do you see?"

Sunny peered at the page, eyes moving. "'That same day, two of them were walking to the village Emmaus.'" She tilted her head. "It's the gospel. The part right after the resurrection. Is this your Bible?"

"You don't see anything else?"

"Am I supposed to see anything else?"

"You don't hear anything?"

"I hear you asking me some pretty strange questions. You sure you're all right?" She put her hand on my forehead. "You still have a fever."

"Trust me, it's not a fever," I said. "Thanks for bringing this."

"Is that my signal to go away and leave you alone?"

"No," I said. "My signal for go away and leave me alone is 'Hey, Sunny. Go away and leave me alone.'"

Sunny pulled her eyebrows together. "You must be feeling better. You're getting ornery again."

I realized as she left that I actually did feel better. Maybe an inch better. Hopefully RL would take me further.

The warm page wasn't hard to find, and the words began as if they'd been waiting with fingers drumming.

So—you gave everything you had.

That wasn't what Sunny had read.

This is about you. Do you want your next story?

I do.

Yeshua has been killed, just as he predicted, and he has risen from the dead three days later, also as he promised. But his disciples seem to have forgotten that. They've gone into hiding, terrified that they're going to be next. You can't really blame them.

No, I couldn't.

But what they can't forget is him and the impact he had on their lives. It's all they can talk about. You know how that is, when something big goes down, nobody can focus on anything else.

It didn't matter how many times it happened, I still got a chill when this book seemed to be reading my life.

So that Sunday, the day of the resurrection nobody really knows about yet, two of Yeshua's friends are walking to the village of Emmaus, about seven miles out of Jerusalem. Like everyone else who was involved, they're going over and over what's gone down. Right in the middle of the conversation, Yeshua joins them. But they have no idea who he is.

Yet another thing I'd always had a hard time understanding. They'd been with him for, what, three years, and they didn't even recognize him? By the time I'd gotten to that story in Sunday school, I had stopped asking questions.

Yeshua says, "So what's this you're so focused on? Looks like serious stuff."

One of them, a guy named Cleopas, says, "You've got to be kidding me, pal. You must be the only person in Jerusalem who doesn't know what's been going on."

So Yeshua plays along. He asks what he's missed, and they tell him the whole story, including how confused everybody is by what the women have told them about not being able to find his body and seeing angels who say Yeshua is alive. "Who's gonna believe that, right?" Cleopas says. He goes on to tell how some of the men went back to the tomb and, son of a gun, it WAS empty. If Yeshua is alive, nobody knows where he is.

I was still working on why they couldn't see that he was standing right in front of them.

Oh, and get this. Yeshua says to them, "Why can't you just believe what the prophets said?" And he starts at the beginning, with Moses, and he goes through all the prophets, bringing up every reference to him in the Scriptures.

And they still didn't see who he was.

Not even. They get to Emmaus and Yeshua starts to walk on, and they say, "No, no. Have dinner with us." Still totally oblivious, they sit down at the table with him, and then—are you getting this?

I'm working on it.

Yeshua takes the bread, and he breaks it, and he gives it to them—is this sounding familiar?

I could see myself taking the bread from Valleri—I could hear her whisper, *Tyler, this is for you, from Jesus.*

They saw it too. Their eyes opened wide, and they knew who he was.

Yes.

And then he was gone.

"What?" I said out loud. "Just when they recognize him, he just disappears?"

Ever felt that way?

"Ya *think?*"

I pressed my lips together and watched the door. I was going to have the nurses running in here in a minute. When I didn't hear white tennies squealing down the hall, I turned back to RL.

I feel that way right now. I went to Valleri's church. I felt like something happened and I started praying and things were turning out right and then—

I put my hand to my mouth, because I was crying and I was talking straight to God.

And then You just seemed to disappear, and all this horrible stuff happened. I mean, what is the point in coming to You if You're not even here?

The story isn't over.

The warmth of the page touched me. Like Valleri's mother kissing my forehead. Like Sunny holding my face in her hands. I couldn't turn away from any of it.

"Tell me," I whispered.

The men Yeshua had just broken bread with were finally able to speak. And this is what they said to each other: "Didn't we feel like we were on fire when he talked to us out there on the road? Didn't it burn in us when he opened up the Scriptures for us?"

They said that? Please tell me they said that.

They said that.

And then what did they do?

They knew it was true—that Yeshua really was alive.

But what did they *do*?

They did what you do when you know. They ran and told the others.

I don't—

Tell the others what you know is true.

RL was then silent. I closed it and hugged it to my chest until the glow went deep inside. And then I rang for the nurses.

*

It took some convincing to get them to let me go see Valleri. They finally relented when I said I'd go in a wheelchair and would only stay five minutes. The truth I had to tell wouldn't take longer than that.

Her room was right across from the family lounge, which was standing room only when I rolled past. I recognized some of the faces I'd seen at Valleri's a week ago. I guessed if Valleri couldn't get to the church, they brought the church to her.

Mrs. Clare was sitting next to her bed, flanked by two bouquets of balloons, chatting away. My heart leaped—for the first time I realized a heart could really do that—and I thought Valleri was awake.

But she wasn't moving, except for the steady rise and fall of her chest that took a confused tangle of tubes and lines up and down with it. Her blue, blue eyes were closed.

Mrs. Clare looked up and smiled at me. "We do not know what can she hear. So I talk to her soul."

"That's—what I was thinking of doing," I said.

"Then come."

She put out her hand to me, and I rolled toward it, to a space by the bed.

"Remember," she whispered. "She loves you."

It was no longer a mystery to me how Valleri could be the person she was.

I slid to the edge of the wheelchair so I could fold my hands on the mattress. After using up one of my precious five minutes insanely hoping that she would sit up and say, "All better," I knew I had to start talking.

"First of all, I want to tell you that I'm sorry I got you into this mess."

I blew out some air.

"No, first of all, I want to tell you that I love you too. I never said that to a friend before. I never even *had* a friend before. Okay — you know all this."

I pressed against the bed and stared at her closed eyes. I needed the blueness. It always made me feel like somebody got me.

"You know everybody's praying for you. I am too. Seriously, I am. I don't know what I'm doing — it just comes out."

I looked at the clock. Two minutes left. Get to the truth.

"I've been thinking and thinking — no surprise there, huh? — and even though I still believe I'm responsible for your accident and Yuri's breakdown and Matthew being arrested, I think I'm responsible for some other things too, some good things. I just wanted to run them by you and see what you think. That's the way we work, right? You and me behind the scenes, and then I take it to the mob?"

She didn't nod her mass of bouncy curls. But I pretended she had, and I told her what I was thinking. What I wanted to go and tell them.

When the nurse came in and pointed to her watch, I knew what to do next. Before she rolled me out, I turned to Valleri and whispered, "Please come back. I need you."

*

If it hadn't been for Sunny, I couldn't have pulled it off. Well, as it turned out, Sunny, Ms. Dalloway, and Mr. Zabaski. They convinced Mr. Baumgarten that a meeting of interested juniors and seniors in the hospital lobby Tuesday after school should be announced in the morning bulletin. He conceded that it wasn't a school function, but the school wasn't *going* to function if there wasn't some closure on "this whole thing."

My mom helped too. She arranged it with the hospital for us to use the chapel, one of the perks of being supernurse. She had a harder time persuading my doctor to let me. He wasn't happy about my lingering fever, even though my blood tests didn't show an elevated white blood cell count and my incision was healing nicely. I didn't waste my breath telling him my temp had nothing to do with infection, but I did present him with a pretty impressive argument for the application of emotional support to healing. He gave me ten minutes.

These people were tight.

My father was the only one who said I was "carrying this thing too far."

"This is as far as I can carry it," I told him. "And then I'm done."

"All right—and then that's it," he said and shook his head. "I should have listened to you about that private school."

I let that go for the moment. I could only handle one truth at a time.

As three thirty approached, I experienced a smaller version of the what-if-nobody-comes attack I'd had before the pre-prom party. But I tried to pray that away and came out with, "Tell the truth to whoever shows up."

"Whoever showed up" was just about everyone in the junior and senior class. A hundred people were packed into the chapel, and my dad and Valleri's were setting up chairs in the back. I figured the man in the policeman's uniform must be Noelle's father.

The only person who seemed to be missing—besides, of course, Matthew and Yuri and Valleri—was Patrick.

This isn't about that, I told myself. I had to focus on what it *was* about.

Even though Mr. Baumgarten was there, running his hand

over his pink scalp by the door, it was Sunny who got the crowd settled. When she turned the podium over to me and I leaned on it for support, the same nurse who'd escorted me to Valleri's room held up ten fingers to me from the back row.

"Thanks for coming, everyone," I said.

"Go, Ty-*ler*!" someone called out. Probably my cousin Kenny.

Someone shushed him. Probably my cousin Candace.

"I'm sure you've all heard some rendition of what happened on prom night, and I know those of you who are so inclined are praying for Valleri and Matthew and Yuri."

The crowd rustled.

"So why pray for Matthew, when he hit an innocent person with his car and then ran away? And why Yuri, when he planned to take down all our hard work with his paint gun? I'm sure Egan wants to know that. He gave everything he had to make the prom amazing."

In the fourth row, Egan mouthed a watery thank you.

"Why pray for them, or even give them a thought? Because they're victims too. Victims of the kind of bullying and harassment and class snobbery that brought about the need for a Prom for Everybody Campaign in the first place. Even though they made some bad choices in the way they responded, we are all partly responsible for the results."

The chapel was breathless and silent.

"But not all of the results of the campaign were bad," I said. "Because what if we hadn't done it? What if we hadn't had a dress shop, and a tux contest, and a pre-prom party, and a place to do our hair and nails together and another one to make corsages? We would never have broken down the barriers enough to see that money separates people, and equality brings them together."

I swept my eyes over the group that looked back at me—Ryleigh nodding, Graham rubbing his thighs, Alyssa trying to toss her head and failing.

"I don't know what you personally have found out. I wouldn't know that Graham Fitzwilliam was a hero. Or that

Hayley Barr has enough enthusiasm for thirty-seven people. Or that Deidre Proccacini really does care about something."

I only glanced at her startled face before I went on.

"It was a rite of passage for us—and American kids don't have too many of those anymore. We made it a real one. We saw in it the kind of people we can be. People with integrity and character."

I sought out my father. He gave me a misty smile.

"Yeah, a horrible thing happened on prom night—to someone who bears no responsibility for any of it. And I understand that a lot of people think that means we failed, that it was all for nothing. I felt that way too."

I ignored the two fingers the nurse held up, and the weakness that was creeping into my knees.

"But the way we handle this crisis is a rite of passage for us too. If we have become new people, we have to handle this like new people—with faith, and with support for each other and for Valleri's family. You are the people that *I* want standing beside *me*." I looked again at my father. "I love this school and what we stand for now."

I didn't need the nurse's closed hand to tell me I was done. My knees were buckling, and my friends' faces were full enough.

"Thank you," I said.

"No." Egan stood up, face pale beneath his freckles. "Thank *you*, Tyler."

He started the clapping. Fred picked it up. As everyone rose to their feet, I wobbled on mine. Amid the cheers, my mother took one elbow and Sunny took the other, and I sank gratefully between them. We headed for the side door, which opened as if by magic.

But it wasn't magic. It was Patrick.

"Are you—is she okay?" he said.

"She will be," Mom said.

She backed me into the wheelchair that waited in the hall, and Sunny pushed it forward.

"I want to talk to him!" I said.

"Right after you talk to Valleri," Mom said. She squeezed my shoulder. "She's awake, and she's asking for you."

CHAPTER TWENTY-ONE

They all warned me before they rolled me into Valleri's room that although she was lucid, she couldn't move her legs yet, and she might fade in and out.

"Just a few minutes," said the nurse who had become my personal timekeeper.

Mrs. Clare gave her a look with her Valleri-blue eyes. "She can take as long as Valleri needs her."

"I want to get to know that woman," Mom whispered to me.

The minute I saw Valleri, I discarded everything they said about her "fading." She was so there, I was surprised she didn't sit up and bounce her curls at me.

"Well," she said. "Did you tell them the truth?"

"How *are* you?" I said. "Are you okay? Of course you're not okay—you're in a hospital."

"You're not making any sense."

"I know—I can't even think."

"No way," she said.

She licked her lips and I dove for the ice chips.

"No," she said. "I have to give you a message before they make you leave."

"What message?" I said.

"From Patrick."

I shook my head at her. Maybe they were right. Maybe she *was* fading in and out.

But her eyes were growing brighter by the minute.

"Saturday night," she said. "He was bummed out when he got to the prom, and I got him to talk to me a little."

"Of course you did."

"He was depressed about you."

"Me? Why?"

"He wouldn't tell me that — but I told him he should tell *you.*"

She coughed. I looked nervously at her monitors, although I had no idea what I was supposed to be seeing.

"We should stop," I said. "We can talk later."

"I want to tell you."

"So give me the short version."

"I said I would find you for him. And he said if you would come and dance with him, he would talk to you — really talk to you."

"No," I said.

"That's what happened."

"No — you weren't coming to find me when Matthew hit you. Please tell me no, Valleri."

She closed her eyes. All the fear I thought I had put to rest rose in me, and I had to clench the arms of the wheelchair to keep from screaming, "Don't fade now! You have to tell me no!"

"I wasn't coming out."

I pressed against the bed. "What, Valleri?"

"I wasn't coming out of the prom. I was going back in."

"From where?"

"From praying. I went outside to get quiet because it was all so much, and then I started praying. Then I saw Matthew's car so I ran to wave to you — " Her eyes fluttered closed again. "I shouldn't have stepped out in front of him. It was my own fault — "

"No," I said. "No, it wasn't."

"Just so you know," she said as she faded away, "it wasn't yours either."

*

I was a wilted version of my former self when Sunny wheeled me back to my room. But when Patrick stood up from the chair in the corner, I revived like I'd just been shot with caffeine. And no amount of clock pointing and finger counting from Nurse Watchdog dissuaded me from parking the wheelchair next to him and staring at her until she left the room.

"I don't know how she expects to get that fever down if she doesn't stop holding court all over the hospital," she said to Sunny and Mom as she bustled out of the room. "She's just a little queen, isn't she?"

"Oh, yeah," Mom said, eyes twinkling at me. "She's a queen."

With them gone, I turned to Patrick. For the first time, I saw that *his* eyes weren't dancing. In fact, the circles under them were so dark and deep, he looked like he'd just arrived at a funeral. My heart sank. "Depressed about me" could only mean one thing, and I just didn't want to go there yet.

"Were you sick yesterday?" I said. "Sunny said you weren't in school."

"I sort of was," he said to his lap. "I had to go see—somebody."

"I don't think it helped," I said.

His head jerked up.

"You're obviously still sick or bummed out or—"

"I'm depressed."

"Well, yeah, I think everybody is right now. But Valleri's out of the coma and—"

"Not that kind of depressed. This is, like, clinical. I get these—I don't know—moods where I feel like I'm suffocating and I have to go see my therapist."

"Well, do you want to talk—"

"Yes." He raked a hand through his hair. "I just don't know if you're gonna want to hear."

"It sounds like maybe I have to."

"If you don't feel like it—I mean, they said you had surgery—"

"Patrick," I said. "Talk to me."

He nodded. Miserably.

"It started after eighth grade. It was like I woke up one morning that summer and went, 'I hate myself.'"

"Why would you hate yourself?" I said.

"Because of the way I treated people. I was the ringleader back then. YouTube and those guys would do anything I told them to do."

I grew very still, as if something familiar were creeping up behind me.

"What did you tell them to do?"

"Torment kids I thought were weird—just so I didn't have to face that I was weird too. That we were all 'weird.'"

"What kids?" I said. But I knew. I knew because Matthew had practically told me.

"Kids like Yuri Connor," he said in a voice I could barely hear. "Mostly him. We made his life—"

"A living nightmare."

"It was like all of a sudden I couldn't even look in a mirror. I'd stay in my room for days and pretend I was sleeping, but all I could do was think about all the stuff we did to him, and the way he'd look when we stuffed him into a trash can or threw him out of the locker room half naked. It was like he disappeared a little more every time we did something to him. And that summer, I wanted to disappear too."

He stared at the window, even though the blinds were drawn. I was sure he was seeing it all, just the way it was then.

"At the prom, when I was carrying him outside, it was like I was doing it again."

"You weren't."

"It didn't matter. I went to bed that night hating myself as much as I ever did." He pulled the miserable, danceless brown eyes to me. "And now you must hate me too."

I closed my eyes.

"It's okay," he said. "I don't blame you. You're always so honest—"

"Why would I hate you, Patrick?" I said. "Because you used to be a stupid kid, and then you changed and became somebody I like as much as I've ever liked anybody?"

I opened my eyes to see him rock his head back. His face worked as he searched the ceiling.

"I hated *my*self before this all started," I said. "Only I didn't even know it. Do you hate me because I used to be superior and disdainful and insufferable?"

His laugh was thick. "No. I don't even know what half of that means." He looked at me, eyes red. "I don't hate you," he said. "I even wanted to ask you if I could be your escort—"

"And then I announced that I was only going with a group—because, of course, I didn't think anyone was going to ask me—"

"—And then you showed up with Matthew—"

"—Because I thought you'd asked somebody else—"

"—Which I didn't do because I didn't want to be with anybody else." Patrick reached across the wheelchair and grabbed my arm and pulled my hand up to his face. "I *don't* hate you, Tyler. I think I love you."

When Nurse Watchdog burst in, she found him kissing me on the nose.

"She needs to rest," she barked at him.

But I pulled him close so his ear touched my mouth. "Next time you come," I whispered, "bring me a latte."

His eyes danced again.

*

I finally got out of the hospital the next day. Everyone decided that in spite of my fever, I didn't have an infection, and that I was healing enough to go home.

I visited Valleri before I left. Her eyes were bright, this time with pain. She said the doctors told her she only had a 50 percent chance of walking again. We both cried—and I promised to be there for her during physical therapy—and she made me tell her about Patrick. It felt like friendship.

When I walked into my room at home, though, there was a sense of everything-is-different-now.

My makeup and hair stuff and unchosen jewelry were still strewn where I'd left them the night of the prom.

My cell phone, which I found on the table in the foyer where Matthew had put it, was dead. When I charged it up, there was a text message from Deidre. It just said IM SORRY.

My wastebasket was filled with brochures from private schools. My father and I hadn't talked about it yet. I was sure he was saving it for a dinner table debate. I was going to win, but I'd let him have his fun.

The schoolwork I'd missed had been stacked neatly on my desk by Sunny, but I didn't start in on it. I pulled RL out of my bag and went to the window seat. The warmth made some things feel the same. The things I wanted to keep.

The rest of the disciples finally saw Yeshua, the warm page told me. And they believed it was him—although some of them had to have hard evidence. They had to touch his hands and feet. You can relate to that, I'm sure.

Yeah, yeah. Go on.

He went through the Scriptures with them too, and he was majorly clear that all of it meant a total life change for them, through the forgiveness of all the wrong they'd done, and would probably do in the future.

I could relate to that too.

Then he said to them, "What's going to happen next is huge."

I held my breath. I was waiting for that.

I'm going to send you what my Father has promised.

Which is?

You will feel it when it comes. A Spirit will fill you—

"A Holy Spirit," I said.

And my peace will be with you.

I sank back into the pillows. "I think it already is," I said.

Good.

I looked down at the empty space.

Yeshua then made his exit, into heaven, and they returned to Jerusalem, ready to tell the world.

Tell them the truth.

I let myself sit with that for a minute, and then I turned the page. It was the last one. The only thing written on it were some email addresses.

"Is that the end?" I said.

That's the end of the story as it's written here. It's not the end of your story.

Which I'm going to have to live out in baby steps.

Yes. But I am going to give you one specific direction.

No way. You?

Way. You are to take this book and leave it in a place where someone else who needs it will find it and take it into her heart.

"How do I know where—"

Just leave it. It will fall into the right hands.

I ran my fingers over the addresses. "I always wanted to ask this—was I supposed to have you? Or were you left on the bus for Candace?"

Maybe both.

I nodded. I knew just where I was going to take it.

I tried to close the book for the last time, but its heat still drew me in. The warmest page was the one I was on. The one with the three email addresses.

harleyjess@yahoo.com was one.

dramaqueen@gmail.com the second.

cassroid@hotmail.com was the third.

Who were these girls RL had spoken to? I had no idea, of course. But the warmth that brought out the glow on my forehead told me we had something sacred in common, no matter who we were.

I took the book to my laptop and logged on to my gmail account. I typed in their addresses and closed my eyes and prayed.

And then I wrote: Dear HarleyJess and DramaQueen and CassRoid, You don't know me, but I know you through RL. I think we need to be friends. Because a girl on a Yeshua journey needs all the friends she can get.

Yeah. And now? Now I knew how to be one.

Didn't I tell you I'd make it worth your while?

ABOUT THE RL BOOK

It took Tyler no time to figure out that when she opened the leather RL book, she was reading stories from the Bible—but, then, she's pretty smart that way. I'm sure you were right there, too. They aren't the actual Scriptures, of course, but they *are* inspired by what Eugene Peterson did in *The Message*, which was to use modern, everyday language that makes you realize the Bible is for and about you. Jesus spoke in the street language of his day, so it only makes sense that we should be able to read his words that way. In fact, Eugene Peterson was inspired by a man named J.B. Phillips, who in 1947 wrote *The New Testament In Modern English* so his *youth group* could understand the Bible and live it. How cool is that?

Of course, no matter what translation of the Bible you read, it doesn't actually "talk" to you the way RL carries on a conversation with Tyler. Or does it? Scripture is the Word of God and a Word is meant to be spoken. When you really settle in with the Bible:

- *doesn't it make you ask questions?*
- *doesn't it answer the questions that pop into your head?*
- *doesn't it seem weirdly close to the exact things you're going through now, even though the stories were told thousands of years ago?*
- *doesn't it sometimes say something you didn't see the last time you looked at that very same part?*

Reading the Bible really is like having a conversation with God, and I hope RL helps you open up your own discussion with our Lord, who is waiting for you to say, "Can we talk?" Comparing what Tyler reads to the actual passages in the Bible might help you get started. All of them are found in the Gospel of Luke, who even more than Mark, Matthew, and John showed the love and sympathy Jesus had for the people who didn't fit, the people who others said were weird, sinful, and not to be hung out with. Luke also shows how much Jesus respected women. It seemed like just the thing for our RL girls—and for you.

THE SCRIPTURES

pp. 110–116: Luke 19:1–10

pp. 177–182: Luke 19:12–27

pp. 196–198: Luke 20:1–8

pp. 235–237: Luke 20:20–26

pp. 273–277: Luke 24:13–32

pp. 289–290: Luke 24:33–53

WHO HELPED

One of my favorite steps in the process of writing a book is working with experts who know things I don't. I mean, seriously, how long has it been since I went to a prom or did a chemistry experiment? These are the pros who helped me make *Limos, Lattes & My Life on the Fringe* feel like real life.

Winnie, Armenak, and Yervant Kutchukian, who opened up their home and their town—Castleton-on-the-Hudson, New York—to me. Although Tyler's Castle Heights is a made-up village, many of its details came from my delightful stay with them.

Destiny, Meg, Kaleb, Sean, Kristina, Blake, Austin, and Heather—a very cool group of students at Maple Hill High School in Castleton. Their school is way more open and accepting than Tyler's (I wanted to immediately start teaching there), but they helped me shape what *could* happen if ...

Mariah, who shared what it's like to be an outsider.

Candace, librarian at Maple Hill High School, who made it possible for me to hang out with them.

Charles Beverly, physician and homeschool dad, who gave me the chemistry experiments. I'm thinking he's a far better teacher than Mr. Zabaski.

Megan Lee, intern extraordinaire from Cumberland University, Lebanon, Tennessee, who found out all the little stuff I couldn't come up with—like the right slang and the perfect clothing brands and the hip actor references, and found more than a person could want to know about proms and student government. Next to the word "real" in the dictionary, there is a picture of Megan.

Lauren, Melody, Katie, Victoria, and Paige, blogging friends on "In Real Life" who gave their authentic comments about prom and student government. And for ALL the bloggers, who gave me great names like Candace, Frederick, Graham, Noelle, and Ryleigh.